I0597025

A PECULIAR SCHOOL

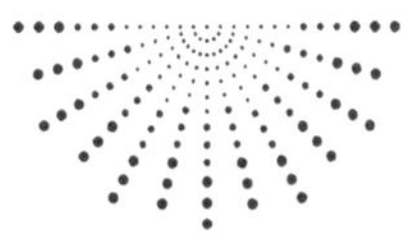

J. SCHLENKER

Binka Publishing, LLC

To Opa and Wynn

The clearest way into the Universe is through a forest wilderness.

— JOHN MUIR

For most of history, man has had to fight nature to survive; in this century he is beginning to realize that, in order to survive, he must protect it.

— JACQUES-YVES COUSTEAU

Man's heart away from nature becomes hard.

— LUTHER STANDING BEAR

PART I

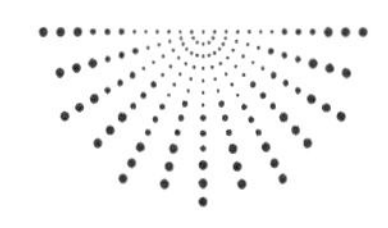

THE GREAT ESCAPE

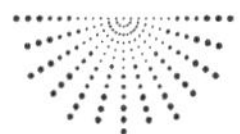

Miss Ethel Peacock strutted and proudly displayed her plumage as she paced around the waiting room of Mr. Densworth Lion. She had come unannounced, but she was so excited about the idea she had received in a dream, that she dared not lose any momentum. She could have called ahead, but what if he refused to see her? No, she decided not to risk it.

With the first light of morning, Ethel had roused from her nest feeling exhilarated. It was more than a dream. It was a vision. She breathed in the cool crisp air of early spring. Everything about the morning was perfect. The words of her grandmother, who was considered a sage by many, echoed in her mind, "Ethel, bold steps are needed if one is to accomplish great things." Sharing her vision with a lion, and asking him to help her make it happen, was definitely a bold step.

"A peacock? A peacock, you say? What is a peacock

doing here?" Mr. Densworth Lion asked his secretary in disbelief.

"Technically, she's a peahen. Her husband is a peacock. That is if she has a husband. I don't think she does, She introduced herself as 'Miss'. But together, they would be peafowl," his secretary corrected.

Mr. Densworth Lion uttered a slight roar of impatience.

"She's a teacher at the aviary," his secretary added.

"And she wasn't afraid to come here?"

"No, not that I could tell. Walks around like she owns the place. A proud one, she is. You know what they say, Mr. Densworth Lion."

"No, Miss Roberta Lion, I don't know," he retorted gruffly.

"'As proud as a peacock.' That's what they say, sir."

"They say that, do they?" he said, arching his eyebrows above his glasses. He rearranged some papers on his desk in an effort to tidy up. He moved the candy jar to the far edge, out of temptation. "Do you know what else they say, Miss Roberta Lion?"

"No, sir."

"'As hungry as a bear,' and that is what I am as we are coming up on lunchtime."

"Oh, Mr. Densworth Lion," the secretary said with a snicker. "But you're not a *bear*."

"No, Miss Roberta Lion, I am not, but I am as hungry as one." He inhaled deeply through his nostrils. "Is that duck I smell?"

"No, sir. It's chicken."

"Again? Didn't we have chicken yesterday and the day before that?"

"Yes, sir. We did."

"I guess chicken will have to do. My office is too close to the cafeteria," he sighed and rubbed his expanding waistline. "Too much temptation. But back to the peacock. What business does she think she has with me, anyway?" he roared and then slumped with an air of resignation. "Can't one day around here go smoothly without distractions or interruptions? Well, she's here. I can't very well walk out into the waiting room past her. She's standing outside the office door, right?"

Miss Roberta Lion nodded her head and said, "Yes, sir."

"Hmm," he sighed. "Well, let's see what she wants. If I think she is worthy of my attention, I will try not to eat her. Though peacock might be a nice change from chicken."

Miss Roberta Lion wrinkled her brow and scowled. She had been employed by Cub Academy for ten years and had worked under Mr. Densworth Lion for five of those ten years. If she had learned anything during that time, it was that his roar was worse than his bite—not that he had much of a bite these days, having had extensive dental work because of all those jars of candy he kept on his desk. Nor would he risk biting anyone now with all those bridges, fillings, and root canals. Embarrassed by them, smiling was not one of his strong suits.

She shrugged him off, as she so often did, and said, "She spoke rather highly of you. Said you carried a lot of weight in the area. Said she had a rather novel idea, for your ears only. She used the term *enlightened*."

"She did, did she? Well, let's not dilly dally. Send her in. Let's get it over with. The quicker she's in and out of here, the quicker I can eat my lunch." He motioned his secretary out.

Miss Roberta Lion turned, smiling to herself, and opened the door from Mr. Densworth Lion's office to the waiting room.

THERE WAS AN ART TO HANDLING MR. DENSWORTH Lion, an art that Miss Roberta Lion had come to master. Although she was usually on top of her game, she knew today would require extra finesse. She had arrived early to see the card and package with the frilly pink bow from yesterday still laying on his desk.

As any good secretary would, she made sure he remembered his mate's birthday. Where was his mind these days? For that matter, where was hers? She shouldn't have to remind him of his mate's birthday. That was not in her job description. The total lionesses' liberation movement had somehow passed her by, along with finding a decent and hard-working male. She had made this school and its cubs her life.

MR. DENSWORTH LION SHUFFLED MORE PAPERS AROUND his desk. Would the paperwork never end? This is not what he envisioned when he proudly roared to his father. Well, it was not quite a roar, more of a slight burp and *ahem* as he danced around and stammered that he wanted to go into education.

"Education, education?" his father retorted, flabbergasted, giving him an incredulous look. "We come from a proud heritage. You are king material, my son. Leave education to the lionesses."

"But, Father," he protested, "times are changing. We are on a progressive path, and education is where I can make a difference."

"Politics is what you want to go into," his father replied. He rested his paw on his son's shoulder, relaxed his pose, and let out a heavy sigh, his way of indicating the matter was settled, and that Densworth's future as a politician was carved in stone.

Young Densworth tried pleading with his father, but his father put his paws over his ears and shook his head, letting his auburn mane fall over his paws, further muffling any attempts Densworth might make to reason with him.

If only his father had lived, he would have seen just how political the school system was. And now dealing with a peacock? Of all things.

The day, which was still young, had been a disaster at every turn. His mate, who did the hunting for the family, had slept in. The nerve. She said he should get the food himself this morning. What had he done to deserve this? It wasn't until he opened the door of his office and saw the card and package still on his desk that he knew.

. . .

"Mr. Densworth Lion will see you now," his secretary said.

Mr. Densworth Lion eyed the proud bird as she walked like a queen into his office, something he admired, although he wasn't about to show it. He sat erect in his chair, gaining a few inches over the bird. It was a game—a game all animals played. When she spread her feathers, she had to be at least five feet tall. And those beautiful feathers, although not as glorious as those of her male counterpart, would throw anyone off balance.

She would not get the better of him. He was king here. Cub Academy was his jungle, and he was the ruler. At least that is what he kept telling himself amid piles of paperwork and unruly cubs. He cocked back his head, letting the curls of his thick mane cascade down over his back.

"Won't you have a seat? Won't you have a piece of candy?" he asked, pushing the jar closer to the edge. *No reason in being rude*, he thought. His mate kept telling him he needed to work on his manners. As with most things, she was usually right.

"No, thank you. I haven't had lunch yet. And I feel I'm losing my taste buds for it. Such a foul smell coming from your cafeteria," she said, remembering the words her grandmother said, trying not to lose her resolve.

"Neither have I, had lunch that is, and a *fowl* smell is right." He glared with saliva dripping from his lips.

Miss Peacock, not taking her eyes off him, brought her feathers in close to her body, folding them as gracefully as a geisha might fold a colorful silk fan, while she took a seat. "I know you are a busy lion. I will not take up a lot of your time."

A gurgling growl came from behind the desk where Mr. Densworth Lion sat. "My stomach. Excuse me. It's the aromas drifting up the hall from the cafeteria."

"I apologize I came so near lunchtime. Smells meaty." Miss Peacock cringed. "I eat grains, seeds, and fruit. I pride myself on being a vegetarian."

"Yes, I've heard peacocks have a lot of pride. I thought you ate insects," he said while swatting at a fly buzzing around his head. "Oh well, a shame. I thought you might try consuming this fly that has annoyed me all morning."

Miss Peacock walked over and raised the window. The fly made its way out. Mr. Densworth Lion grunted and scowled. "I guess that is one way to do it."

His secretary, standing just outside the door, snorted a chuckle.

"You may close the door now, Roberta," he said.

Miss Peacock let out a stifled squeak before regaining her composure.

"Oh, I used to eat worms and such, but then realized they are creatures as ourselves. So…"

He interrupted her. "Perhaps another day we can

discuss the plight of the worms. Surely that is not why you are here?"

"Why I am here, sir, is…"

"Yes, why are you here?"

"I had a most enlightened idea. It's grand. It came to me in a dream. An idea that comes in a dream is most auspicious."

"Do say, Miss Peacock? Myself, I have dreams of standing on a high cliff, overlooking lush green trees and beautiful waterfalls. There are no piles of paperwork or disagreeable cubs. I must be dreaming of retirement."

"But you are yet young, sir."

Flattery. Couldn't she see he wore bifocals? Had his secretary given this Miss Peacock pointers before she entered his office?

"My dream was not about retirement, sir. In it, I dreamed of a school. A *most* magnificent school."

"Miss Peacock, you are in a school, a most magnificent school. A grand one, I might add," he roared and rose from his chair.

"Yes, sir, that is why I'm here. I've heard about your school. Everyone has heard about it. Everyone has heard you are a most magnificent principal."

Mr. Densworth Lion became more relaxed, sitting back down and leaning back in his swivel chair.

"Do I call you Mr. Densworth or Mr. Lion?" she asked.

"We are formal here. Putting on airs is in our nature.

I am addressed as Mr. Densworth Lion," he said. "Always."

"What I propose, Mr. Densworth Lion, is that we use your school as a model—a model for a bigger school, a university of sorts, one that houses all animals."

"All animals?" he roared. "We teach cubs here—lion cubs. Such a proposal is ludicrous."

"But sir, all animals could learn to work together in a spirit of cooperation."

"Preposterous, Miss Peacock. It is not in animals' natures to work together. In fact, it is quite the opposite. We all serve a purpose. There is a certain pecking order. If this hierarchy were to break down, all manner of chaos might ensue."

Mr. Densworth Lion once again moved a stack of papers across his desk while standing on two legs, towering above her.

"Mr. Densworth Lion, that is easy for you to say since you are at the top of the ladder."

"Rightly so, Miss Peacock."

"But sir, animals can be taught to work alongside each other. Why, look at humans and dogs."

"Surely you are not suggesting we would include domesticated animals in this so-called school of yours? That idea is even more absurd. Why they're…"

"Beneath us? Is that what you were going to say, Mr. Lion? I'm sorry, Mr. Densworth Lion, but…"

He roared, moving in her direction. "What I'm saying is that dogs and cats have cast their lots in with the humans. And what of humans? Are you also suggesting we work alongside them? Even lions fear the humans. If that is all, Miss Peacock, I'm famished."

She shuddered at seeing the drool drop from his mouth but stood her ground. "Then, sir, we will save this for another day."

"No, madam, we will not." He walked her toward the door.

Miss Roberta Lion removed her ear from the other side of the door and retreated to her own desk.

"Whatever they are paying you to work for that lion, it's not enough," Miss Peacock said to Miss Roberta Lion before she bounded out of the waiting room of Mr. Densworth Lion and down the hall past mischievous little cubs who were throwing spitballs.

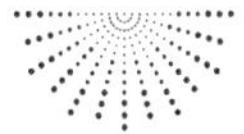

*E*thel had a turbulent night. She tossed and turned, clawing at her pillow until it was in shreds.

It was the dog that lived at the house across the lake that disturbed her sleep on most nights, but tonight was different. No barking. Not even a whimper. How odd. The dog barked for a good solid hour almost every night. What was he trying to say? Since dogs had taken up with humans, their language had become garbled and unrecognizable. It was obvious the humans didn't understand them either. Every night the human came out on the porch and yelled something to the dog in the scrambled tongue of humans. This banter went back and forth between them until the human got frustrated and went back into the house, slamming the door. Still, the dog continued to bark. But tonight, the dog remained silent. Why was she worried about an animal she didn't even know?

Ethel wondered what the dog was trying to convey. Mostly dogs were a peaceful lot, although wild animals labeled them as traitors or inferior creatures. Were dogs beneath them because they bowed to humans—thinking humans could do no wrong?

Then there were the cats. Cats were an entirely different matter. They were aloof creatures, subservient to no one. The man also had cats. His felines came and went as they pleased.

The man was an anomaly, too, living so close to the forest and away from other humans. On most days, he wore a green uniform, and she knew his job had something to do with the forest and all the animals who lived within its boundaries. She had seen him plant seeds and observe the animals from a distance. Sometimes, she and others had observed him taking hurt animals away.

Some animals came back. Some didn't. The ones who did reported being taken to a building in a van. They were in a room, placed on a table, injected with something or rubbed with ointments, sometimes bandaged, and most always put in cages after the fact. Sometimes, they saw someone they knew on the other side. They were checked on daily, and when they were well, they were put back into a van and returned.

The man had kind eyes, and Ethel sensed there was nothing to fear. Each day the man set out food in bowls. The dog was so thankful, bouncing around, wagging his tail; while the cats turned up their noses like kings and queens. She didn't know what sex his cats were. She might have known if he had dressed them in little human outfits as humans had a tendency to do with their pets. At least he had spared them that humiliation.

Observing the man interacting with his pets had been a pastime of hers. She watched as he stroked each animal's back and smiled at them. She watched as he picked up his two cats the way a lion would carry around cubs and rubbed their noses in the food. They would saunter around, examining the dog's food at which time the dog would growl, before beelining it back to their own bowls. It appeared to be a ritual with them.

She couldn't blame the cats for not wanting it. The little stamped out pieces in different shapes that fell into the cats' bowls were something made from human machines and not natural at all. The cats seemed to be content pursuing and feasting on mice and moles all day, of which there were plenty around.

For some reason, the cats and dog stayed. The cats purred when rubbed, and the dog wagged his tail and greeted the man every evening when he returned from his job, whether it be in the forest or elsewhere. The dog also went jogging with him. They always ran alongside the outer rim of the forest while the cats engaged in their own exercise ritual of chasing a ball of yarn.

The one time she saw the man and cats connecting was when he directed a beam of light in a random pattern. The man offered a challenge they considered worthy of their attention.

Could there be some unspoken language between them, or were the cats and dog stupid? Was Mr. Densworth Lion right? Had they cast their lot in with humans? Perhaps the dog had succumbed, but those cats were a different story. There was definitely something suspicious about them. Were they on the side of animals or humans? More than likely, they were plotting against everyone. She would have to keep a better eye on them.

Ethel tried to clear her head, but no matter how hard she tried, Mr. Densworth Lion's rebuffs would not leave her mind and give her the peace she desired. The full moon stared down at her through her window. She could see Mr. Densworth Lion's face plastered across it, peering down into her very soul. He looked over his wire rims not roaring at her but laughing at her. She blinked her eyes as she could not believe what she was seeing. A myriad of animals took his place, all laughing.

The hyena had a nightmarish squeal. She did not even know any hyenas. Then there was a badger and a tiger. What an odd combination. A polar bear grunted a deep, throaty laugh. An orangutan had a peculiar smile, almost sympathetic to her plight. But no, she couldn't read it. She shut her eyes and looked again. They had all vanished. Had the dog seen this too? Had the scene taken away his bark?

Tomorrow her good friend, Luce, was coming for a visit. It was Ethel's spring break from teaching. They planned to spend the whole week together, catching up. Luce would take her mind off the situation. She had a way of making all things seem trivial. Miss Luce Pigeon was a city hen, not an old hen, but a close to middle-aged one with lots of experience. Never married, although she always had a new beau to report. Yes, Luce had been around the block, a hen of the world. Luce could advise her on these matters. At the very least, provide a welcome diversion.

Stretching her legs was what she needed—a good brisk walk to tire her out. Ethel ventured out into the night air and took a stroll around the lake, gazing periodically up at the moon. The faces she had seen earlier through her window were a blur. The blur melted into something resembling Swiss cheese which was making her hungry. This whole idea was making her crazy. Perhaps it was preposterous. Perhaps Mr. Densworth Lion wasn't so mean and grouchy after all, only logical.

At any rate, the walk was the exercise she needed to put her mind at rest. She returned to her home, hoping to finally drift off to sleep. She punched down her tattered feather pillow. Tomorrow she would have to mend it. It was a treasured heirloom containing bits and pieces of the feathers of her esteemed ancestors. Her grandmother had saved the feathers and given them to her. Ethel hid them under her own feathers when she left India and made them into a pillow. The pillow of feathers helped her to forget the troubles of the day.

She always had a troubled mind, or so her mother had said. Her grandmother begged to differ. Because of that, she tended to bypass her mother and go to her grandmother for advice. Back in India, her grandmother was looked upon as a sage. A lot of peacocks went to her for advice. She had said to her, "Ethel, your mind is not troubled at all. You are merely a big thinker. All great minds are big thinkers. You will accomplish much. Don't let the naysayers and critics get you down."

Grandmother also told her to pay particular attention to dreams. "Dreams will only come true if you pursue them," she had said. That was exactly what she was doing concerning her dream about the school.

Her grandmother presented her with the feathers, saying they contained bits and pieces of all the wisdom of those who came before her, but she needed to piece those bits of wisdom together for herself. Life was a jigsaw puzzle.

Ethel turned the pillow over so as not to disturb the rip she had made and gently lowered her head down upon its soft billowiness, hoping to awake to some answers, or at the least, the right questions to ask her good friend, Luce. Luce was a different kind of sage, a practical sage. Yes, Luce was indeed a rare bird.

Her eyelids began to feel heavy. Just as they fully shut, the dog commenced barking.

BACK IN HIS DEN, MR. DENSWORTH LION WASN'T sleeping any better, much to his mate's dismay. "Densworth, if you are going to disrupt my sleep, you can move to the couch."

Usually, his mate helped him work out his problems, but she was not yet over his faux pas in forgetting her birthday, even though he had stopped on his way home and picked her a fresh batch of daisies to go along with the card and gift. On his way to the couch, he noticed they still lay on the table, wilting. He dug out a vase from the closet, arranged the flowers in it, filled it with water, and placed the vase on the table. They continued their droop. They were as beaten down as he was.

The couch was lumpy. His wife had complained, wanting a new one. He had told her they couldn't afford one, not on a principal's salary. Perhaps he should have gone into politics like his father wanted him to. They would have been able to afford a grand den with all the trimmings that kickbacks and bribes could buy. *No*, he told himself. That is why he went into education—to make a difference, that someday all the corruption might be eradicated.

Miss Peacock's words kept ringing in his ears. *All animals working together.* That old busybody. That old hen. Why couldn't she leave well enough alone? Status quo. He was nearing retirement. Well, another five years. Then he and the missus could do all that traveling they had talked about. Visit their cousins in Africa. Why, they could sell this den and its lumpy couch. It would make a nice starter den for some young couple. A fine place to raise cubs.

He and his wife had no cubs of their own. Glenda assured him there was still time. Maybe time for her, but not for him. Marrying a young lioness seemed like a good idea years ago. He was the envy of all the lions his age. Even his father nodded in approval. Densworth smiled, remembering one of the few times he had pleased his father.

He was glad his father hadn't lived long enough to see how stagnant his life had become and at how inept he had remained.

His father prided himself on being a handy lion. Densworth barely knew a wrench from a hammer. Glenda was always complaining. Gutters needed fixing. The roof needed patching. Their den had never progressed beyond a starter den. Sure, he had plans to build onto it, a fine study with built-in bookcases to hold his precious books, some of which were first Owl Headquarter editions, *Animal Farm, Black Beauty, Alice in Wonderland, All Creatures Great and Small, Call of the Wild, The Wind in the Willows,* and *The Life of Pi.*

The Life of Pi was one of his favorites. Now there was a book to ponder. A lifeboat full of wild animals: a tiger, a zebra, an orangutan, and a hyena, pitted against a scrawny human, Pi. Perhaps if the animals had worked together? Pi had already worked everything out in his mind. Instead of adhering to one philosophy or religion, he combined Hinduism, Christianity, and Islam.

Mr. Densworth Lion threw off the cover, his fur in a sweat, his mane drenched and matted together. What was Miss Peacock suggesting? He didn't know for certain as he hadn't given her a chance, didn't hear her out. More importantly, why was her visit and the idea of a school for all animals playing so heavily on his mind?

Was she recommending the animals cooperate in order to defeat humans? She made no mention of humans. Was she theorizing animals were of different religions—that they could achieve great things like Pi if they combined their religions?

His own mind was so scattered. That's what came with administration. If only he could be a teacher again… As a teacher, he started out with so much hope, the hope of guiding young cubs toward a brighter future —one in which they could achieve anything they wanted. He once was like Miss Peacock, bursting with ideas—ideas that would change the animal kingdom for the better. How had he become so jaded? Had he turned into his father?

Perhaps he would give Miss Peacock another chance. Hear her out. He could invite her to their den. Glenda loved entertaining. Would she welcome a peacock?

He could hire someone to fix the gutters and patch the roof, make the house presentable. His mate couldn't protest after that. She might even forgive him for forgetting her birthday.

Glenda could show her the garden. She loved working in her flowers. Miss Peacock would surely be impressed by all the different varieties and bright colors. Glenda might be appalled that she would have to serve something vegetarian, but then again, being younger, Glenda was more open to such radical ideas as vegetarianism.

Yes, his mind was made up. His life had become so

dull and monotonous, and he was dragging his mate into this downward spiral with him. This strange turn of events might be what he needed to get his life back on track. At any rate, it would be an entertaining distraction, something to take his mind off work. He punched down the pillow and began snoring.

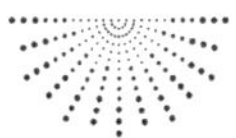

CHAPTER THREE

At hearing the peck at the door, Ethel scurried around, checked her feathers in the mirror, and did some quick facial yoga stretches to reduce the bags under her eyes from such little sleep.

She opened the door in a frenzy of anticipation, not bothering with the peephole. At long last, there stood her dear friend. They strutted around each other; Luce cooed, and Ethel squealed.

"It's been ages. How was your flight?" Ethel asked.

"It feels like ages. As far as my flight, first-class all the way," Luce cooed. "Good weather. Didn't rain one drop the entire trip. Only a slight breeze. No tailwinds."

"Well, your feathers certainly show it. They are glistening. Or could that be because you're in love? You said there was someone new in your last telegram. I want to hear all about him."

Luce cooed in embarrassment, unusual for Luce. "Not in love, but he is special." Luce eyed her longtime friend up and down. "Ethel, I'm sorry I can't say the same for you. You're looking a little worse for wear. Have you been getting proper sleep? You're not ill, are you?" She raised her right wing to her friend's head. "You don't feel hot."

"Oh, Luce," Ethel said, breaking into sobs.

"Now, now, tell old Luce all about it," she said, entering the nesting area.

"I will. I will. But first a nice cup of tea. A hearty chai. And, Luce, please don't call yourself old. We both still have a lot of bird years left."

"I hope so, Ethel. Oh, I almost forgot." Luce reached into her bag and pulled out a mesh pouch tied with a red ribbon.

Ethel untied the ribbon, examining an assortment of tea bags: Earl Grey, Oolong, Jasmine, and Darjeeling. "Some of my favorites, in particular Darjeeling. It comes from my home country."

"I know. The minute I saw it, I thought of you. Sorry it couldn't have been more, but when you're flying, you have to travel light."

Ethel hugged her dear friend. "This is perfect."

Luce's head did a few quick turns, examining her surroundings. "Ethel, I have to say, I like what you've done with the place. Such a cozy little reading nook you've fixed in that corner, all bright and cheery. I see you've added more books to your collection. The owls must stay busy."

"Yes, they do indeed."

"I like this fabric you've used to decorate the bench. What do you call these again?"

"Saris. I thought they would make nice throws."

"You have an eye for interior decorating." Luce choked on her words as soon as her eye caught the one bleak spot in the room, the one Ethel tried to hide by pushing an eyesore off into a darkened corner. What looked to be an outline of a chair was covered by an old tattered cloth and a pile of *Owl Gazettes.* It was so unlike the surrounding festive atmosphere. She noticed Ethel saw her staring in that direction and glanced elsewhere. "And that statue on the bookcase? The blue man with the flute?"

"Lord Krishna."

"Oh, yes," Luce agreed.

"It's a little piece of home," Ethel said.

"I have to say, I love having a friend from India. Growing up in that culture gives you a certain edge. What do you call it?"

"I think you are referring to enlightenment," her friend said. "But far from it, I'm afraid it all went to my head, being the national bird and all. All the meditation, yoga, mantras, and admiration made me think anything was possible, but now, I don't know. I had such a good life there. And I miss my…"

"Yes, dear, I know you do." Luce placed her wing on Ethel's shoulder. "I'm sure your hatchlings turned out to be fine birds. Thinking of the past will do you no good. I don't think I've ever seen you so down. What's troubling you, Ethel, besides missing your loved ones?"

Before Ethel could respond, there was a peck at the door. "Are you expecting anyone else?" Luce asked.

"No." Ethel looked through the peephole. "A carrier pigeon," she exclaimed, opening the door.

He tipped his hat and handed her a note. Luce cooed and strode up beside him, batting her eyes and cooing, almost grabbing the letter from the carrier pigeon's wing herself, but Ethel beat her to it.

"Thank you," Ethel said, closing the door. She turned to Luce. "Luce, such outrageous behavior. Do you have no shame in flirting with the delivery bird in that manner?"

"Can you blame a hen? Who can resist a uniform, and that fine leather briefcase he had? Besides, he was cute."

"It wasn't a briefcase. It was a pouch and a rather threadbare one. Also, he was much too young."

"So is Santiago."

"Santiago?"

"My latest beau. From Cuba. A bongo player."

"Ooh, la, la. How exotic," Ethel teased.

"Actually, it's good to get away from him for a while. He's a womanizer if there ever was one." Luce sighed. "But then, I'm no different, flitting from one cock to the next. I long to settle down. Just haven't found the right one. If only I had been born a dove. I could mate for life."

"We are born who we are for a reason, Luce. We all question our purpose in life. I have certainly been questioning mine as of late." Ethel did a slight flutter of her feathers. "The note. I haven't even opened it. Whoever could it be from?"

"Some old bird. That is for sure."

"Why do you say that?"

"Ethel, darling, young birds use computers. They send emails."

"I guess you're right."

Ethel opened the envelope, taking out the note. She read it out loud.

YOU ARE CORDIALLY INVITED FOR DINNER AT THE HOME OF MR. AND MRS. DENSWORTH LION NEXT SUNDAY AT SEVEN O'CLOCK.

"A lion," Luce exclaimed. "Who in the world are Mr. and Mrs. Densworth Lion?"

"Currently, the source of my troubles. You see, Luce, I had a dream, a most incredible dream about starting a school. It would be a school for all species of the animal kingdom. I thought Mr. Densworth Lion could help. He is the principal at Cub Academy. I went to see him."

"A lion? You went to see a lion?"

"Yes."

Luce raised the feathers above her eyes. "Aren't you the brave peacock?"

"Perhaps. But when you have a revelation such as I had, well, I saw no other choice. If a lion can't bring all animals together, then who can?"

"So, why so sad? He is inviting you to dinner. It must have gone well."

"No, it did not go well at all. He was quite gruff with me. This note comes as a surprise. A complete surprise. It is most peculiar."

"Oh dear, oh dear. You shouldn't go. You have to be careful, Ethel."

Ethel squawked and rolled her eyes. "I'm sure it will all be civilized. What if he has had a change of heart?"

"And what if you are the main course?"

"I'm not. I'm sure," she hesitated, stuttered, and then regained her composure. "Please sit, Luce, while I get the tea. We must catch up."

Ethel carried in a tray with a white teapot, two white teacups, and several macarons. As she poured the tea, the rich aroma of Darjeeling, cinnamon, anise, and cardamom drifted throughout the room. "Macaron, dear?"

"I shouldn't, watching my figure, but how can I resist?" Luce said, grabbing one. "They look so good. So, tell me more about your plan, this school you are proposing."

"Oh Luce, I think this could be my lifetime achievement if it could happen. I could die a happy peacock."

"Oh, now, no talk of death. We are both yet young. You said yourself we have plenty of bird years left."

"I had a dream of all animals working together, young animals learning together, combining their strengths and talents to create a highly evolved animal kingdom. An enlightened Yuga."

"Yuga. I'm afraid you've lost me there. Is that one of those sand skirt terms you learned while in India?"

"Sanskrit, Luce, not sand skirt. Yes, it is. The four great epochs in Hinduism are Satya Yuga, Treta Yuga, Dwapar Yuga, and Kali Yuga. They are based on astrology."

"Oh, I love astrology. I read my sign every day in the *Pigeon Carrier Gazette*."

"Not that kind of astrology, Luce."

"Oh."

"No, well, in a way. It does have to do with the cycles of the planets and their relationship to the solar systems. It's rather mathematical like the one hundred eight steps of the earth."

"One hundred eight," Luce squealed. "I know that number. I remember you telling me it was the number in prayer beads, but not all prayer beads. I know because Santiago is Catholic, and he says there are fifty-nine prayer beads. He's from Cuba, you know."

"Yes, you said earlier," Ethel said.

"They're all Catholic down there. Well, I guess most are," Luce said.

"All the religions form a piece of the puzzle. The one hundred eight steps are only a part. Our solar system, along with our sun and planets, are moving around a much larger star. This takes 25,920 years. Whenever our solar system comes closer to this star, all the creatures living in our system rise to greater possibilities."

"Even humans?" Luce asked.

"All creatures, even humans," Ethel replied.

"So, we are in this enlightened cycle?" Luce asked, perking up.

"No."

"Oh," Luce said, slumping and taking a bite of macaron.

"Likewise, when our solar system moves away from it, we are at our lowest level of possibility or dumbed down."

"Oh, so we are in the bad Yuga?" Luce asked.

"There are different philosophies of thought on that," Ethel said. "Some say Dwapar. Some say Kali."

"Could we get to the point, Ethel? I was never very smart in school," Luce sighed. "In your opinion which one are we in?"

Ethel blushed. "Well, right now we are in the dumbed-down period, what is known as the Kali Yuga."

"Is that the reason there are no good cocks out there?"

"Could be. But that's oversimplifying it. Even during the worst cycle, there are small periods of enlightenment. Krishna said so."

"The man in blue?"

"Yes."

"Santiago saw the Blue Man Group in concert once. Any relation?" Luce asked.

"No," Ethel said flatly.

"Oh, a shame. I thought you might have connections to some free tickets. Anyway, back to your school, or are we floating out in the universe now somewhere far away from schools and other earthly matters?"

"No, fully grounded," Ethel said. "Such a school would certainly be an enlightened thing." Ethel sighed. "Maybe I'm just a silly old peahen. Mr. Densworth Lion said it was not in an animal's nature to get along, in fact, quite the opposite."

"He's wrong there," Luce said, reaching for another macaron.

"I would truly like to believe that is so. Do you really think so, Luce?"

"I don't think so. I know so," Luce said with a satisfied smirk. "I do love these macaroons. They are so French. I don't know any French pigeons. I hear they are quite the lovers."

It was coming back to Ethel about how a conversation with Luce, regardless of the subject matter, somehow always reverted to the male species.

"I don't understand. What do you mean? How do you *know* so?" Ethel asked with a puzzled look on her face.

"There is a whole group of animals, different ones, living and working together where I live in the city—some old, some young—a badger, a tiger, a hyena, and an orangutan."

Ethel sat motionless for a full moment, not believing her ears. These were the animals she saw staring down at her from the moon. Truly this was a sign, but erring on the side of caution, she asked, "Is this gossip, hearsay, some wild fantasy, something perhaps made up during a drunken spree with the bongo player?"

"Ethel, you wound me. No, I met them, twice, well once for certain. The badger, upon several occasions. I see him on the streets, mostly in the park, from time to time. The others don't get out much. In fact, I don't think they get out at all. I mean, how could they? Could you imagine a tiger or orangutan walking down the city streets? I feel sorry for them. You and I are fortunate we can come and go as we please."

"I'm sorry, Luce. I didn't mean to imply you were making the whole thing up. It all sounds so incredible."

"No more so than your idea of a school," she retorted.

"Of course, you are right. This isn't a joke, is it? You can't joke with me on these matters. You wouldn't joke with me, would you, Luce?"

"No, dear, I'm not joking. Like I said, I've met them. They live underground. And I mean that literally. They make their home in the tunnels under the city. Come to think of it, there is a polar bear in the group. How could I have left him out? How he tolerates the heat, I'll never know." She took a bite of macaroon and another sip of chai. "Ethel, you must instruct me on how to make this tea."

"I will, but back to the animals, Luce."

"Ooh," she shuddered, crinkling her feathers and shaking her head, spraying macaroon crumbles from her beak. "They are a haggard bunch. The polar bear is no longer even white. Did you know polar bears are not white at all but translucent? That means clear."

"Yes, I know what translucent means."

"Something about the way the light hits the fur that makes them appear white. Their skin is black underneath the fur. The black is showing through now. But then, there is little light in the tunnels. You would not know him from a brown or black bear.

"Oh, and scrawny. All of them. My lord, they are skinny. I hear they feast on rats. Not much else in those tunnels. And how Orangutan tolerates that, I don't know, being a vegetarian like yourself. Well, Badger brings him bark and leaves from time to time."

"Why?"

"What do you mean why? Why is he a vegetarian?"

"No, why are they in the tunnels, living together?"

"Hiding out, I suspect."

"From who?"

"Those who wish to capture them—the zookeepers. Or humans. They're the same, you know."

"Yes, I know."

"They escaped from the zoo at some point. I couldn't tell you when. Oh, it was in all the newspapers, a big deal. I saw the pictures, but since I can't read or speak the language of humans, I couldn't tell you an exact date. But it was during a big storm. Lots of lightning. I remember that night well. It was a couple of boyfriends before Santiago. A lot of cuddling going on that night, inside those big strong wings of Elijah.

Wonder whatever happened to him?" Luce said with stars in her eyes.

"Luce, Luce?"

"What?" she asked with a jerk.

"You said you met the badger several times?"

"Yes, he's the youngest one I believe," she said, adding more sugar to her tea. "He may be the youngest, but he is their leader."

"A badger leads such fearsome animals?"

"Oh, don't underestimate Badger. He's a smart one. Besides, he is the only one who can move freely about the city. Roams all night. Sleeps during the day. Badgers don't much like the daytime. The others are entirely at his mercy."

"Why doesn't he just leave?"

Luce paused. "He has grown to love them, I suspect. It's like you talked about, the cooperation thing, all animals working together. Living under the conditions they do, they are more alike than different."

"Luce, do you think I could meet Badger? I would like to meet the whole group."

"I suppose I could arrange it."

"I should pack. We could leave first thing tomorrow morning."

"Whoa, Nellie. I just got here. You really know how to make a girl feel welcome."

"Oh, Luce, I'm sorry. It's just that this is the evidence I've been looking for—something I could take to Mr. Densworth Lion, proof that my dream could work. Why, if I could provide evidence that a badger, hyena, polar bear, orangutan, and tiger are living together, well, that is the proof I need. I must take my camera." She smiled smugly. "We'll get a good night's rest, leave first thing in the morning. Oh, I'm so excited. And, we'll be back in time for dinner on Sunday. When we return, you can go with me to dinner. You don't have plans, do you? I'm sure they, Mr. and Mrs. Densworth Lion, wouldn't mind one more."

"Me? You want to take me?" She paused. "Oh, I see. You want me served up for dinner as well." She cooed a laugh. "Well, I guess we could go talk with the animals in the tunnels. I have been trying to entice you into trying city life again. Who knows? You may not want to come back to this rustic existence." Luce finished her cup of chai.

CHAPTER FOUR

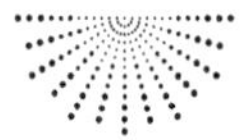

*L*uce, with baggy, half-opened eyes and ruffled feathers, staggered from her bed into the kitchen.

"Oh, you're up?" Ethel greeted her friend in a cheery voice.

"Who could sleep with all of that racket? Pots and pans banging, a teapot whistle going off. It took me forever to get to sleep. The city is noisy, but it's a different noise. I look at it as one harmonious blur, the way you feel about chanting. This forest noise is scary. And my back has a horrible kink. However do you sleep on such a soft nest? I'm used to stone window sills. My back will never be the same." Luce arched backward, rubbing her backside with her wing.

Ethel rushed over and pushed forcibly on her friend's back. There was a pop.

"Oh, Ethel, you're a lifesaver. I think that did the trick. Where did you learn that move?"

"One doesn't practice yoga in an ashram for years and not learn a few tricks."

"Now that my back feels better, is there coffee? A full cup. All I ever get is the remnants humans leave at the green mermaid store, and believe me, they rarely ever leave anything."

"There's tea, but I'll put a pot of coffee on."

A few moments later, Ethel handed her friend a steaming cup. Luce sighed, breathing in the liquid's aroma before taking a hearty gulp. She coughed, spewing the liquid from her beak. "What is this?"

"Coffee," Ethel said.

"What's in it?"

"In the forest we use acorns."

Luce frowned.

"You'll get used to it," Ethel said.

"Hopefully not. But it did wake me up." Luce uttered a sigh of relief and fully opened her eyes. "It's still dark out. What time is it?"

"A little after five."

"In the morning?"

"Of course, in the morning. I've been up since four, getting everything together."

"Together for what?"

"Our trip."

"Trip? Oh, trip. I almost forgot." Luce looked at her friend perplexed. "You're serious about visiting Badger's little band of ragamuffins?"

Ethel looked at Luce in utter disbelief. "Yes, I'm serious. It's coming back to me how you never were a morning person. A hearty breakfast should put you on track."

"Ethel, you also may remember I don't do breakfast."

"Nonsense, dear. You're in the forest now. Everyone here does breakfast. We have biscuits and honey. Brandon Bear, down the way, has the best honey."

"I'm sure it's great, Ethel, but it's too early for me. A dip in the lake might wake me up."

"Okay, whatever you wish."

LUCE HOPPED BACK AND FORTH, SHOOK HER FEATHERS, and toweled herself dry.

"You look much better," Ethel said.

"I feel better. But it's still awfully early."

She watched curiously as Ethel put various covered plates in a box before volunteering. "Let me help you with that."

Together, they loaded up Ethel's culinary concoctions. The most pungent aromas filled the tiny kitchen. "We'll move this box out to the front of the cottage and then onto the cart."

Ethel looked around and double-checked that everything was in order in her cottage. "Are we all set?" she asked.

"I was set a good hour ago," Luce said with a roll of her eyes. "I'm not sure why we need all this food for a day's trip."

"Where I come from…"

"India?"

"Yes, India," Ethel continued, "everyone packs sufficient food for outings."

"Sufficient? I would say far more than sufficient. Why, this is enough for a human buffet. Have you seen the portions of food that humans eat?"

"Yes, I have."

"And what they throw away." Luce shook her head. "Humans waste way too much. You don't see animals wasting. Hmm," Luce said, eyeing over the food. "The good news is that we will have plenty of leftovers—enough to take to our friends."

"The badger, polar bear, hyena, orangutan, and tiger?"

"Yes, them. Packing all this food is a good idea. They could use it."

"I hope they will be our friends, my friends that is, as I haven't yet met them. They are already yours."

"Badger is a friend. The others are more like acquaintances."

"Luce, do you think they will see us? I would hate to travel all the way to the city only to be turned away."

"Of course they will, especially since we come bearing gifts."

"Gifts!" Ethel shrieked.

"Yes, the food."

"No, I mean, we should take gifts."

"I'm sure the food will be enough," Luce said.

"No, no, a good guest always takes something. Oh

my, oh my. What do I have on such short notice?" Ethel looked around. "I don't know what I have they would like. We will have to make a stop. We will take a little side trip to Squirrelly Emporium. It's on the way. Well, nearly on the way."

"The squirrels have an emporium?" her friend asked.

"That's what they call it. It's not as big as the shops in the city, but it winds in so many different directions. They have been squirreling away various trinkets for years. They have a rather large inventory."

"An inventory of what?" Luce asked.

"Oh, of this and that. Mostly that. Things discarded by humans, a lot of art and crafts, a lot of things made from nutshells. Believe me, you can find anything there. Things you would never expect to find."

"Oh, I love places like that. I dare say, though, with all the cooking you did this morning, and with stopping to eat, and now with stopping at Squirrelly Emporium, we will do well to make the trip by nightfall."

"Yes, yes. We must get going. This cart will make things easier."

Luce observed it wasn't a cart at all, but a small red wagon, something a human child used. They loaded the dishes from the box into the wagon, leaving enough room for any purchases they might make at the Squirrelly Emporium. She watched as Ethel tied a rope to the handle and around her waist.

They walked along the path taking in the fresh air and breathing in the aroma of the newly formed spring flowers shooting up from the rich compost provided by the rotting leaves from the previous season. Animals were going about their business. Ethel waved to those she knew. And she seemed to know everyone. They stopped every few moments to exchange hellos with this or that animal.

Ethel introduced Luce to the swans on the lake as well as to the oldest resident of the forest, Mr. Thaddeus Tortoise. Ethel remarked at how surprised she was that Thaddeus engaged in conversation.

"It's not usually his custom. He mostly abides within his own little shell," Ethel said.

Luce heaved a heavy sigh. "I think they all smelled the food and thought there was a picnic they hadn't been invited to. Whatever was in that last dish? It was heavy. I had to muster all of my energy to heave it into the cart."

"It was gulab jamun."

"Gulab what?"

"It's a dessert. It's the sugar syrup that makes it heavy."

WITHIN A COUPLE OF HOURS, THEY CAME TO A GNARLY old chestnut tree with a rounded door bearing traces of blue paint, now in peels, with a rickety, rusty sign tacked to it that said SQUIRRELLY EMPORIUM—almost. Both an l and an m was missing.

"Are you sure they haven't gone out of business?" Luce asked.

"It may look bad on the outside, but I assure you they are still here. It's a family run business. Sebastian Squirrel manages it, and he is getting old. I'm afraid his son, Sam, is not all that interested in the business."

"What is he interested in?"

"Teenage stuff, I guess. I think he is what you call a nerd."

"Oh," said Luce. "Should I stay out here with the food?"

"No, whatever for?"

"We can't leave the cart unattended. Someone will steal it with all its contents."

"Why we haven't had a theft in this area for, well, I can't say we've ever had a theft in the forest."

Luce raised the feathers above her eyes. "No theft? Why that is unheard of! You wouldn't dare leave this alone in the city."

"There was one incident, but it was long ago. I don't think he would dare resort to thievery again." Ethel looked off into contemplation before saying, "It will be fine. Besides, I wouldn't dream of you waiting by the cart. There is so much to see inside."

"It doesn't look that big."

"Oh, the entrance is misleading. It leads to an under-ground cavity. Every nook and cranny is packed to the brim with the most delightful finds. One could stay in there for a whole day and still not see everything."

"Ethel, we don't have that much time. You told me we would reach Squirrelly Emporium within an hour. Yet, it took two hours."

"Yes, but you met so many of my friends along the way."

"They were all delightful, but at the rate we are going, we will never make the city by nightfall."

"Not to worry, Luce. We will pick up what we need and be on our way as soon as possible."

A bell rang as they entered the shop. A gray squirrel making notes in a ledger looked up as they entered. "Welcome, welcome," he said. "Miss Ethel Peacock, I haven't seen you in the longest time. Been staying out of trouble, I hope."

"That is what she has me for," Luce piped in. "I mean trouble."

"Oh, Mr. Sebastian Squirrel, this is my dear friend, Luce, from the city. Her middle name *is* trouble."

Luce's feathers turned a slight shade of pink.

"Oh, you do say. We don't get many city critters around here. I have cousins who live in the city. Haven't seen them in ages. I get word from them through my delivery squirrels. Always sending invitations for them to come for a visit, but I guess park life keeps them busy."

"You must go visit them," Luce said.

"Yes, yes, my wife and I often talk about it, but this place keeps us both hopping. So, what brings you here?" Sebastian Squirrel asked.

"We are on a mission, or perhaps a quest is more like it," Ethel said.

"A mission? A quest? Either one sounds utterly spectacular. You have piqued my curiosity."

"Yes, we are headed for the city to see friends, and we must take gifts," Luce said.

"We definitely have gifts," Sebastian Squirrel said. "Do you know what you are looking for?"

Ethel sighed. "No, might you help? We need one gift each for an orangutan, a badger, a polar bear, a hyena, and a tiger."

"Oh my. This trip to the city you are taking is getting more interesting by the minute."

"While it is a quest, in some ways it is more of a business trip," Ethel said.

"Yes, Ethel wants to see them about starting a school," Luce said.

"A school? How fascinating," Sebastian Squirrel said. "Follow me, and while we find the perfect gifts, you must tell me all about it."

They went down a great way before reaching the first room. Roots protruded from the dirt above them. All roots were utilized. Ethel ducked and dodged so as not to bump her head on the objects hanging from them. Luce had no problem. Some of the objects were made by animals, but most were man-made. Luce strained her neck looking up. Items stacked on top of each other resembled the skyscrapers back home. "Why, I wouldn't know where to begin," she said.

Just then, the shop bell sounded. "That must be Oliver Owl, my accountant. I must go over the books with him. You know how hard it is to get an appointment with the owls."

"I do, indeed," Ethel said. "Cornelius Owl promised

I would have one of the first editions of the *Harry Potter* book he is translating. He tells me owls figure quite prominently in the story."

"Sam is ready to camp out by the owls' study in anticipation of the books. I hear Cornelius has all the owls working furiously on the translations. I've also heard they have run into some snags— some new language he is not used to humans using."

"I have every faith in Cornelius and his apprentices in solving it."

A loud *ahem* sounded from above. "I must go. I so wanted to hear about this great expedition. Oh well, another time," said Sebastian Squirrel. "One does not want to make the owls angry."

"No, one doesn't," Ethel said.

"I will send Sam to help you. In the meantime, please look around."

"Thank you, Sebastian," Ethel said.

"Nice to meet you," Luce said.

"Likewise."

"An old rusty key," Luce said, examining the odd shape of the incisions. "Wonder what it could open? I bet it could tell some stories."

"I'm sure it could if it could talk," Ethel said.

"You're the psychic one, Ethel. What does it tell you?"

"It tells me some human discarded it because they forgot what it opened."

"I would like to think of it as a key to the city. It would make a perfect gift for Badger. If anyone deserves a key to the city, it is Badger."

"Why, Luce, that is a great idea."

"I could shine that up for you." A shaggy, unkempt young squirrel entered. He wore a plaid shirt sporting two pockets bulging over with pens, a smartphone, a music pod, all stuffed into slightly yellowed pocket protectors. One earplug remained in his ear while another dangled down his shirt. A jumbled, muffled sound of drums and guitars echoed from the unused earbud.

"You must be Sam," Ethel said.

"Yep, Samuel Squirrel at your service. My friends call me Sammy."

"Well, Samuel…" Ethel said.

"Sammy's fine. Or Sam," he said while reaching for his music pod, turning it off. "I'm getting a little too old for Sammy."

"Sam, your father said you could help us with gifts. We seem to have found one. It is for a badger. But we will need something for an orangutan, a hyena, a tiger, and a polar bear."

Sam's eyes grew big.

"It's a long story," Luce said.

"I love stories. I'm only working in my dad's shop to save up for a computer. My dream is to become an author."

"An author. My, my," said Ethel Peacock. "Usually, writing is reserved for the owls."

"But who's to say a squirrel can't write. Squirrels read. So, why can't we write?"

"Why, no reason at all. I think it is a fine aspiration," Ethel said.

"My friend has a dream of a school where all animals work together. Sam would be a fine candidate for your school. Don't you think so, Ethel?"

"Yes, I think you are right, Luce."

"That's why we are going to see Badger, Orangutan, Hyena, Polar Bear, and Tiger," Luce said.

"Wow. Usually, those guys don't get along with each other."

"These do," Luce said. "They escaped from the zoo and are living underground in the city."

"Wow. Hiding out? Like gangsters?"

"Yes, hiding out. But not like gangsters. More like refugees. And that is why…"

"You must find gifts for them. To make their lives more tolerable."

"You are a perceptive lad," Ethel said.

Sam smiled. "I know something a polar bear might like. Right this way." Sam stopped at a display case covered in dust. With an embarrassed grin, he wiped it off with the edge of his shirt. He raised the lid and pulled out a tiny, battery-operated fan. "It must get hot in the city. Polar bears like the cold. This might help."

"Indeed, it might. What do you think, Luce?"

"I think it would be a wonderful gift."

"And the batteries are included. Can you tell me about the others?" Sam asked.

"I haven't met them. Luce, what can you tell us?"

"Orangutan smiles a lot, showing all of his teeth. He is by far the most agreeable. Hyena might be the comedian of the lot. He is rather loud and boisterous as I remember. Tiger, hmm, what can I say about Tiger. I believe he comes from India, like you, Ethel. He is rather proud, I think."

"Let me see, let me see," Sam said, his paw to his chin, his eyes moving up and down over the items on the shelves. "A nice hat to go with the orangutan's smile? Something to make his smile stand out. This way, ladies." Sam stopped at a rather tall shelf. He climbed up a ladder and pulled down a baseball cap. "Extra-extra-large should fit."

"I wonder what the hawk stands for?" Luce asked.

"I don't know, but I like that it has a hawk on it. The hawk is a messenger from the divine. Okay, Sam, we'll take it. Three down, two to go."

"Hmm, and you say the hyena is a comedian. I have just the thing. I love this one. He will too." Sam went behind a counter and came back with a canister.

"What is it?" asked Luce.

"Open it and see."

Luce pulled off the lid. Both she and Ethel shrieked and jumped back. Sam was rolling on the floor with laughter.

"It's a gag. A snake in a can."

"Yes, I think Hyena might appreciate that," Luce said, fanning herself with one wing.

"One left—Tiger," said Ethel.

"Yes, and I've already thought of something." Sam went behind the counter again and returned with a small box. He opened it to reveal a gold medal. "It's for bravery," Sam said. "And it is attached to this colorful ribbon. He can wear it around his neck."

"It's perfect," said Luce.

"Down this corridor, we have some nice things for ladies," Sam said.

"Maybe next time," Ethel said. "We must get going. We have a whole day's journey ahead of us. You are quite the sales squirrel I must say."

"Dad lets me keep a percentage toward my computer. He says I'll appreciate it more if I earn it myself."

"Your father is a wise squirrel."

"Do you want these wrapped? Wrapping is free."

"Normally, I would say yes, but we really are in a hurry," Ethel said.

Sam put the items in a bag and handed it to Luce while Ethel counted out what she owed.

"You won't forget me when you start your school, will you? You'll have a writing course, I hope."

"No, Sam, I definitely won't forget you, and yes, I hope we will have a writing course, among many other subjects."

They made their way back toward the front of the store. Sebastian Squirrel and Oliver Owl were busy pouring over the books. Sebastian looked up. "Did Sam take care of you?"

"Yes, you have a fine boy."

Sebastian smiled with pride. "I was telling Oliver that you wanted to start a school."

"Oliver, this is my dear friend Luce," Ethel said.

"Pleased to meet you. Who is this school for?" Oliver inquired, dragging out the word *who* as most owls did.

"Why, for all animals," Ethel Peacock said.

"All animals?" Oliver Owl put his wing up to his chin as if in deep thought. "What a splendid idea," he said after some consideration.

Ethel squealed in delight, thrilled to get the approval of an owl which was a rare thing to come by. "We could use someone strong in numbers," she said.

"I will definitely give this some thought—your school," he said.

"Oh, not just my school—a school for all animals."

"Sebastian, I think we are finished." Oliver Owl gathered up his accounting books and tucked them securely under his wing. "Good day to you all." He looked at Ethel. "I will run this school idea by my associates." The three of them watched in awe as Oliver Owl departed. The owls gleaned the most respect in the animal community, being regarded as the wisest.

"We must also be on our way as well," Ethel said.

"Good luck to you and a safe journey," Sebastian said.

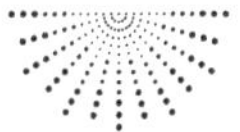

CHAPTER FIVE

"That was most delicious," Luce said. "Especially the dessert. But I feel the heaviness of the syrup has weighed me down. I don't know if I can walk another mile. Flying is my preferred mode of travel, you know. I don't know if I could even lift off now."

"Yes, I fear I slow you down, but as you know, flying is not my strong suit. Not over long distances."

"Being on the ground has thrown me off."

"I regret we have made little progress," Ethel said.

"I have to say, the springiness of the grass is much easier on the claws than city concrete."

"That's good to hear since we should step up our pace if we are to make the city before nightfall."

"I think that would mean ignoring everyone we see. You know everyone in this forest, I think."

"Hardly everyone, but when I see someone, I can't be rude."

"I take it you are referring to me," Luce said in indignation. "Interrupting that woodpecker in the middle of his lecture on what woods were the best to peck was not being rude."

"Oh, Wendell, he *is* a bit of a windbag."

"A bit?" Luce exclaimed. "Why, if I hadn't said anything, we would still be there, listening to him rattle on about all the various aromas and textures of the trees in the forest. He acted as if the trees were fine wines to be savored."

"They are," Ethel said. "Where would we be without the trees?"

"No trees?" Luce exclaimed. "I tell you where we would be, the city already."

"You have a point, there," Ethel confirmed.

"And Rhonda Rabbit. I thought we would never get away from her."

"She is one of the kindest creatures in the forest. All the rabbits are for that matter."

"One compliment after the other. I thought they would never end."

"I didn't see you wanting to get away when she was singing your praises. All that stuff about being such a sophisticated bird from the city. If you are so eager to get back to the city, why don't you fly ahead without me? I can meet up with you there."

"No, no, I wouldn't dream of that. I apologize for being cranky. It's just that when I came to see you, I was thinking of a peaceful, relaxing stay, not hiking through a forest without end. I'm surprised you know the way with all the little side paths and forks in the trail. How you maneuver on the ground the way you do, I will never know."

"Do you see that side trail to the right?"

"Yes, what of it? Please tell me it's a shortcut."

"On the contrary. It's where the foxes live. It's called Fox Hollow. Mostly, the foxes are okay, but Filbert Fox is a different story. No, no, you want to steer clear of him."

"Something tells me Mr. Filbert Fox has something to do with the incident you referred to earlier."

"You are right, but please don't ask me. It depresses me to dwell on it, let alone talk about it. Do you see the path ahead, the one veering off to the left?"

"Yes, is *that* the shortcut?"

"It's where the owls live." Ethel gave her friend a mischievous smile.

"No, no, no, Ethel. We will never reach the city by nightfall at this rate."

"We must pay our respects. Besides, aren't you curious about how the translations are coming along for *Harry Potter*?"

"Not in the least. You know I'm not one for reading novels. I thought you were impatient to talk to Badger's crew?"

"I am, but it's all about the journey, not the destination."

"What is that? Some Hindu mumbo jumbo?"

"We will just be a moment, honest," Ethel said, looking at her friend with pleading eyes. "I know you enjoyed conversing with the beavers about their dam project."

"I enjoyed it because they were all about the work and not talking about it."

"That dam was a sight to behold, though. Wasn't it?"

"I will give you that."

Ethel set the cart off the path that led to the owls' treehouse, lest its presence should block anyone that needed access. The structure was a massive conglomerate of various species of trees, mostly evergreens, a wise location for the owls as the greenery provided camouflage year-round. A young owl passed them in a blur, totally unaware of their presence. The owls were notorious for their couriers darting back and forth, gathering much-needed information for the projects they took on. Although translations were their main forte, they excelled in many others: graphic design, interpretation of laws in the forest, psychology, and mysticism, among others. Mainly, they were the keepers of the sacred knowledge.

"We must be very quiet," Ethel said as she lifted her train and flew up several stories to the owls' offices with Luce right behind her.

"We are here to see Cornelius Owl if he could spare a moment," Ethel told the receptionist.

The receptionist looked up. "Miss Ethel Peacock,

you are just the person I hoped to see. A courier went out for you earlier. He came back reporting you weren't home and that your place looked all locked up. And as for Cornelius, he is out of town on business."

"A courier for me?" Ethel fanned herself.

"Yes, I believe you ran into Oliver Owl earlier this morning?"

"Why, yes, we did."

"He sent a courier out to find you."

"But we told Oliver Owl we were traveling."

"Wires obviously got crossed. The courier was our newest trainee." The receptionist shook her head ever so slightly. "This young generation. Sometimes I fear… well, enough of that. Ola Owl would like to speak with you."

"Ola Owl," Ethel shrieked.

"Who is Ola Owl?" Luce asked.

"WHO is Ola Owl? WHO is Ola Owl?" the receptionist repeated, alarmed at the pigeon's ignorance.

"Luce is new to the forest. She is from the city."

"Oh, *well,* that explains it," said the receptionist, rolling her eyes. "Please follow me." She led them through a complex network of offices spread about the large branches of about thirty trees, all housing owls busy at work, hardly looking up to acknowledge their presence. "So many deadlines. We are always up against deadlines it seems."

They came to the last office, larger and more decorated than the previous offices which housed stacks of books, reaching sometimes to the ceiling amid papers and computers. A few owls had pictures of loved ones on the desks and diplomas scattered along the walls, the blank spaces that didn't have stacks of books against them. Ola Owl's office was posh in comparison. Only one bookshelf lined the back, and the books looked to be rare and old. Off to the side were scrolls encased in glass. Among them were clay tablets with small markings in neat rows.

Ethel stood in the doorway taking it all in before entering with Luce in tow. She didn't know quite what to do and fumbled about awkwardly. To gain an audience with Ola Owl, especially one she didn't seek, was extraordinary. Should she bow at Ola's claws like the monks did when coming upon someone holy? She took a few steps forward and stood transfixed for a moment and curtsied and introduced Luce.

"I'm most happy to make both of your acquaintances," Ola Owl said.

Ola moved with an ease and down-to-earthiness Ethel didn't expect. If anything, she was informal and plain, dare she say it. Yet, she ran this intricate nexus. Ethel couldn't help but ogle her collection of articles which resembled that of Squirrelly Emporium except with the touch of an interior designer as each piece was given due reverence in its positioning in Ola Owl's office.

"I see you are admiring my accumulation of treasures," Ola Owl said.

"Yes, they are all quite remarkable," Ethel said in awe. Luce acquiesced.

"Some have been handed down for generations from my family. Others were gifts."

There were pictures of wonders of the ancient world, some in black and white, dating back to when photography was first invented and others in color. Off in the corner was a small mummy. It looked to be a human child, one with an elongated skull. There was something most curious, although all of it was unconventional—a crystal skull given a prominent place on a pedestal. Off to the side, a bouquet of peacock feathers shot from what appeared to be an ancient vase.

"Dorothy, please prepare some tea. Darjeeling, if we have it and some light refreshment," Ola Owl said to the receptionist who stood in the doorway. "I believe Darjeeling is a favorite of India. And please, won't you both take a seat?"

Ethel noted the various sizes of chairs surrounding Ola's desk.

"We get all sizes of animals here," she said. "However, still we cannot accommodate them all. The giraffes will have to peep through the window, and no doubt they will still need to duck." Ola burst out laughing. "Giraffes ducking! I do believe I made a joke. Giraffes and ducks are about the most opposite as animals can get. Wouldn't you agree?"

"Why, yes, I would agree, but giraffes? There are no giraffes in the nature preserve," Ethel said.

"Not yet, but they will arrive soon. Coming on a boat from Africa sometime this week. We have eyes and ears everywhere."

"Giraffes? And from Africa."

"Perhaps even elephants. I think there was talk," Ola added.

"Elephants!" Ethel exclaimed. "We have elephants in India. I do miss my old home."

"I feel I have been remiss in not welcoming you to our forest abode sooner. How long has it been since you moved here?"

"Nearly one year ago," Ethel replied.

"My, my, time flies." She laughed, sputtering out a few *who's* before gaining her composure and putting on a serious face. "Well, as you can see, there is always so much to do. You saw how hard the owls work as you passed their offices. There is a lot to overseeing our little forest."

"Yes, everything is remarkable," Ethel said.

"I saw you eyeing the peacock feathers. I want to assure you no peacock was harmed in collecting them. They were part of the ones shed as your species does every year."

"Not many know that," Ethel said.

"They don't call us wise for nothing," Ola laughed again. "Sit down, sit down. You must be weary. You have been traveling all day. I hear you are on a quest."

Ethel gathered her feathers and became comfortable in a wicker chair. Luce flew up to the chair beside Ethel's and nestled in.

"Yes, how did you know?" Luce asked.

"Remember, Luce, Oliver Owl," Ethel said.

"Oh, right, right. Oliver Owl." She looked at Ola.

"This whole trip has been a whirlwind of an experience for me."

"I think it may turn into a bigger experience than you might ever have imagined. We, the owls, find this whole concept of a school to be enchanting."

"How so?" Ethel asked.

"We have conferred and agree a school for all animals would be a good thing. We are ready to give it our full support."

"You are? You will?" Ethel almost toppled out of her chair. The backing of the owls could make her dream a reality.

"And you met with Densworth?"

"Yes," Ethel said, surprised that Ola only addressed him as Densworth and not Mr. Densworth Lion. "But that meeting did not go well at all."

"So, I hear. But not to worry. I can handle Densworth if need be. But for now, I think you are doing quite well. Tell me about this school you propose."

Dorothy returned with tea and shortbread cookies. Ola Owl expressed intrigue with Ethel's aspirations of a school where all animals worked together, nodding her head off and on, as much as owls can do, before seeing them off.

"YOU HAVEN'T SAID A WORD SINCE OUR LAST STOP," Luce said.

"It's just that this journey has been so extraordinary. I never dreamed I would be invited to Ola Owl's sanctuary."

"Yes, it was astounding, but it wasn't her home, only her office."

"Can you imagine what her home is like?"

"My guess is it is rather drab, not like her office at all."

"Why do you say that, Luce?"

"I have a feeling she isn't one to take her work home with her. She was one down-to-earth owl if you ask me."

"That is precisely what I was thinking," Ethel concurred.

The sun was shining low through the trees. "We will not make the city by nightfall," Luce said, resigned.

"Yes, I know. And I am surprised you are not complaining about it."

"I apologize, Ethel. I have a confession to make."

"Oh?"

"I missed you, my dear friend, but the main reason for my visit was to get away from Santiago for a while. I didn't even tell him where I was going, hoping he might become jealous, thinking I might have run away with another pigeon. I know I have a reputation for being flirty, but I would settle down with Santiago in a heartbeat. I also dream of having little hatchlings."

"You, Luce?"

"Don't act so surprised. It won't happen though. Oh Ethel, one day I saw him with my best friend, my best pigeon friend, as you are my *best* friend. It was the last feather. I didn't even confront him. I immediately sent word to you asking if I could visit. I was so relieved when you said yes."

"How could you possibly think I would say no?"

"I didn't know. I was on shaky ground. I thought Santiago loved me. I doubted everything, even *our* friendship."

"Luce, never doubt that. We will always remain friends. I will never forget how you saved me that day."

Luce smiled. "When you sent back word, I immediately packed my bag, and well, here I am. I can relax and let off steam with you. I can do that with Santiago as well, or could until I saw him with Gloria. The day I saw them together, I felt as if my feathers were on fire. I knew if I stayed in the city I might do something I would regret. But after one night, I missed him so. And although I was perfectly content to spend the week in the forest with you, forgetting about city life, and even letting you try to teach me to meditate again, the way you used to do, I was inwardly happy when you said you wanted us to travel back to the city together. I knew with my best friend by my side I could face him again. At least that is what I thought at first."

"Ah," Ethel cooed, hugging her friend. "But now?"

"Feeling the earth under my claws, breathing in the fresh air, being greeted with such friendliness from so many animals, squirrels and owls in particular, and not being around humans, has given me a new perspective. I think I could even learn to like that woodpecker.

Rhonda Rabbit was a bit much to take. She is so nice. Niceness is not something you encounter much of in the city, especially from humans. I suppose in time I could get used to it. You are blessed to have such a community of caring fellow-creatures around you."

"Indeed, I am, but I wouldn't put humans down. It was humans who made this into a nature preserve and made it off-limits to most of their own kind. Occasionally, you will see a forest ranger, in particular the forest ranger with the dog and cats. Sometimes, there is a younger one with him, someone who is almost a man, but not quite. Fortunately, they are the ones who respect our way of life."

"Since we will not make the city by nightfall, what will we do?" Luce asked.

"Betsy Bear's Bed and Breakfast is up ahead. We can spend the night and commence our journey in the morning all refreshed."

"A nice dip in a pond or lake would be good."

"Oh, Betsy boasts of having all the amenities. We will have a delightful breakfast before leaving. She procures her honey from Brandon Bear. She is too busy with running the inn to get it herself. Also, you will meet an array of animals. It's hard to say who might be there at any given time."

"That sounds nice. While my wings have been properly rested on this journey, my claws are killing me. They need a nice soak." Luce sprang backward, perking her ears. "Ethel, did you hear something?"

"Yes, and I see something, or rather someone. I have smelled his presence for some time."

"Who is it?"

"If my eyes are not deceiving me, I believe it is Filbert Fox."

"You mentioned him once before."

"Yes, and we want to avoid him at all costs."

"Why is that?"

Ethel shoved her friend back. "Sorry, Luce." Ethel pulled the cart up behind the bushes. "Let's wait here until he passes. Try not to make a sound."

They waited, breathing shallowly until Filbert strode past them, talking to himself in low murmurs.

"I think he is no longer a threat," Ethel said.

"He seemed distracted by something. Hardly a threat at all."

"Maybe not a threat. But one can never tell what Filbert might do. Better not to engage with him. We have this cart full of food and gifts. I would like both us and the cart to make it to the city intact."

"Such a bad dude," Luce cooed. "Whatever did he do?"

"It happened when I first arrived. Sometime I will tell you about it, but not today. I would like to stay on track regarding our mission. Be assured, Filbert Fox is not one you want to mess with. Let us hurry. Betsy Bear's place is not far."

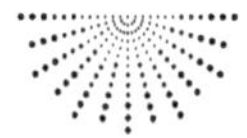

CHAPTER SIX

"Guests, how nice. Ethel, I haven't seen you in ages. Are you traveling?"

"Yes, Betsy, headed to the city. Please tell us you are not booked up."

"Almost. I hope you do not care to share a room? I don't believe I know your travel companion."

"This is Luce, my dearest friend. Luce is from the city, and we are traveling back to her home."

"You're not moving out of the forest, are you? I, for one, would hate to see you go."

"No, I wouldn't dream of leaving this community."

"I'm glad to hear it. Well, well, come in, come in. We've already served dinner. But I'm sure we could rustle you something up from the kitchen if you like."

Ethel looked at Luce, whose eyes where drooping. "No, I think we both would like to get to bed and get an early start."

"Are you sure? A spoonful of honey might make you sleep better."

"Believe me, we won't have any trouble sleeping. It's been a long day."

"Okay then, if you insist. Let me show you to your room. Do you want to leave your cart downstairs? It will be perfectly safe in my office."

"That would be fine," Ethel said. Ethel and Luce followed Betsy Bear up two flights of stairs. She led them into an attic cove with a set of twin beds.

"I hope this will do. I know you both like to nest up high. It's the only room we have left."

"This will do nicely."

"Breakfast is from six until nine. Do you have a preference?"

"Six will be fine," Ethel said. "We want to get an early start." Luce turned her head from the pillow she was staring at and shot daggers at Ethel through slit eyelids.

"Perhaps eight will be better," Ethel corrected. "We do need to catch up on some much-needed rest."

"Eight it is, then. Good night." She closed the door behind her.

Ethel looked over to see Luce had already tucked herself under the covers of one of the twin beds. She did the same.

"Good night, Luce."

"Good night, Ethel."

~

"THAT LAKE WAS AMAZING—ZEN-LIKE. I'M NOT SURE why, but I feel so calm," Luce said.

"Yes, the fresh water of the forest is far superior to the chlorinated water in the city fountains."

"I have to agree," Luce said. "I am starved. Is it time for breakfast?"

They walked into the dining room to find Betsy Bear serving biscuits and scones with an assortment of marmalades, jellies, and honey. A fresh bouquet of daisies in a cracked honeypot adorned the center of the table. A pot of steaming tea rested on a bamboo tray with eight cups circling the pot.

"Welcome. I hope you got a good night's sleep. You are the first to arrive for the eight o'clock seating." No sooner than Betsy spoke, a family of three raccoons entered. An older badger and his wife followed them. "Oh dear, we are missing one. Well, I'm sure he will arrive shortly. Please take a seat. There is one for each of you."

They each pulled out their chairs. Betsy Bear had seen to it they all had chairs that would accommodate their different sizes, including a stack of pillows for the young raccoon who was a toddler. The one empty chair next to Ethel's was also stacked high with pillows implying the absentee guest was small in stature.

Betsy Bear began a round of introductions when an out-of-breath owl, looking at a pocket watch suspended by a chain around his thick neck, entered. It was none other than Cornelius Owl. "Am I late?"

"No, Cornelius, you are just in time. Now that we

are all here please go ahead, eat up. I know you must be hungry. I will make introductions. We have Ronald and Rita Raccoon and their little one, Ronald, Jr., Bradley and Bertha Badger, Ethel Peacock, and her friend Luce Pigeon, and our esteemed guest, Cornelius Owl. It is always so good to have a visit from our owl community. We appreciate so much what they do in our little forest." Nods and hellos echoed around the table.

While all vied for Cornelius Owl's attention, he immediately turned his head in a clockwise position and said to Ethel Peacock, "Back at Owl Headquarters we are much in awe of this idea of a school you have."

"A school? A school?" they all questioned.

"A raccoon school, perhaps? Will there be sports at this school?" Ronald Raccoon asked. "My boy, Ronnie, will make a fine guard. He's strong like his old dad." Rita Raccoon held her head down in embarrassment. Her son had not yet mastered coordination. A pile of biscuit crumbs surrounded his plate and the floor below. The table occupants held back snickers, observing the kit had biscuit crumbles stuck to the honey surrounding his mouth.

Ethel cleared her throat in an effort not to laugh out loud. "The school is yet a dream. I would hope it would take into consideration the various talents of each individual student, whether it be sports or math, so we might develop that talent."

"But you didn't say. Will there be a school for raccoons, in particular?" Ronald Raccoon asked.

"It will be a school for all animals." Luce piped in.

"All animals!" Betsy Bear exclaimed, almost dropping the teapot while refilling Mr. and Mrs. Badger's cups.

Cornelius Owl offered a knowing smile. "I, for one, think it is a marvelous idea."

"Thank you, Cornelius," Ethel said.

"It doesn't matter either way to us," Bertha Badger said with a sad expression. "We lost our only son a while ago."

"Oh, I'm so sorry," Ethel said. "Was he ill?"

Bertha burst into tears. Her husband withdrew a handkerchief he kept in his vest pocket and handed it to his wife. "It's best we don't talk about it. The mere mention of his name always evokes this reaction in her. Please, please continue. Tell us about the school."

Feeling bad because of her faux pas, Ethel looked in the other direction of the table. "it is only a dream at this point. I have talked to Mr. Densworth Lion about it. He did not take too kindly to the idea."

"The lions," Betsy Bear growled. "No, the lions wouldn't. The lions think they are better than everyone else in the forest."

"But we still have hope," Luce chimed in. "He has invited Ethel to come to his home for dinner this coming Sunday."

The others *oohed* and *ahhed*, but Ethel couldn't place whether it was due to fear or hope.

"I think it is brave of you. All animals working together. In the city, it was every animal for himself. One would think we could have banded together as we all had one common threat—humans," Bradley Badger said.

"Ethel, tell them why we are traveling," Luce insisted.

"Yes, yes, tell us," they all echoed.

"We are on a mission, or a quest, to visit animals who are living underground in the city. Luce told me about these animals."

"Yes, there is a polar bear, a hyena, a tiger, an orangutan, and a badger. They escaped from the zoo," Luce said.

At the word badger, Bertha Badger's sobbing commenced again. "Now, now, Dear," her husband consoled. "If you will excuse us, I think we might retire to our room for a little while longer before taking that hike through the forest we were planning after breakfast. It has been a pleasure meeting all of you. My wife and I wish you safe travels. The best of luck with this school idea," he said.

Everyone said goodbye to the Badgers and watched quietly as they left the room.

When they were out of earshot, Ethel said, "I feel so awful. If I had known, I would never have said anything."

"Nor I," said Luce. "I would have omitted there was a badger in the group."

"It couldn't be helped," Betsy Bear said. "The Badgers are spending the entire week. Retired now, they are looking for a new home. I'm certain our little forest community will give them what they need. Who knows?

Perhaps volunteering at your school and working with young ones may help heal the hole in Bertha Badger's heart."

"Yes, that might be nice," Ethel said. "But the school is only an idea at this point. I only presented the idea to Mr. Densworth Lion a couple of days ago, and already everyone seems to think it is a done deal, everyone but Densworth Lion, that is."

"Everything is born from an idea," Cornelius Owl said. "We must not let the idea die. We must bring it to fruition."

"Exactly what my wise grandmother would have said," Ethel agreed.

"Here, here," the ones remaining at the table shouted.

"It won't be long, now. I see the skyscrapers in the distance. Are you okay? The contents of that cart look like they have doubled in size."

"Betsy Bear insisted I take several jars of honey as an offering. She said it was the least she could do to further the cause."

"Oh, we have a cause now, do we?" Luce asked.

"I suppose we do."

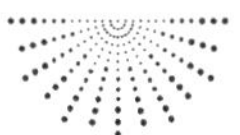

CHAPTER SEVEN

The foliage changed from wild and gnarly to manicured and symmetrical. Ethel recognized it immediately as the park, her former abode. Bridges curved over artificial streams. Various sizes of fountains spurted water.

"We're here," Luce said. This was after Luce's insistence at veering off course and stopping at a small café where humans ate under green umbrellas on the sidewalk. Ethel hid behind the boxed shaped bushes as she knew the sight of a peacock would cause a disturbance. Thoughts of her brief time in the city crowded her mind; she traveled undercover mostly at night, ducking in and out of the seediest of places for fear of being captured. Luce, on the other hand, could roam freely. The park was where Luce called home, although she spent most of her time perched on the windowsills of the high-rise apartments across from the park. How Luce could stand living in such proximity with humans, Ethel would never know.

Ethel let down her guard in the park as humans would think she was part of the ambiance, like the swans on the lake. Most humans seemed friendly enough to her, *ooh*ing and *ahh*ing, and pointing their cameras and phones every time she spread her feathers —even wanting to get into the picture with her. But Luce was a different matter. No one was taking her picture. They shooed her and kicked at her in disgust. How could she stand such prejudiced behavior? However, it didn't seem to faze Luce.

"You see that woman?" Luce asked pointing to a haggard lady on a bench.

"Yes, who is she?"

"A true friend to the pigeons. We call her the pigeon lady. We talk to her and think she understands us. At least she appears to. The other humans steer clear of her. They think she is ready for the looney bin. The men in white coats have taken her away several times, but she always comes back. She sits on the same bench every day, feeding us what she can scrounge up and reading her book. Sometimes she hums to herself, like now."

"That's not humming," Ethel said. "It's a chant. And that book she is reading, I know it."

"But it is a human book," said Luce.

"'Tis so, but the man on the cover is an important saint, revered in India."

"The dark man with the long hair?"

"Yes."

"That's odd," said Luce.

"What's odd?"

"She doesn't have her bicycle. She has an old rusted-out bicycle she rides around on. It's always somewhere near. It's her pride and joy. I hope someone didn't steal it, although I can't think why someone would. It's in such bad shape."

"Maybe it's behind the bushes for safekeeping," Ethel replied.

"Maybe. We should move on," Luce said. "The tunnel entrance is not far."

Ethel looked back at the woman who was waving at them. Both Ethel and Luce raised their feathers to wave back. Ethel's glorious spread of plumage caused the woman to smile.

"Here we are," said Luce. "This is one entrance." They were in a back alley that smelled of fish as the fish market was around the corner. A broken grate covered a hole in the pavement. "I will drop down first and let you know if the coast is clear. No one will think anything of a pigeon down there. Be prepared to get your claws wet. There is always water."

Ethel grunted and wiggled, squeezing her larger body through and floated downward but not before lowering the cart down when Luce let her know it was okay.

If Ethel had thought the city above ground was dirty, the tunnels were a different matter altogether. How could these animals live in such conditions? How could Luce think creeping through stinky, slimy, dark passageways beneath the rumble of heavy trucks and beeping horns would entice her to give up the rustic charm of forest life? She would take the barking dog any day over this. But her friend seemed at home here.

They had been walking through this underground maze for what seemed like forever, trudging toward the bowels of the earth. No sign of the animals Luce told her about. Ethel was beginning to doubt the authenticity of her friend's story. "Maybe they left," Ethel suggested. Luce assured her they hadn't.

Each time Ethel asked if they were getting nearer, Luce told her they were almost there. Was her friend out of her mind? Had she been breathing in exhaust fumes for far too long? However, the smell of the exhaust fumes above ground was nothing compared to this enclosed space. The stench was overbearing. The odors had nowhere to go. They only doubled back on themselves. Luce said you got used to it. Ethel could never get used to it. And if all of those things weren't bad enough, the gas her friend was emitting in her wake was enough to make a rat gag, although there were plenty about, and they were not gagging, but thriving. Luce turned and blushed. "Sorry, something I ate at the green mermaid store went horribly wrong. Usually, I can eat anything."

What could Ethel do? She graciously accepted her apology and said while holding her beak, "Happens to all of us as we age." She realized that wasn't perhaps the most appropriate response and countered with for about the tenth time, "Are we almost there?"

"Almost," Luce said while looking back and giving her friend a dirty look.

Just as Ethel was thinking this was a wild goose chase, that the animals had moved on, she beheld him or what was left of him. She stared at the creature in disbelief. What she saw was a massive piece of grimy brown-streaked fur. It was the backside of an animal she wouldn't have recognized as a polar bear at all.

Luce had warned her. She thought her friend had exaggerated, as Luce had a tendency to do, but if anything, she had understated his condition. His thinning fur hung in shredded tangles down his body, exposing sporadic patches of black. It was the black skin underneath the fur that Luce told her about. She held in a shriek upon seeing a hideous scar at the back of his head. How could that have happened, she wondered? More so, how could such a long gash have closed up on its own? This bear had once been a magnificent specimen, but no more. Living in this environment had taken a toll. Luce, however, didn't seem the least bit alarmed by the beast's appearance.

"Ted E. Bear. My word," Luce exclaimed. "It's been a long time."

The bear turned. What Ethel saw was all that remained of what was once a grand creature, now beaten down by the confines of his horrible underground prison. His eyes bore the defeat as there was no trace of gleam left in them. Ethel did her best not to stare.

"Luce, is that you?" the bear asked in a hoarse voice.

"Yes," she said, cooing and lighting on his back, and then coming back down to the wet ground. "This is my friend, Ethel Peacock."

"Yes, I can see she is a peacock," the bear said with a hint of insult.

Luce whispered to Ethel, "Not to worry. It's his manner." She spoke up, "We are on a mission."

"What sort of mission? I love a good mission, but then those were in the olden days."

"Is there somewhere we could speak? We would like to sit and talk with all the gang."

"I can take you there, but Badger is out. On a *mission,* you might say." He attempted a wink, but his crusted over, reddened eyes fought him. "He is the only one that can move around in the city unnoticed. I would stand out like a sore paw as would Tiger and Orangutan. As for Hyena, well he has grown untrustworthy. Has become a loner of sorts."

"I am so sorry to hear that. I always liked Hyena," Luce said.

The bear grunted and scowled. He walked with a slow sway to his movements. "Follow me," he said. "And as for what I said about Hyena, keep it to yourselves."

"Of course, of course," they both replied.

Shouting and laughter resounded in the distance. Ethel yelped, "Those voices sound human."

"Human children," the bear said.

"What are they doing down here?"

"It is a game to them, a dare you might say. They enter through the storm drains."

"And they don't report you are down here?"

"No, we have an understanding."

"You can communicate?" Ethel asked, surprised.

"Somewhat. Badger has been working out a system of deciphering their language. He almost has it cracked, or so he tells us. Sometimes I think he is bluffing to keep us from eating them, although they wouldn't be worth the trouble, a scrawny, homeless lot, all but one. Occasionally they bring us food which causes me to think he is making progress with them, at least one of them, the one that is different—the outcast."

"An outcast? How sad. How do you know they are homeless?" Ethel asked.

"Badger says it is so. He sees them on the outside. Well, here we are."

Ethel looked around. It was a side entrance to another tunnel that had been blocked, filled in with rubble, what they called home. There were old blankets strewn about along with piles of litter. However, on closer examination, Ethel realized it must be their possessions, a collection of human discards from above, something to make it home. "It is nice," Ethel lied.

The bear growled, "Do not pity me, hen."

Ethel shut her beak.

Ted E. Bear lay down and invited them to do the same. "The others should be here shortly," he said.

Then a most ungodly racket began. Ethel jumped,

spreading her feathers to their full extent as she danced around. "What is that?" she shouted.

"Men in hats," Ted E. Bear shouted back at her.

"Men in hats?"

"Follow me," he yelled. He stood and removed rocks from the back wall. He displaced just enough for himself to squeeze through. "Two stones less this time," he said. Ethel and Luce followed. After they were on the other side, he placed most of the rubble back which muffled the loud sound.

"So, who are these men in hats?" Ethel inquired.

"They work in the tunnels. What you hear is the sound of their machinery, jackhammers. We will have to wait it out. Badger, Orangutan, Tiger, and Hyena cannot make it through without being seen. We may be here a while."

"No matter, right, Ethel? Ted E. Bear comes from a most noble line of kings. I never tire of hearing the story. If you would be so kind while we wait, Mr. Ted E. Bear?" Luce asked.

Ted E. Bear growled, a rather defeated, subdued growl.

"But first, Luce, we must give Mr. Ted E. Bear his gift."

"Gift?" he asked.

"Yes, and food," Luce said.

Ethel reached into the bag and brought out the small fan.

"What is it?" he asked.

"Push the little button to the side," Luce said.

"Ah," he sighed. He held the fan next to his face. After a moment, he asked, "Food? You mentioned food."

"Yes, please, take what you like. There is enough for everyone."

After Ted E. Bear ate his fill which wasn't much as his stomach had shrunk, he expressed his appreciation and began, "I was a small cub, destined for greatness, before the ship pulled up. My friends and I were out swimming. We were catching fish and seals, showing off for the females. There was one in particular," he said, smiling and looking off to the corner for what seemed like a full moment before his lips turned downward.

"We heard thunderous sounds. I now know the sounds came from guns. I felt a sting on my right side. It was nothing. Just a prick, I thought. I even laughed at the fragile humans trying to take me down with something so small.

"All the others ran off. I tried to follow, but I heard a loud thud. It was the sound of my own body falling onto the ice. I looked up. I could see the others off in the distance. They were calling for me. Their images and voices were distorted. I tried to look up. Everything was in slow motion. It was then I realized I was hurt more badly than I had first thought. Everything went blurry and then black. The last thing I saw was humans standing over me. I thought I was at the end of my life, my short life. I later discovered it was not a bullet at all, but a dart, one that filled my bloodstream with a tranquilizer that induced sleep.

"When I awoke, I looked around. I was in a strange place. There was no ice or snow. When I saw the bars, I knew there was no going back. I had no idea how to get back. The enclosure I was in imitated the Arctic area from which I came. But it was a poor substitute. It was not right at all. There were rocks, but not real rocks—something the humans molded from something liquid coming from trucks. I often saw the trucks there, men in hats, different men from the ones in the tunnel, making the fake rocks and fake jungles, our captors appeasing their consciences of putting us behind bars and on public display.

"There were other enclosures with other animals. I could hear their screams. I was in a deep pit with other bears, not all my own species. They were both black and brown. And above us were the humans, all forms, shapes, and sizes, their cubs squealing and shrieking and pointing at us, while the grown ones pointed their cameras. A man or woman always sat in a chair by a sign, talking to them, explaining, answering their questions. I didn't know what he or she said, but I know they knew only a small picture of what we were all about. How could they know? Why would they enslave us? Were they trying to make us like the dogs? My friends and I sometimes saw the dogs when we lived on the ice. They pulled the sleds of humans, the humans who mimicked us, wrapped in our furs, only their bare red or white faces showing.

"Oh, the heat." He picked the fan back up, running it for a while before continuing, "I thought it was hot, even though giant fans blew on us all the time. As you can see, I've grown accustomed to the heat."

Ted E. tugged at his fur with his paw. As he did so, a heavy chunk fell out.

"I was once fat with a lustrous coat. Now, look at me. My skin sags. My hair falls out. I dined on seals and swam all day, hunted, ran, got into all kinds of mischief with my friends. My life was great. My father was a king, and I was to succeed him.

"In the enclosure, I spent my days with the other bears, lazily. There was not much room to roam, not like I was used to. There was a small place to swim. The humans wanted us to swim. I wanted to swim, but I was obstinate. I would not be their slave. The other bears knew no better. They had all been born there. They knew nothing of the outside world."

"Like *The Allegory of the Cave,*" Ethel said.

"What?" asked Luce.

"From *The Republic,* a work by Plato. There are people in a cave, somewhat like this. In this case, though, the bears are kept in a zoo. The zoo is all they have ever known. This is their reality. In the allegory, the people in the cave watch shadows projected on the wall from objects passing in front of a fire behind them. The people or prisoners give names to the shadows. Socrates explains how a philosopher is a prisoner until he discovers the truth that the shadows he sees are not reality at all."

"You said Plato, and now you say Socrates," Luce interrupted.

"Socrates was Plato's teacher," Ethel said. "Anyway, the cave or the zoo is the prison, but the inmates don't see it as such since it has been the only reality they know, what they have been born into. They don't question. The philosopher questions. The philosopher thinks there must be something better out there. Yogis would say in here." Ethel pointed to her heart. "But one day, the prisoners break their bonds and discover it was an illusion."

"As we all must do," said Polar Bear. "But the zoo was no illusion. I lived there, if you could call it living, for many years. And this tunnel, or cave, is also no illusion. I feel its hard walls. There is no fire behind me casting shadows on the wall. And if it were so, for the sake of argument, then you, Miss Ethel Peacock, and you, Miss Luce Pigeon, must be a part of that illusion."

"You may be right, Mr. Bear. I find I question everything," Ethel said.

"Polar Bear, Ethel comes from India, from an ashram, no less. She has been brought up to think this way."

The bear grunted. "I hope you will not say the love of my life was an illusion. There was a female cub from my home—Fay. I can still see her face. At night, I dream of her. I would have made her my queen. I wonder if she is waiting for me. And what of my mother and father? I had a younger brother. It pains me to think Fay might now be married to him. It is the memory of her that keeps me going. So, please do not tell me that Fay was an illusion."

"I am only speculating, philosophizing. Pay no heed, Mr. Bear."

"But you escaped from the zoo," Luce interrupted, trying to keep them on track.

"Yes, some of us did. Something happened. It was in the middle of the night. There was a fierce storm. Some malfunction with all the enclosures. Gates were opening and shutting. I saw my chance and ran. A lot of animals did. Only a few of us made it out of the main gate. We hid for the longest time at a construction site. We disagreed over which direction to go. I wanted to go north. I knew north was my home. The others, south, but it didn't matter. Humans were all around us.

"Badger discovered a small opening in some rubble alongside the construction site and went inside. Badger is a natural burrower. He returned and told us to remove the pile of rock which we did. To hide our whereabouts, we put them all back. That is where we are now. This is where we come to hide when the need arises. On the other side of this wall is the construction site. Badger burrowed through another small opening and found the tunnels.

"We removed thirty-three rocks in all on that day. I was the largest. It took thirty-three stones before I could get through the entrance. Orangutan counted them. He is a born mathematician."

"You said two less rocks today. Is that because you have become smaller?" Ethel asked.

"Yes, a brilliant observation. I have become smaller —four rocks smaller in all. Anyway, the second rock pile led to these tunnels, and here we have been ever since. Every day, we plan and plot our escape, or so we did at first. Now, we only talk about the days before we came into hiding. We have lost hope." He hung his head down. "Humans are our worst enemy, and they surround us. Badger, ironically, the least fearsome of all of us, keeps us going in the hopelessness. But then, Badger loves tunnels. Sometimes I think he keeps us here on purpose."

Ethel and Luce sat motionless with sad expressions. Finally, Ethel spoke, "What does the 'E' in your name stand for?"

"Einstein. My full name is Theodore Einstein Polar Bear."

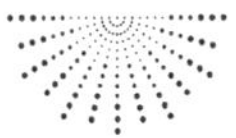

CHAPTER EIGHT

The jackhammering ceased. The three sat in the enclosure with only the sounds of scurrying rats and dripping water. And then, the sound of paws against the damp and water-pooled floor of one of the passageways came nearer. "Bear, are you in there? I detect you have company." They had long stopped calling each other by their first names, using only surnames when referring to each other.

Ted E. removed the rubble from their hiding place to form a doorway big enough for himself. His new companions followed him through.

"Why as I live and breathe," Badger exclaimed. "If it is not Luce Pigeon. I thought you might have eloped with the bongo player. That was the word on the street."

Luce cooed a chuckle. "Oh, I think you know me better than that. Too many cute pigeons out there to restrict myself to only one."

"I see you brought a friend. At least I hope she is a

friend," Badger laughed. "To what do we owe the pleasure?"

"This is my fine friend, my best friend," she corrected, "Ethel Peacock." She paused and then stated, "We are on a mission."

"Oh, I love missions," Badger said. "You have met Bear. Please meet Tiger and Orangutan." Tiger let off a growl of acknowledgment while Orangutan extended his hand. "Hyena should be along soon." Ted E. Bear snarled at the mention of Hyena. "Please, please, tell us about your mission."

"First, though, we come bearing gifts."

"And food," exclaimed Polar Bear, rubbing his belly.

"Luce, do you want to do the honors?" Ethel asked.

"I would be thrilled. First, we have a medal for bravery. We thought this would be a nice gift for Tiger. If you will bend down, please." Tiger crouched low, and Luce put the medal around his neck.

"For Orangutan, we have this nice cap." Orangutan took it, eyeing over the picture of the hawk and placed it on his head. Even though it was an extra-large human size, it only covered Orangutan's balding spot. Still, a smile erupted across his face.

"If only I had a mirror," he said.

"And I'm extra proud to say I picked this gift myself." She pulled from the bag the key that Sam Squirrel had meticulously polished and handed it to Badger.

"What is it a key to?" he asked.

"Why, a key to the city," she said. Badger appeared pleased.

Badger took the key and pulled a chain from underneath his coat of fur. "I'm honored by your gift. I will put it on this chain along with my locket." He opened his locket for Ethel and Luce. "It is a picture of my parents on their wedding day."

Ethel studied the picture. "What are their names?"

"Mom and Dad."

"No, their given names."

"Why, I don't know. I only ever called them Mom and Dad. I was so young when they died."

Ethel wanted to make a further comment, but the picture was so worn and faded, and even if it wasn't, you wouldn't know if they were a good-looking couple or not, as she had no standards by which to judge badgers. She merely said, "It is so nice you have something to remember them by." Luce agreed. Ethel then changed the subject, "We brought food. I hope there will be enough. You must dig in."

"Yes, you must eat while Ethel tells us of her mission," Luce said.

Ethel Peacock cleared her throat. "I would like to start a school. A unique school. Some might find it peculiar."

"A school?" Orangutan asked, removing his hat and scratching the diminishing orange fur on his head.

"I hail from the school of hard knocks," said Tiger. "Shouldn't you be talking to fish?"

Luce chuckled, batting her eyelashes, "Oh, Tiger, always the smart-aleck."

"Pigeon, do you flirt with every species on the planet?" Tiger teased.

"Well, certainly not humans," Luce retorted.

"Oh, don't mind him," Badger said. "His pride is wounded. One of the rats got away. Hyena is still chasing him down. That one has a determination. He is driven, I tell you."

"The rat or Hyena?" Luce asked.

"Both," Badger said, laughing.

"We will need determination and animals with motivation if we are to start this school," Ethel Peacock said.

"We, we," Tiger exclaimed. "You have told us nothing about this school."

"I am the one that told Ethel about your group, how you heroically escaped the zookeepers, working as a team even though you are all so different."

"Yes, the story greatly inspired me," Ethel Peacock said.

"Tell them. Tell them, Ethel, more about this new school you propose," Luce urged.

"What I would like to achieve is a school for all animals regardless of species, one in which the talents of all animals can be combined. The animal kingdom will no longer be divided."

"Do you really think that would work? I don't know," said Tiger.

Orangutan nodded his head. "I think it will work. I

can see it now, our statues on the campus lawn. I will wear a cap and gown and hold a diploma."

"It will be your embalmed statue since the humans will most assuredly pierce you with one of their bullets if you try to leave this place," Bear scoffed.

"Always the pessimist," Tiger roared. "I, myself, am sick and tired of this dark existence."

"Oh, so now you have changed your stance? A minute ago, you questioned this school. How do you propose we leave?" Bear asked. "Walk out boldly as if we are humans? Badger is the only one who can come and go as he pleases, because of his size, and because he is cunning."

"I am cunning," Tiger growled.

"Yes, yes, you are," Badger said. "We must study this, give it some thought."

"That is all you do, Badger," Bear said angrily. "We have been in this cavern for nearly a year, growing weaker by the day."

"But you like caverns," Orangutan said.

"No, I dislike caverns," Bear retorted. "Do I look black? Do I look brown?"

"Well, actually…" Tiger said.

"I was once a proud Polar Bear, a prince, the son of a king, destined to be a king myself one day. And rule beside my queen, the sweet Fiona."

"Oh, her name is Fiona, now? Last week it was Flora. I don't think you ever caught the name of this elusive female. One thing we can all agree on is her name started with 'F' as in a figment of your imagination," Tiger said.

Bear used all of his strength, letting out a ferocious growl which turned into a cough.

"Here, have some honey, Polar Bear," Badger said. "It is good for coughs." Polar Bear took it, polishing off the jar in one quick swoop.

"And what about me?" Tiger glared. "Having mates are the least of our worries. I am nothing if not the symbol of power. *Was* the symbol of power. I have keen eyesight. I *had* keen eyesight. Since being in here, my eyesight has weakened. I could barely see that rat."

The bickering continued. Ethel and Luce moved off to the side. "Is this how they work together?" Ethel asked. "If so, it all seems so hopeless." She looked at the almost bare cart. "I do hope they leave some food for Hyena."

"I do too. They once worked together. I'm afraid their patience has worn thin by being in this dungeon for too long. Can you blame them? We must get them out of here, Ethel."

"But how?" Ethel asked. "And look at them." Ethel shook her head in despair. "Except for Badger, they all look as if they have been stricken by a plague. And did you notice Badger is not eating anything?"

"No, he wouldn't. He always puts them first."

"That is commendable of him." Ethel sighed, "Even if they were to get out of here, how could I present them to Mr. Densworth Lion in their current condition?"

TIGER STRODE OVER TO THE CORNER WHERE LUCE AND Ethel sat. "Why do you two look so down? You are the lucky ones." He let out a half-hearted growl. "Forgive me. Where are my manners? We have guests. Guests who have been extra kind to us, bringing us food and gifts." He traced the engraving on the medal. "Do you know what it says?"

"No, I'm sorry. We don't," Ethel said.

"Even if you had brought nothing, I am so glad to see you. We rarely, if ever, have visitors. I'm so tired. I want to leave this place so badly. I will do anything. The zoo was bad, but compared to this, it was heaven. At least I saw the light of day, and food was thrown at me twice a day."

Tiger sucked in the air, smiling, remembering the aroma of the fresh meats, before choking on the stale putridness of the tunnel.

"Sure, I longed to hunt the food myself, but at least I ate. My nerves are as raw as the meat they threw in our cage. I see what this place has done to the others as well.

"Orangutan, a cap, and gown, and diploma," Tiger exclaimed. "He once was smart. Sat around, calculating all day. And once, I thought his plans had merit, but now, they border on the ridiculous. He is yet young, but I fear he is now senile. He has a bunch of books and pretends he is reading them.

"Bear has become jaded, as have we all. He talks of

nothing but his royalty, his birthright, and of his lost love. Why, he hardly knew the cub. At most, they only exchanged glances. That is what he told us at first. Didn't even know her name. But the stories grew. If the bear only had paper and pen. He could write a romance novel.

"Hyena is aloof. He was always the prankster, but he no longer knows the real from the unreal. Driven? Driven mad, if you ask me.

"Badger may be the only sane one of the lot of us, but then, he is not so far removed from his element as the rest of us are. He burrows about the city, coming and going as he pleases. I have a lot of respect for Badger. He is a born leader. He takes his role as our protector seriously. He could have easily deserted us, but he hasn't. Why he has stuck it out with our ragtag group, I will never know. I fear we depend on him way too much. Whenever he is gone, we worry something will happen to him. If something happens to him, what will happen to us? Worry is a human trait. We never worried before."

Tiger let out a sigh and gave a pensive look. "This school you speak of, it goes against natural law. But then, if there is a chance it might work, I am all for it. Anything is better than this. This place has taken away my spirit."

"I fear you may be right about it going against natural law. That is what Mr. Densworth Lion said. Maybe I didn't think this entirely through," Ethel said.

"Ethel. May I call you Ethel?"

"I would be honored."

"Ethel, do not let our own hopelessness get you down. I fear it may be contagious. Anyway, a lion, you say? Who is this lion?"

"He runs Cub Academy. He once was a teacher like me. Now he is a principal. I think he once had high aspirations, but administrative duties have deadened his ambition. We all have things we let dampen our spirit."

"Not Luce," Tiger said.

"What, what?" Luce perked up at hearing her name mentioned. "I'm sorry. I must have nodded off. All the recent traveling has taken its toll."

"Do you mean the nightlife?" Tiger chuckled. "Perhaps it's time you settled down."

"Oh, poppycock," said Luce.

"Exactly," said Tiger. "Find yourself a nice cock and settle down."

Luce scoffed.

"But I have gotten off track. I am so very sleepy. We spend a lot of our time sleeping. Nothing else to do. Have to preserve our strength," Tiger said, eyeing Luce as she sat slumped in the corner, yawning. "I said previously this place has taken away my spirit. It has taken all of our spirits and drained us of hope. I look at the others and see a reflection of my own disheveled soul in them."

"What you just said," Ethel said, her feathers rising. "That is why I want to start this school."

"I don't understand," said Tiger.

"Look at your group. Look how far you have gotten. You are alive. You have managed not to eat each other."

"I'm ashamed to say it crosses my mind on a daily basis, but we've all become so pathetic, not much meat on any of our bones."

"But you haven't. That says a lot. You've taken each other's strengths and made them your own. Would you have survived if you had been alone? More than likely not. You would have wildly darted out among the humans and their vehicles, getting hit, or badly mangled. You would have damaged or killed some of them in the process.

"They would have come after you with a vengeance, hunted you down, made you suffer the worst kind of death, maybe even put you on public display for all to see. They have done it to their own kind, for being a different color or of a different belief. Having spots, stripes, or fur, and not pink skin would have been your death sentence for having killed one of their own. Even humans band together when there is an outside threat. I know there are animal activists, but not even they would have been able to save you.

"And what of those poor creatures in the zoo? They would suffer the consequences of your actions. You left behind friends, did you not?"

Tiger nodded his head and hung it down.

"If it were not for Badger's quick thinking, finding holes, burrowing, and your willingness to listen to him, you would all be back in the zoo or worse, dead. Even now, humans go on hunts for wild animals for trophies.

And what they do to domesticated animals such as cows, chickens, and pigs, well, I shudder to think. Working together is what can save us all."

"We must devise a plan," Tiger said. "We may not all walk out of here in one piece, but we must try."

"Yes, we must all put our heads together. It can be done. I know it can. You have gotten this far. It cannot all be in vain. We will walk out together. We will travel back to speak with Mr. Densworth Lion."

"And he will help us?" Tiger asked.

"Oh, I don't know about that."

"But you said…"

"I did not say," Ethel Peacock interrupted, "that he was on our side. In fact, it is quite the opposite, but he invited me for dinner this coming Sunday. So, there may be hope. If we all confront him together, he may have a change of heart. We only have a few days, so we must act fast. I also have to say speaking to him as a group will relieve my fears of being the main course."

"It would be a sad end to escape from this place only to be eaten by a lion."

"Yes, indeed it would," Ethel said. "What is your given name, Tiger?"

"Thor. I was named for a god. I was born on a thunderous night. My parents thought it appropriate. "

"I think it suits you well. It denotes strength."

A smile came across Tiger's lips. The smile turned serious. "We will need all the strength we can muster."

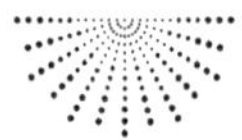

CHAPTER NINE

The den had grown quiet. All the quarreling had tired them and put them in a deep slumber. Ethel was a little worse for wear herself and took the opportunity to doze for a bit. However, that did not last long as they all were awakened by a boisterous racket.

"I caught him. I caught him," Hyena lauded.

Tiger stood at attention and growled, "Where is your proof?"

"The proof is right here." He rubbed his belly

"That is no proof," rebuffed Tiger.

"Then smell my breath," said Hyena. He opened his mouth wide and blew out a heavy puff of air. Tiger instinctively turned away. "See, my breath smells of freshly consumed rat," he bragged.

"I will have to pass and take your word for it," Tiger conceded.

"Who do we have here?" Hyena asked, eyeing Ethel and Luce, licking his lips.

"No one for your dinner or rather dessert since you already feasted on the rat," Badger barked in.

"He did not catch the rat," Tiger whispered to Ethel.

"How do you know?" she whispered back.

"He would have brought it back whole and dangled it for us all to see. That is his way."

"Would he have shared?" she asked.

"Probably not. That is also his way."

"And you don't begrudge him for lying about it?"

"No, why should I? We would all do the same. It's the only pride we have left. Besides, Hyena is my best friend. Do you see why we have to get out of this place?"

Ethel nodded with downcast eyes.

"Hyena, you remember me, don't you? I'm Luce?"

"Oh, yes."

"And this is my best friend in the world, Ethel. I was paying her a visit at the nature preserve and told her about the lot of you, and she had to meet you. So, here we are."

"So glad to meet you," Hyena said, distracted. "What is that smell?"

"Oh, I almost forgot, the food," Ethel replied.

"Yes, our dear friends brought us food," Badger said.

"But you must be full after consuming the rat," Polar Bear said.

"Nonsense," Hyena laughed. "If anything, it will help me digest the rat."

"Please, help yourself," Ethel said, pointing to the almost empty cart. "But first we must give you your gift."

"Gift, gift?" Hyena cackled.

"Yes, Luce, once again, will you do the honors?"

Luce handed Hyena the canister.

"What is in it?"

"See for yourself," Tiger encouraged him.

"Yes, yes, we are all eager to see what is in it," they agreed.

As Hyena struggled with the lid, Ethel and Luce moved back a few steps. When he finally got it off, they all stepped back, Hyena, in particular, howling and covering his eyes as he fell to the floor. Laughter echoed throughout the tunnel.

"That was the best gift of all," Tiger squealed, rolling on the damp surface of the passageway with laughter. "Oh, to see the expression on your face, Hyena."

"I wasn't scared," he protested. "It was all for show, to give you a much-needed laugh."

"That you did," Polar Bear said.

"You must eat, now," Luce said, hoping to veer off any argument that might start.

"I smell something delicious."

After watching him take the last bite, Bear exclaimed, "I am ready for a nap."

"We all are," said Badger.

"Not me," said Hyena. "I am pumped after the chase and after all the food."

"As you wish, Hyena. The rest of us will rest now, and when we wake, we will plan our escape," replied Badger.

Ethel watched as all, including Luce, retreated to their various corners and settled into deep slumbers.

"It is the air in this place, if you could call it air at all," said Hyena. "It is easier to sleep. We forget the smell when we sleep. We sleep a lot and dream. In my dreams, I am outdoors, running in the grasslands. I was born in captivity, but the stories were handed down. They were told with such exuberance I could feel the blades of grass beneath my paws. I imagine Bear is swimming in the icy Arctic waters and no doubt showing off for Fiona or Flo, whatever her name is this week. I suspect Orangutan is dreaming of painting a great masterpiece. Did you see the drawings he has done on the tunnel wall?"

"No, I haven't," replied Ethel.

"Well, you must. Simply delightful. As for Tiger, his dreams will consist of breathing in the fresh night air under a full moon. He prefers hunting at night. Badger more than likely dreams he is free from the worry of us. But enough of our problems. What about you, Ethel? How did you meet Luce? You seem an unlikely pair?"

"We met at an airport. I had just arrived from India with my owner. India is my homeland. I was revered in India, the national bird. I lived on a property with a beautiful lake. I had a mate and five beautiful hatchlings. Grown now, probably with hatchlings of their own." Ethel sobbed.

"Oh, I did not know," Hyena said sympathetically.

"Yes, we have all left others behind. I lived in an ashram. Monks, with heads bowed, walked around the lake with their beautiful orange robes flowing. It was serene and peaceful. I came and went as I pleased. They would even stop, put their hands together, and bow saying, 'Namaste.' What it meant, I don't know, but it was something that warmed my heart. They always smiled when they said it. All was provided for me.

"Then a man came. Rupees were exchanged. Although the lake and grounds were beautiful, the buildings where the monks lived needed repair. I assumed my sale would help with those repairs. Although monks were not supposed to be concerned with worldly affairs, even *they* needed money to exist. The next thing I knew, I was put in a cage and loaded into the cargo bay of a plane along with other animals, mostly cats and dogs. After a rather turbulent trip, we were unloaded and put in an area where we awaited the humans who owned us.

"I looked up to see an owl perched on the top of the building. Only, it never moved, but the bird next to it did. It was Luce. She looked down and saw me. The next thing I know, she was on the ground, walking back and forth in front of my cage.

"After she paced about for several moments, she spoke. 'I have seen parrots and other birds in cages here before, but never one as exotic as you. You must be hungry. Almost everyone is after these long flights. I can tell your flight was long. The ones with the bigger planes always are. The people getting off them look worn and tired and are all different species of humans. I can tell from the different shades of their skin and different outfits.'

"She brought me over some tidbits that had been inside of a wrapper with a yellow arch on it. Even though I am a vegetarian, I voraciously wolfed it down and thanked her. I broke down into tears."

"'What's wrong, my dear?' she asked.

"I told her about the family I had left behind. She told me she had no family of her own. Did you know she was orphaned?"

"No, I didn't," Hyena said.

"Yes, her parents were killed in an effort to rid the city of pigeons."

"No wonder Luce is always looking for love," Hyena said.

"Yes and in all the wrong places."

"But you are a good influence on her," Hyena said.

"I don't know about that. I think, if anything, Luce is a good influence on me. She has the best of hearts you know."

"Yes, I have always seen that in her."

"After my cry, I asked about the owl on top of the building. She laughed and said, 'It is supposed to scare us away.' I asked her who us was.

"She said, 'Us birds. The owl is a fake, not real.'

"Then she said, 'I have never done this before. But, a bird as beautiful as you should not be caged. Birds of a feather flock together. Well, that may be stretching it since we are definitely not of the same feather, but I feel we are kindred spirits. And kindred spirits should stick together.' She pecked at the lock until it came open. I followed her, and we have been friends ever since."

"That is a beautiful story," Hyena said, looking over at Luce, snoring away. "But you said Luce came to visit you. So, you are not together anymore?"

"No, I found that even though we are joined by our souls, our personalities differed greatly. I like to say opposites attract. I mean, look at Luce and me, and look at us two, talking like this. Who would have thought? Well, on with my story. Luce loves the nightlife. I do not. And me wandering around in the city was out of the question. It was with reluctance I ventured out to somewhere more secluded. I traveled until I came upon an aviary. It is part of the nature preserve where I now live. I missed my family so. I found young hatchlings at the aviary I could share my knowledge of the outside world with. I became a teacher. I love teaching, but I missed Luce so. She comes to visit as often as she can. I think my friendship with Luce, us being so different and all, may have been what spurred this idea or caused the dream of all animals working together." Ethel paused. "And what of you, Hyena?"

"I, too, like you, hail from India, although unlike you I've never seen it, being born in captivity, but the stories have been handed down. The humans are different there I've been told. They are not so keen on killing animals."

"Yes, they believe in reincarnation. Many are vegetarians for that reason. They fear eating their ancestors. Cows are also greatly revered, and they walk the crowded streets freely. Do you have a name, Hyena?"

"Hyena is my name."

"No, I mean do you have a first name."

"Hiram. I had almost forgotten. I haven't used it in so long."

The other animals began to stir.

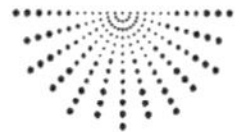

Orangutan stretched his arms and yawned. "I think I may have dreamed of a plan we can use to escape. We must do it at night and travel through the park."

They agreed. "The night is a given."

"The park is a block from here," Badger said.

"A block?" Ethel asked. "We walked much further. We went past a fish market."

"Isn't the fish market Santiago's territory?" Badger asked.

Luce hung her head down. "We came in through the entrance I thought would be easiest for us. There are many entrances to the tunnels," Luce said, humbly.

"Easy? You call that entrance easy?" Ethel exclaimed.

"Easy or not, we must take the closest one. Not the one by the fish market," Tiger said, winking at Luce.

"We may be okay once we get in the park. We can take cover behind the trees, but the construction site is open and well-lit at night."

"Yes, but the workers will have gone home for the day," Hyena said, optimistically.

"What if it is no longer a construction site? We haven't heard the sounds of heavy machinery in a long while," Bear said, putting a damper on Hyena's enthusiasm.

"But we do still hear noise from time to time," Tiger said.

"You are right," Badger said, nodding his head. "There is no longer a construction site there. What you hear are delivery trucks behind a new building. Fortunate for us, the building is an office. There shouldn't be anyone there at night."

"What about guards?" Tiger asked. "Humans always feel the need for guards for all of their buildings."

"Yes, but they are usually at the front entrance," Badger replied. "There could be another obstacle. In my ventures out, I have seen men in hats assessing the situation of what to do with the rubble covering the tunnel."

"Then it is all for naught. We are blocked in," Hyena said with downcast eyes.

"Not necessarily. If I have learned anything from watching humans, I've learned their decision-making process is fraught with indecisiveness, much arguing back and forth and many paper cups of their hot brew, that smelly stuff they drink," Badger said.

"The drink that comes from the green mermaid store," Luce chimed in. "I'm rather partial to it."

"The only thing we know for sure is that we have to act fast," Ethel said. "Besides, I'm due back on Sunday. That is when we must all go see Mr. Densworth Lion."

"Oh, so that is where we are going?" Bear interjected.

"Yes, the lion king will save us," Tiger said.

"No, no, I didn't say…" Ethel said, but the rest of her words were drowned out by their sudden newfound fire and commitment to work as a team in leaving the wretched place. Ethel, seeing a light had returned to their eyes, said, "Yes, yes, the lion king will save us." With Ethel's confirmation, they all applauded. She looked over to see Luce's wink of approval.

"Back to business. There is not a moment to spare. We must have a map," Orangutan said.

"Luce and I can venture out—draw one up," Badger said.

"And Luce, while you are out, you must contact your friend, the bongo player. He will be instrumental in this plan. Tell him to bring his bongos," Orangutan said.

Luce remained silent.

"I'm afraid Santiago and Luce are on the outs," Ethel said.

"But Luce, you must," Badger said.

"All right, I can rise above it for the good of the group. I will not ask what you have planned, but I know Santiago will agree if it involves a performance."

"It will. Santiago, the bongo player along with the boy, will be our distractions," Orangutan said.

"The boy?" Ethel asked. "A human boy?"

"Yes, the different one. The one who understands us," Orangutan replied.

"The outcast that Polar Bear mentioned? The one that came down through the storm drains?" Ethel asked.

"Yes, he is always escaping from his parents. He is the one I am working with to understand their language," Badger piped in. "He differs from the other boys. His mother takes him for walks in the park every day. He doesn't talk, at least like normal children. But he understands me and I him. I hide in the bushes near the bench where they sit. We converse. He has his own special language. He can understand the humans, but they can't understand him or not much. He tells me he has something called autism."

"I once saw human hatchlings like that," Ethel said. "There was a group they brought to the aviary. It's the only part of the nature preserve where humans come, and it doesn't happen often. There was something in their eyes. I never even thought about trying to communicate with them. That was a smart thing for you to do, Badger—establishing communication."

"Do you think he would help us?" Orangutan asked.

"He loves the zoo. He has a special affinity with all the animals there. I know he would. The only problem is that I only see him during the day. The humans keep a close guard on him at night, but I know where his den is. I have watched from the park as he enters one of the brownstone buildings with his mother. I have waited and watched. He is on the second story. I know because he often looks out and waves at me."

"If they keep such close guard on him, how does he end up underground with the other boys?" Ethel asked.

"His mother keeps a close watch on him. His father doesn't. He escapes from him," Badger said.

"If it could be on a day when he is with his father, we stand a better chance," Luce offered.

"I'm not sure if that is possible. The other day I saw the father leave the building. He had a suitcase. The mother was standing in the doorway, yelling at him."

"Oh," said Ethel. "It happens in the animal world too."

"Whatever it takes, we must find a way," said Tiger.

"I love nothing better than perching on windowsills. Perhaps we could break it. He could escape. Two stories are not so far to fall," Luce said.

"Oh, but it would be for a human boy," said Bear, who had been quiet until now.

"I don't know," said Ethel. "His mother hen would worry something frightfully. I have lost my own hatchlings. I could not in good conscience do that to another mother. Even a human mother. Besides, he can hardly fly down two stories, like us, Luce."

"If we could find a way to get him out, it will not be for long. And, it will be at night. His mother will think he is sound asleep," said Orangutan. "I am an excellent climber. I would bring him down safely. I would even return him. His mother would never know."

"Perhaps getting him might not be so dangerous, but returning him would," said Badger. "You would put your own life in danger." The others murmured and nodded in agreement.

"It has to be so," said Orangutan. "It is the only way. Look around us. Do we want to die slow, decrepit deaths in this place?"

"We will either succeed or die trying," said Polar Bear.

"Here, here," said Tiger, pointing with his paw to his medal for bravery. "It may be our last adventure together, but it will be a grand adventure."

They all agreed.

"Then we are off to make a map," said Badger. "Luce, are you with me?"

"Right behind you."

"We will rest to conserve our energy," said Tiger. Hyena and Bear yawned. All gingerly sauntered off to their usual corners except for Orangutan who picked up a piece of chalk and began some calculations on one of the few bare spaces left on the wall of the tunnel.

"Orangutan, are these your drawings on the wall?" Ethel asked.

"Yes, how did you know?"

"Hyena told me about them. But I would have known your work anywhere. There were several clues. First of all, I see likenesses of Badger, Bear, Hyena, and Tiger, but none of you. That was the first clue. Considering there are no places of reflection where you could behold your own image, how could you do a self-portrait? Secondly, there is a perfection to the portraits, a mathematical precision, and I have heard you excel at mathematics. Thirdly, it is easy to see you are the gentlest of the group, and I only mean that as a compliment. I see your gentle hand in the renderings. The mathematics of the drawings are reminiscent of Picasso. I like Picasso. I hope you do. And, the gentleness reminds me of Mary Cassatt."

"I don't know them. You are so smart, Miss Ethel Peacock."

"Oh, I don't know about that. I've traveled a lot. You pick up things."

"At the zoo, they took a few of us, trying to teach us sign language, and they gave us paper and crayons for drawing."

"They are remarkable."

"Thank you. I have had plenty of time to hone my skills. Getting lost in the drawings relieves my growling stomach, and it passes the time."

"It is a shame we will have to leave them behind when we depart."

"I can do more at your school. Perhaps teach a class."

"That is a fantastic idea."

Orangutan smiled, showing rotting teeth, no doubt from the conditions of living underground for so long. Still, he had one of the most adorable, innocent smiles. Of the entire group, he retained the most of his spirit.

"Orangutan, may I ask your name?"

"Owen," he said smiling.

"Tell me more about your life while at the zoo."

"I was born in captivity, but my parents weren't. They longed for the freedom they once had, swinging from tree to tree. Nesting in trees. Still, my parents told me we had a lot to be thankful for, being together, for one. They were forever hugging, cleaning, and grooming me, and I miss them greatly.

"They told me, although they had a good life, their numbers were dwindling and being in the zoo protected us. They were happy I was working with the humans. My parents are progressive thinkers like you. They told me apes have a lot in common with the humans." Owen held up his hands. "We have opposable thumbs and can use tools."

"Yes, I know you do. Sometimes these feathers can be so awkward, but then I have never experienced anything else," Ethel said.

"Your feathers are beautiful, and your neck, such a rich hue of emerald. I can't help but notice colors. It is the artist in me. I would love to do your portrait."

"I would be greatly honored."

"It could hang in the school. After all, you will be the founder. I must have paints to do you justice. Now, I only have this chalk." He held up a much-used yellow stub. "I'm thankful Badger brought me some colored chalk. He stole it, although he used the term borrowed, from some girls who were using it to write on the side-walk. They were so busy drawing hearts and plus signs with words of their language they didn't even notice he had taken the box from the steps. There was no red.

"Badger is good at bringing us all kinds of discarded objects and food. He says he is not stealing since the humans throw so much away in something called waste cans. He knows where all the food stores are. There are mountains of feasts behind them. Lots of fruit—what I mostly eat. Not fresh from the tree but perfectly good. Humans can't tolerate anything misshapen or with brown spots."

Ethel squeaked a giggle.

"The others don't always have to subsist on rats. Badger finds raw meats and fish behind these food stores, a little on the smelly side, but Hyena, Tiger, and Bear hungrily wolf it down. I don't know what we would do without Badger. We would unquestionably have died of starvation."

"Yes, you have a good leader and friend in Badger."

Orangutan smiled. "They called me Hector at the zoo. I had learned the alphabet there. They gave me lettered blocks. I once tried to spell out my name, my real name, but didn't know the proper letters. I placed O, E, and N on the table in front of the scientists who were studying me. They didn't understand."

"And they call us the dumb ones," Ethel said.

"I was only beginning to understand the letters, what they meant. They gave me paints, and I drew pictures. I was in my abstract stage then. Again, they didn't understand."

"What phase are you in now?" Ethel asked.

"I would say impressionism," Owen answered.

"Hmm, I can see that," Ethel said, nodding her head

and turning it from side to side. "Mary Cassatt was an impressionist."

"I would like to see her work," Owen said.

"We will get art books for the school."

"I love books. I discovered them through the humans."

"The owls supply us with all kinds of books—not human books, per se, but translations of the human books. We learn so much about the humans through their books."

"The owls?"

"Yes, they will want to meet you. Please tell me more about your life before the tunnels."

"I was in the lab, separated from my parents, on the day we escaped. I went looking for them, but it was pure chaos. All the animals darted in every direction, screaming and howling about their stroke of luck in being freed. I didn't see them back in their cage. I went in the wrong direction at first. They were probably looking for me. I didn't know where to go, but then I saw Polar Bear and followed him out through the front gate. The bears were across from us. I thought he might have seen my parents. He hadn't. I went back, hoping to find them, but by the time I got back, the front gate was closed again and locked.

"Polar Bear took pity and said, 'Come on, little ape. It's too late. We can't get back in, even if we wanted to. I, for one, don't want to go back.'

"Little did he know how badly I wanted back in. But under the circumstances, what could I do? I followed

Polar Bear. A little way down we met up with Tiger and Hyena. We all stood there, not knowing which direction to go in until Badger came along and told us to follow him. We have been following him ever since."

"I am so glad you have Badger."

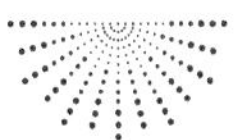

Badger, out of breath, with Luce close behind, burst into the subterranean section of tunnel his friends occupied. "It won't be easy, but Luce and I walked and flew over every square inch of the park and have it mapped out. Luce took the high road, getting the aerial perspective, while I took the low road."

"Let me see," said Orangutan, as they all gathered around. He studied the drawing and bombarded Badger and Luce with every question he could think of regarding the logistics of escaping through the park, scratching his head with each answer. He had removed his hat as it was a hindrance to his work in the poorly lit tunnel. Taking his yellow chalk stub, he said, "I will study this and scribble out proposals of how we can pull this off. A lot depends on the boy and Santiago. Did you discuss this with them?"

"I sent word to Santiago and will meet him later tonight," Luce said. "But I'm sure he will help."

"The boy is definitely game," said Badger. "He was excited when I told him an orangutan would escort him to the spot. Do we have the spot?"

Owen deliberated and examined the piece of paper Badger and Luce had brought back, giving every aspect careful consideration. "Yes, by the fountain. It is the perfect place. It is there we will create a diversion, something to throw everyone off, while we make our escape. We must carefully plan, study it like a script, set up a miniature from this map, get our roles down. It will be like a rehearsal before the big performance. The only drawback is that the boy… What is his name?"

"Michael," Badger said.

"Is that Michael will only have one chance at it, as will Santiago."

"We all only have one chance at it," Tiger corrected Orangutan.

"You are right, my good friend," Hyena agreed.

"Badger, you will have to make sure Michael knows his role, and Luce, you will have to instruct Santiago." They both nodded.

"How long, Orangutan?" asked Hyena.

"Five days, less if we all feel like we have our parts down."

"Five days," roared Tiger. "I don't know if I can handle five more days in this place."

"It has to be three," Ethel said. "I'm due back— make that we are due at the home of Mr. and Mrs. Densworth Lion on Sunday."

"Make that two days. Ethel gets distracted easily. It's

the journey, right, Ethel? Not the destination. We must allow for getting sidetracked as Ethel so often does," Luce said.

Ethel sighed.

Bear chimed in, "If we practice almost non-stop, we can make it two days. Can you show me north on the map?"

"North would be here, no here," Orangutan pointed. "But we will be headed west out of the park."

"I was only curious," Polar Bear said. Hyena looked at him suspiciously.

"For now, I will have to study this over. Give me some time while I calculate. I must go to work," Orangutan said.

"What can *we* do?" Ethel asked.

"Nothing for now. Perhaps rest. We will all need our strength."

"I, for one, don't know if *I can rest*. I am feeling pumped," Hyena said.

"We rest too much," said Bear. "We have all become sluggish. What we need is more food and lots so we can build up our strength."

"And exercise," said Tiger.

"Rest, exercise, do whatever works for you, but let us all keep a clear mind. We will need it. There is still much work to do," Orangutan said.

Out of habit, they retired to their corners while Orangutan poured over the piece of paper devising various contingency plans.

Before long, snores drifted throughout the tunnel.

Ethel and Luce sat huddled together in a far corner, giving Owen plenty of room for his calculations. They watched as he periodically scratched his orange thinning hair and made low guttural sounds before each chalk mark to the map.

"Ethel, do you really think this will work?" Luce whispered.

"It has to, Luce."

"I will leave soon to meet up with Santiago."

"Do you mind if I go with you? I could use some fresh air. I'm suffocating and going stir crazy in this environment. How they have lasted this long, I don't know."

"Yes, please go with me. I need you with me when I face Santiago."

THE AIR HAD A CHILL, SOMETHING THAT WOULDN'T HAVE been obvious before spending so much time in the passageways beneath the city. But Ethel knew she would adjust and become one with nature in no time. She wondered what effect it might have on the others who had been confined underground for so long. The sudden change might wreak havoc on their deteriorating bodies, but then again, it might give them the spark of life they lacked.

They stood by the lake where the humans would most likely think Ethel was a permanent fixture of the park. The plan seemed to be working. Ethel sauntered behind a bush to draw less attention in case someone of authority might question the presence of a peacock while Luce nibbled at a discarded bag of peanuts.

There were benches around the lake and a fountain across the way. A concrete curb by the fountain housed a human with long stringy hair and a top hat. He was strumming a guitar. His guitar case lay open at his feet. Humans would stop and listen, applaud when he finished a song, and throw coins in the open case. He either bowed in appreciation or glared at those who only listened.

"I suppose this fountain is where Orangutan wants Santiago to play bongos," Luce said.

"A pigeon playing bongos will certainly be a diversion," Ethel replied.

"If we knew how to write in human language, we might make a sign requesting peanuts instead of human money."

"Good idea," said Ethel. "But we don't know how. Orangutan told me some interesting things while you were out with Badger."

"Oh?"

"Yes, before he left the zoo, he was learning the letters of the humans."

"Really? Perhaps we could have Orangutan copy the letters from a peanut bag."

"Luce, you are one smart bird."

"I wonder what part Michael has to play in all of this?" Luce asked.

"Your guess is as good as mine, but I'm sure Orangutan has something brilliant in mind. I watched him while he was working on a strategy to escape, and his whole being lit up. It was as if the whole process of planning the escape revitalized him."

"They all rather perked up, don't you think?" Luce said.

"They were a team, no longer bickering or fighting. It was a good thing to see. That is exactly what I have in mind for the school," Ethel said.

Luce cooed. A male pigeon preened as he walked toward them. The wiry little white and grey bird with a small burlap satchel slung over his wing straddled up beside Luce, pecking his beak against hers.

"And this must be Santiago."

"The one and only," Luce said as he continued to peck on her face.

"Please, get a windowsill," Ethel said. The way Luce was nudging up to Santiago said she had forgiven whatever infidelity he may have committed.

"Santiago, meet my dearest friend, Ethel."

"Pleased to meet you. Luce has told me a lot about you." He turned his attention back to Luce. "Is this where you have been? I've looked all over for you. No one knew a thing. I have been so worried," Santiago said with an accent.

"I almost forgot. You come from Cuba," Ethel said.

"Si, Señora," Santiago replied.

"It's señorita," Luce said.

"How have you not been snatched up?" countered Santiago.

"I had someone long ago, but ancient history."

"Oh, I am so sorry."

"No, no. It was long ago," Ethel said with a flick of her wing indicating it was no big deal.

"Luce, why did you not tell me where you went?" Santiago asked, turning his attention back to Luce.

"We can discuss it later."

"Oh, we will. What is this big plan I hear about? The word on the street is that the zoo animals are planning an exit, a great escape."

Luce rolled her eyes and looked at Ethel. "There are no secrets in this town amongst the animals."

"As long as *the humans* don't find out," Ethel said. "Santiago, since you are such an integral part of the plan, perhaps it would be best if Orangutan explained it to you. He is the mastermind behind the great escape as you call it. Are you in for an adventure?"

"*Am I?*" He looked at Luce, excitement written all over his face.

"Santiago is always in for an adventure. You must tell her about making your way from Cuba."

"Oh, it was nothing."

"Nothing? Hardly! Santiago is the bravest pigeon I know."

"Perhaps another time, my little lovebird. I can see you and your friend have some big plans. For the moment we must concentrate on those."

"Yes, you are right," Luce agreed.

Ethel watched the two lovebirds as they fluttered their wings against each other, cooing and making unrestrained guttural sounds. She was both sickened and envious. "Now, now, you two, I hate to break this reunion up, but we have to get down to business. Lives are at stake."

"Yes, yes, Ethel is right," Luce said, pushing Santiago away.

"We must make our way back through the tunnels. Luce, I believe you know the way much better than me. We will follow you. Lead on," Ethel said.

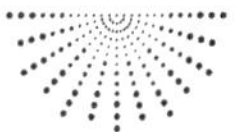

CHAPTER TWELVE

*L*uce and Ethel funneled through the cavernous maze with greater dexterity than before. They had a gallant purpose to their trek. Both continuously reminded Santiago to hurry as the bravest bird that Luce knew felt the need to stop periodically to shriek, gag, and offer commentary concerning the rodents and hideous nature of the city's underground.

They first came upon Badger, who was dragging along a punctured plastic bag filled with mostly brown fruit. "Something for Orangutan to keep up his strength, and some fish for the others," he said.

Santiago jerked his head back in disgust. "Not much of a fish connoisseur myself," said Santiago. "I smell it, day in and day out."

"It's an acquired taste," said Badger. "One acquires a taste for almost anything after living in this place for any length of time."

"I can understand."

"Where are my manners? This is Santiago," said Luce.

"I kind of suspected," said Badger. He wiped a paw against his fur, extending it to Santiago, who winged him a high five. Badger emulated the move with his paw. "We must hurry. Time's a-wasting. Much planning to do."

They found the others pouring over plans and fitting themselves with harnesses, an odd collection of frayed rope, and plastic in which to carry their belongings.

"I told them this won't do. It will only slow us down, but they insisted. During their stay in the tunnels, they have collected an assortment of bric-à-brac. I feel responsible. It was something to take their minds off of their predicament. Tiger, in particular, could not part with his snow globe encasing a forest. He says it reminds him of home although he was born in the zoo. Polar Bear carries a red pouch, the contents of which he has always kept secret. Hyena has a collection of bones."

"Bones?" exclaimed Santiago.

"Yes, the remnants of his prey, his trophies. At least they won't add much weight since they are the bones of rats."

"And Orangutan? What are his possessions? I suppose his chalk since he can hardly carry his drawings from the tunnel walls with him," said Luce.

"A few chalk stubs which he has agreed to leave

behind. But he has a few human books and blocks with human symbols on them."

"Whatever for?" asked Santiago.

"I believe they remind him of home, the zoo that is. He prizes those books above all else. He had scientists who worked with him there. Apes are the nearest to humans, you know. I have seen one book. It is all about a monkey."

"You don't say?" said Luce.

"They've been through so much, how could I deny them?"

"I sense you have little hope for this mission," said Santiago.

"Does it show?" asked Badger.

"Well, maybe not to the others, but…"

"Santiago has been through his own escape," said Luce. "From Cuba."

"Yes, and I made it only by a feather."

"Then you know what we are up against," said Badger.

"All too well. But have hope. I made it. But what about you, Badger?"

"I don't understand."

"You don't have to be here. You can burrow and traipse about the city as you please. Why encumber yourself with this band of outlaws?"

"Oh, I would hardly call them outlaws. More like a hodgepodge of misfits that when you place them together, they make a whole. And I am a piece of the puzzle."

"I see. Like Luce and me. We go together like coffee and donuts." He gave Luce a squeeze as she cooed with delight.

Badger continued, "More than being a piece of the puzzle, the reason goes deeper. I lost my own parents when I was young, and I blame myself for their demise. I wandered off, always the explorer, always disobeying, getting into trouble. They had their hands full with me. You see, I was their only kit, and I was rather spoiled.

"If they hadn't been chasing after me they wouldn't have been picked up by that garbage truck. I was running away from them, teasing, always the mischievous one. I made it across the city street and hid behind a garbage can. They heard me calling and jumped in the can, thinking I was there. Just as I was about to surprise them and say *boo,* a man's gloved hand extended outward and took the can away, with them in it. I waited for days, trying not to go too far from my location, but they never came back. I knew they must have been killed. Have you seen how the garbage is crushed in those trucks? I cried for days, all the while moving onward. That part of the city had such bad memories for me. I still can't go to that section of the city.

"Call this my penance. At least that is how it started. It is no longer a burden but an honor to help them. They are my family—my only family."

"Ah," Santiago murmured. "Quite the story, Badger."

"Call me Billy. It is the name my parents gave me."

"An honor to meet you, Billy," said Santiago.

They walked along together until they saw the others.

"Is that fish I smell?" asked Polar Bear.

Badger laid the haul before them.

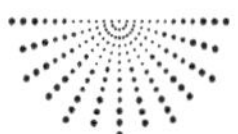

"A lion is here to see me? My oh my! We must hurry. Miss Betty Beaver, follow me. A good builder always has a contingency plan. The bookcase has a secret panel. My grandfather engineered this long ago for just such an emergency. We can escape through there." Bernard Beaver III pranced around, grabbing papers and blueprints off his desk. "Quick, quick, help me, Betty. Grab what you can."

"No, no," Betty Beaver said. "Calm down, Mr. Beaver. He is not here to eat us. No, quite the opposite. He wants to hire our company."

"Hire us?"

"He seemed serious. Do you think I would be standing here in one piece if he had carnivorous intentions?"

"No, no, I don't suppose you would." He scratched his head. "A lion hiring beavers? Most strange. It wouldn't be good to keep him waiting. Send him in,"

Bernard Beaver said in a rather shaky voice. "Didn't bring any coyotes or bears with him, did he?"

"No, sir, he's alone."

Mr. Bernard Beaver straightened his tie and stood behind his desk. "Please hurry, Miss Betty Beaver. Mustn't keep a lion waiting."

"Yes, sir," she said, reluctantly making her way out of Mr. Bernard Beaver's office.

"Mr. Beaver will see you now, sir," his secretary said.

Mr. Densworth Lion ducked as he entered Mr. Beaver's office.

Mr. Beaver grinned an embarrassed smile while extending his trembling paw. "Sorry about the close quarters. We don't get many clients your size. Won't you sit down?"

Mr. Densworth Lion took the beaver's paw, giving it a vigorous shake. He looked back at the rather small chair. "I will stand if you don't mind."

"No, not at all," Mr. Beaver said.

Mr. Densworth Lion looked around. "Nice book-case. You are a reader, are you?"

"When I get time. These days I'm mostly reading blueprints."

Densworth Lion grunted in acknowledgment. "Same here. That is, I don't have so much time for reading these days either, except for budget reports. I am the principal at Cub Academy."

"Yes, yes, I've heard of it. My company constructed

a bridge not too far from it. Dams are our specialty, but we do many projects."

"I know the bridge," Mr. Densworth Lion said. "That is why I'm here. I thought who better to do repair work on my den."

"But, sir, our firm handles commercial projects, much bigger in nature than homes and simple repair work. Might you get a handy lion?"

Mr. Densworth Lion roared. The fur on Bernard Beaver's body cascaded backward like an ocean wave.

"But then, we have been known to take on smaller projects," Mr. Bernard Beaver stuttered, pressing his fur back into place with his paws.

"Do you also offer financing?" the lion asked in a gruff voice.

"Yes, we can do that too. My secretary, Betty, you met her on your way in, takes care of all the financial aspects for our clients."

"I need it done this week."

"Sometimes financing can take a little longer than a week," Bernard Beaver said, wiping sweat from his brow.

"No. The project. I need my den improvements done this week. Everything has to be finished before my wife returns on Saturday night. She will be leaving after her bridge club tomorrow to see her mother. The project can start then."

"This week? Totally out of the question. We have the large clubhouse we are building, and then there is a lodge after that."

Mr. Densworth Lion snarled.

"I'm sure, though, we can clear our calendar," Bernard Beaver said, swallowing. "I guess we better get down to some planning. Can you tell me what you have in mind?"

"I think it might be better to show you. Can you come tomorrow? I would need you to arrive a few minutes after the noon hour as that is when my wife leaves for her bridge club. We will have two hours to get the plans underway. After bridge, she will return to pick up her suitcase before heading to her mother's. The work can start then. She will return late Saturday night. The whole thing is a surprise for her. On Sunday, we have company."

"Oh my, I see you have been busy with your strategy. I do admire a busy beaver, I mean lion. Such a nice surprise for your wife. A birthday or anniversary, perhaps?"

"Something long overdue," Mr. Densworth Lion stated bluntly.

"The company you are having on Sunday. Must be someone important."

Mr. Densworth Lion snarled again. "A vegetarian, like you."

Bernard Beaver cleared his throat and changed the subject. "Yes, yes, back to business. Not a minute to waste. I'm sure all of this can be arranged."

"That's why I came here. Beavers don't waste time."

"Do you want to leave your address with my secretary on your way out?"

"All right, then. I will see you promptly a few moments after the noon hour. Don't be late."

"No, sir, I wouldn't dream of it."

"You can bring me any finance papers you want me to sign, then." Mr. Densworth Lion extended his paw to the beaver to seal the deal and walked out of his office.

Bernard Beaver along with his secretary stared out the window through the etched glass that said *Bernard Beaver and Sons Engineering and Construction, Three Generations of Prestigious Designs,* and watched as Mr. Densworth Lion walked away. Sweat dripped from Bernard Beaver's fur.

"That was different," Miss Betty Beaver said.

"Yes, most unusual," Mr. Bernard Beaver confirmed. "If only my father and grandfather had lived to see this."

"We live in unusual times, sir."

"Indeed, we do, Betty."

"So, will you be going to his den tomorrow?"

"Betty, were you listening at the door again?"

"Isn't that what all good secretaries do?" she asked.

"What choice do I have? I have a wife and nine kits to consider. Well, we must get back to work. That lion totally threw off our busyness. We must step up the construction on the clubhouse. I will have to take two beavers off the project for work on the lion's *repairs.* Shouldn't take any more than two for his job. That way, we can get in and out possibly in a day."

"Repairs? Are repairs all he wanted?"

"I thought you were listening at the door?"

"I was, but since you put up that heavier oak door, it makes it harder to hear. Sir, if he only wanted repairs, why didn't he hire a handy lion?"

"Intimidation wouldn't work on one of his own kind, I suppose. He asked for financing after all. Well, hustle, hustle, much work to get done. Please get my foreman on the line for me and have lunch brought in. Order something from that new aquatic café. What is it called?"

"*The Seahorse Café,* sir."

"Yes, yes. I've heard they make an excellent algae stew. Get something for the both of us. I'll need your help during lunch."

Miss Betty Beaver sighed. "Sometimes I wish I wasn't a beaver, so I could slow down, take a vacation perhaps."

"Now, now, Betty. Beavers have much to be proud of. Sloths on the other hand…"

"Yes, sir, I know. Of the seven deadly sins—pride, greed, lust, envy, wrath, sloth, and gluttony—sloth is the worst."

"And who knows? If Mr. Densworth Lion likes this work we do for him, we may have to expand our business. Yes, I can see it now. A whole complex of offices. Doing design work for a lion? Whatever would my father and grandfather make of it? Why this could put us on the map."

Mr. Bernard Beaver whistled as he returned to his office.

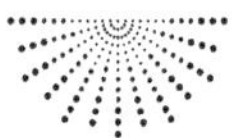

CHAPTER FOURTEEN

"Tonight is when it all happens," Luce said. "Do you think we are ready?"

"As ready as we can be," Ethel said. "There are so many possibilities, things that can go wrong."

"And so many possibilities of things that can go right," her friend reminded her.

"Always my optimistic friend. I don't know what I would do without you." Ethel hugged Luce.

"I sense Orangutan is stressed, more so than usual. He tries to hide it from the others, but I pick up on these things. Ethel, you should talk to him. He needs your wise counsel."

"I will do my best. Won't you talk with him too?"

"No, you would do a much better job. I'm off to see Santiago and go over the plan one more time before tonight."

"That's a good idea."

Ethel sauntered over to Orangutan who was still

pouring over the hand-drawn map. By now, it looked like a chicken had scratched and tore it almost to shreds, but the others had faith in Orangutan and that all would go well—or at least they put up a good front. Ethel looked out into the darkened corners of the tunnel. Her eyes had adjusted to the dim surroundings. She observed everyone meditating in their various spots, lost in their own worlds, making peace with whatever was going to happen tonight.

"Maybe you should rest," Ethel said to Orangutan. "I don't think you've slept at all since we began all of this. I am amazed at the meticulous work you have put into the model." She stared in fascination at the miniature maze with the paper doll figurines of Ted E. Bear, Billy Badger, Hiram Hyena, Thor Tiger, Owen Orangutan, Santiago Pigeon, herself, and Luce, all strategically placed.

"It is adrenaline that keeps me going. Besides, there will be enough time for rest after it is over."

"When we are all safe."

"Yes, when we are all safe," he nodded.

"I'm confused as to what Michael's part in all of this is," Ethel remarked.

"The boy?"

"Yes, the boy."

"Perhaps we don't need him. I fear what might happen by bringing a human child into the equation."

"You could be right," Ethel concurred, noticing an oddity in Orangutan's expression when he said it. She wrote it off as fatigue. "We will tell the others we will not use him. We will do everything else as planned with Badger leading the charge."

"Yes, he has practiced now five times in the park, pretending we are all behind him, me bringing up the rear. Yes, it will work without the boy. The boy was only ever a backup plan if we needed him," Owen said with a nervous smile.

"What is in the burlap bag?" Ethel inquired, going for a change of conversation. All they had talked about for the last two days was the escape. They had discussed and drilled, using the model, wearing themselves down until they eventually fell asleep in their various corners, all but Owen and Ethel. And then there was Luce who resonated a new surge of energy since reconnecting with Santiago. They would need all the energy they could muster since the countdown to the escape was only a couple of hours away. Upon Luce's return, they would put the plan into action.

"Books."

"Books? May I see?"

"Yes. You should have them for the school." Enthusiasm radiated from his eyes as he made the offer.

Ethel untied the rope from the bag and pulled out several worn books. "These are human books," she exclaimed.

"Yes, sometimes Badger snatches them for me, but one I got at the zoo."

"And they have pictures. Of animals. Cartoon-like drawings."

"Yes, *Curious George* is my favorite. That is the book from the zoo."

"Curious George?"

"A monkey who gets into all kinds of trouble, but somehow it always works out."

"Did you give him this name?" Ethel asked as she flipped through the pages.

"No, it is his human name, the name the man in the yellow hat calls him."

"I don't understand. How do you know it is his name? We can't read human, after all."

"Actually, I can."

Ethel gave him a puzzled look.

"The scientists at the zoo taught me."

"Why?"

"Why would they teach me?"

"Yes."

"Because we're related. Apes and humans. And as an experiment. The humans love their experiments."

"They also love experimenting on animals," Ethel reminded him.

"Yes, I heard some unpleasant things from some apes, but the scientists at the zoo wanted to help us, in their own way. I can't fault them. They are ignorant about us. Oh, they know what we eat, our sleeping, and mating patterns, but they don't know our souls. They look at all animals as beneath them.

"I only learned the fundamentals at first. They started with sign language. They used their hands in different gestures to communicate. I remember the first day I understood something. Molly was so excited. Molly was the human who worked with me."

"What was the first thing you understood?"

"Molly. She mouthed her name and kept pointing to herself. I tried to tell her my name, but she didn't understand. I kept saying Owen or tried to mouth the word. For some odd reason, she wanted to call me Hector. And she called Joe and Mac by different names, too. They were the chimpanzees who were sometimes in there with me."

"Humans have this fascination about picking out names for animals. They do it to their pets. Did you learn other words with sign language?" Ethel asked.

"I learned *banana* pretty quickly. Whenever I did something Molly liked, she gave me a banana. And she petted me."

Ethel smiled.

"When the zoo went dark, everyone, including the animals, scattered. The scientists ran out helter-skelter. Fear oozed from their pores. Joe and Mac didn't know what to do at first. They stared at me blankly, scratching their heads. Not much on the ball, those two. How they ever got picked for the training, I'll never know. After some debate amongst themselves, they went off in the opposite direction from me. Maybe they were the smart ones and not me." Owen hung his head down, revealing his bald spot.

"Owen, after seeing your masterpieces, I can't help but think you are a genius."

Owen smiled, showing rotting teeth.

"Only the three of us were left in the lab after the humans fled. I took off, telling Joe and Mac I had to find my parents. Never had a great sense of direction."

Ethel's eyes widened in fear.

"Oh, not to worry. Remember, Badger will be in the lead during the escape. I'll be bringing up the rear."

Ethel gave a sigh of relief.

"The first thing I thought about was finding my parents. The second thing was grabbing the book which was on a shelf near my cage. I didn't have to worry about Joe or Mac wanting them. They weren't nearly as studious as me, to put it mildly. They liked to play. I was what you call a nerd."

"I met a rather nice nerd named Sam before coming here. I think you and he would get along nicely."

"Another orangutan?" Owen asked.

"No, a squirrel."

Owen smiled.

"There's so much time on your hands in here. I read and read, fitting the words together like a jigsaw puzzle in my brain. Sounded them out the way humans would. I practiced until one day the words and what they meant hit me over the head like a two-by-four."

"The others don't know about this? Do they?"

Owen shook his head.

"But why?"

Owen let out a big sigh. "Several times, I almost told them, but they are so dead set against humans. And there was so much fighting amongst us already, I didn't want to add to it. So, I kept my mouth shut."

"But maybe it would help."

"It helps in that I can now read their signs and understand what they are saying. I can warn the others if anything goes awry, but maybe all the humans are like the man in the yellow hat."

"The man in the yellow hat?" Ethel asked.

Owen turned the pages until he came to the picture of the man in the yellow hat. "He helps George and loves him no matter how much trouble he causes."

"Do you think humans are like this—like the man in the yellow hat?"

"Maybe not all humans," Owen said. He pulled out another book, one with a picture of a bear. The bear wore a red hat and carried a suitcase. "His name is Paddington," Owen said. "He traveled from Peru and was helped by a human family. Paddington loves marmalade and has a capacity like George for getting into trouble, but the humans always forgive and love him."

Ethel turned the pages. "I wonder, though."

"About what?" Owen asked.

"Well, everything looks so nice in these books about how humans and animals are best friends. The animals are even wearing human clothes. It's a contradiction, don't you think?"

"A contradiction?" asked Owen.

"Yes, how do you explain the zoo? Animals are in cages there."

"It *is* a dilemma I've puzzled over," Owen said,

scratching his head. "I would love to meet Curious George and Paddington Bear."

"If they are real," Ethel said.

"You mean they are fiction?"

"Yes, I think so. Owen, do you know what I think these books are?"

"No, what?"

"These books are written for children—human children. They are like fairy tales, things that aren't real. I know I told my own hatchlings stories, ones that conveyed a nice peaceful world. We always want our offspring to think everything is right in the world, that it is a safe place. It would appear human adults do the same thing."

"We are not so different, then—animals and humans," Owen said.

"No, I suppose we are not. We always fear what is different from ourselves. We fear the humans. The humans fear us. Certain animals fear other animals."

"But that will all end with your school," Owen countered.

"*Our* school," she corrected. "Yes, I hope the school will change such conceptions. And your knowledge of the human language is invaluable, Owen."

He smiled.

CHAPTER FIFTEEN

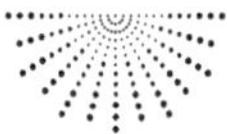

There was a soberness in Badger's voice when he called everyone together—no horsing around, no arguing, nothing but shaky legs, stabilized somewhat by a fierceness of spirit that cut through the thick underground prison. Wanting to make eye contact, Badger stood on the pile of rubble that blocked the tunnel from the outside world. Badger's own eyes sparkled with hope as he began his speech.

"We've gone over it and over it in our imaginations but, more importantly in our hearts. Anything could happen out there. Humans are unpredictable, but we're a team, and I have faith in us. I want to thank Ethel and Luce for being the ones to give us the motivation, or rather, the kick in the butt to do this. And God forbid if anything dire should happen—but it won't—I want each of you to know it has been an honor. Are there any last thoughts or anything that needs to be said before we depart?"

They stood as if frozen in the glare of headlights. It was a first, no one offering an opinion.

Fearing they might back out at the last minute, Luce broke the silence. "Santiago is all set. When he hears my coo, he will take his place near the fountain with his bongos."

"Are we ready?" Badger raised his paw to cheer the group on.

They gave each other nervous looks which melted into indeterminate smiles. Ethel surmised they were having something akin to out-of-body experiences.

Tiger held one paw up and growled, "Now or never."

They cheered, giving each other high fives, all looking to Owen who gave them a final nod of approval. They removed the rocks, creeping out into the alleyway, looking each way. It was devoid of humans.

"So far, so good," Tiger said.

"Fresh air," said Polar Bear sucking it in. He was quickly shushed by Hyena. On wobbly legs, they slowly crept behind Badger who took the lead. One by one they stuck close to the outside wall, ignoring all kinds of signs, none of which they could read, that is except for Owen. The orange webbed fencing around the rubble offered a minor challenge, but they broke through.

The back of the office building on the other side of the alley ran the course of a block. Dimly lit office windows illuminated the back alley just enough. Any more light all at once would have blinded their eyes that had been conditioned to darkness for so long.

"Not much of a view on this side. Feel sorry for the poor schmucks who got the backside," Hyena said in a hoarse voice, trying to lighten things up. "This fresh air will take getting used to," he said with a little more clearness in his voice.

They crept with a caution behind Badger. They moved like railway cars, Badger acting as the engine, followed by Tiger, Hyena, Polar Bear, and Ethel. Orangutan acted as the caboose. Luce served as their lookout, either hovering above them or somewhere out ahead. Badger came to a halt as they came upon the intersection where they would cross over into the park. Huddled down, one on top of the other, covered under a large tarp they had scored from a worksite in the tunnel, they waited until a line of vehicles had moved on. "Do you think anyone in the vehicles saw us?" asked Polar Bear.

"Unlikely," said Luce. "Humans are rather insulated, always distracted by something, mainly those little rectangles they hold in front of their faces. I will fly ahead and investigate."

"Yes," Badger said. "Let us know when the coast is clear."

They each held onto the rolled tarp, carrying it off to their right side like a long log, ready at a moment's notice to unroll it, duck, and cover. They had practiced this to the point of perfection back in the tunnel. However, nerves were coming into play, and getting it back into a roll would have been comical if it wasn't for the danger of being spotted.

"This isn't a good idea," said Orangutan. "We must

abandon the tarp." Since Orangutan was the architect of the plan, they obeyed without argument. Hovering overhead across the four-lane pavement, Luce flapped her wings, motioning them to cross and be quick about it using the sign language she and Owen had devised back in the tunnels.

They all heaved a heavy sigh upon reaching the other side of the street. They hid along a line of trees, awaiting their next instruction from Badger at the head of the line, who in turn awaited Luce who flew on ahead. When she reappeared, saying all clear, they worked uniformly like a bucket brigade passing back information from the head of the line to the back where Owen maintained watch from the rear. Luce continued to levitate above them, sometimes low, sometimes high, providing aerial surveillance.

They eased with caution between a line of trees and the back fence of the park. They halted, one by one, banging against each other, freezing in place, at the sound of voices. Two joggers, a man and woman, came up from behind and passed them, completely unaware of their presence.

"I could have taken them both if need be," bragged Tiger.

Hyena looked at his friend as if he had lost his marbles. "I believe that medal for bravery has gone to your head. It wasn't needed, thank God, and this is no time for heroics. Besides, I'm sure they could have outrun you, outrun all of us for that matter, and warned the whole city. Luckily, they didn't see us at all." Hyena shook his head. "And you thought I was the loony one of the group?"

"You knew?" Tiger asked surprised.

Hyena rolled his eyes.

Luce lit on the back of Polar Bear, who maintained the core of their ensemble. "At the end of the fence, we will come to an open area. Across from it is the entrance of the zoo," she said.

"This all looked so much smaller during the simulation in the tunnels," Hyena said.

"Of course, it did, you knucklehead," scolded Tiger. "Simulations are not the real thing."

"I only wish I could visit my parents one last time before we leave the city," Owen said, looking over at the zoo entrance. The entrance gate was covered in padlocks.

"I see they don't take chances anymore," Ethel said.

"I will get word to them," Luce said.

"Yes," Ethel said. "Luce can inform all of your friends back at the zoo and let them know once we arrive at our destination that we are safe."

"I should have thought of that before," said Owen. "We could have told them of our plans through Luce."

"No, I should have thought of it," said Luce.

"We all had a lot on our minds," Badger said.

"Not to mention the toll starvation takes on the mind," chimed in Polar Bear.

"Let us all take a deep breath and proceed. There is no one here now as the zoo is closed. After crossing the open area and going through one more patch of trees, we will reach the fountain area. There are more walkers in that area at night. Luce, you go on ahead and let Santiago know when he is to commence with his bongo-playing," instructed Badger.

Luce lifted off from Polar Bear's back. The animals all darted in single file across the open way. They breathed a sigh of relief when they reached the clump of trees.

"This has been a piece of cake," boasted Tiger. "We could have left those tunnels months ago."

"I think that bravery medal has gone to your head," Hyena said.

A plethora of voices, young and old, grew louder. The group piled up behind each other. They peeked from the tree line and observed a crowd of humans as big as any special event day at the zoo, or so it seemed.

"Why are there so many?" Hyena asked.

"There aren't so many. Well, not *that* many," Badger said trying to radiate both confidence and a realistic appraisal of the situation. "Our best hope would be a sudden thunder burst. That would send them all scurrying."

Even though they had been cooped up in intolerable conditions for such a long time, being out in nature was rekindling dampened senses and animal instincts. There would be no thunderstorm. It was a perfect spring night, one in which love was in the air, one in which humans came out in droves. Any size crowd would have appeared larger to them and more menacing under the glare of street lamps.

"What do we do now?" they all asked Badger and Orangutan.

"I, for one, wish we hadn't abandoned the tarp," Polar Bear said.

"We could wait it out. They will go to their dens, eventually," Hyena said.

"Most will," Ethel said. "But not all. This city never sleeps. The ones who do stay will more than likely be the most dangerous."

"We have come this far. We will make it," said Tiger.

"The people all have their eyes on the fountain," said Badger.

"Yes," said Ethel. "I can hear a guitar but not bongos. Where is Santiago?"

"He will be here. I have no doubt," said Owen "We must proceed with our original plan."

No sooner had he said that the faint beat of bongos sounded. A swarm of pigeons descended upon the crowd, causing them to scatter and thin out.

One of the pigeons shouted, "Did someone say *party*?" They made an awful racket, drowning out the bongos. The people appeared both annoyed and hysterical, kicking and screaming, motioning for them to shoo, all the while amazed at the pigeon banging on the bongos with his beak.

"It's now or never," said Owen.

They left the cover of the trees, making a mad dash, or what seemed like a mad dash, behind the crowd. The humans had moved around so much, the ragtag band of balding furry creatures ended up darting in every which direction through the crowd, abandoning their soldier-like precision of single-file. A total state of confusion and chaos ensued.

People instinctively pinched their fingers to their noses, while others looked away briefly in disgust only to look back again, aghast at the sight.

"Yuck, what is that odor?" one of them who was holding their nose shouted.

Although all of them understood the gestures the people were making, only Owen comprehended what the man had said. "They are appalled by our odor."

Even though Santiago drummed away and the pigeons did somersaults in the air, mostly at the humans' eye levels, all eyes were now on the pathetic creatures who could have in their more glorious days been the forerunners of *The Greatest Show on Earth*.

A little girl holding a chocolate ice cream cone, the chocolate dripping down her arm, pointed with her free hand and shouted, "Look, Mommy," although it was unnecessary as a hypnotic trance settled over the crowd as they gazed at the strange creatures.

"What is the meaning of this?" asked a man, staring in disbelief. "It looks like animals fleeing from a concentration camp."

There were murmurs and screams from the crowd, not out of fear but pity from what they saw.

"Are they from the zoo?" a woman asked.

"Don't they feed them?" another one wondered.

"No, no," the woman said. "I'm talking about the

ones who escaped almost a year ago. Don't you remember? It was in all the papers."

While the other animals listened and sensed the bafflement of the crowd, Ethel gave Owen both a questioning and nudging glance.

"They know who we are. They know we are the animals who escaped from the zoo," he said. "And they pity us."

"Yes, I can see they pity us," said Tiger, deflated.

"It's not real. It's some kind of projection. They can do remarkable things with technology these days," the man said, holding up his smartphone, making his own video. "I hope I am getting this. That is if it is real."

"Projection or not, someone is getting this," said the woman standing next to him. "This is already live on Facebook."

Everyone had their phones and cameras pointed at the ensemble of escapees. A few of them were holding them so they could get in the picture with the ragtag band of weary travelers.

"They're not real. It's costumes. They can do amazing things these days," someone else said. "They must be shooting some kind of movie. That has to be it."

"Where are the cameras? The movie cameras?" another voice asked.

"Or a PETA documentary," said the woman they had seen jogging earlier.

"Why are they doing nothing?" asked Hyena. "They don't seem frightened by us at all."

"They question whether we are real. They think it is a movie," Owen said.

Tiger and the others shook their heads in disbelief. Orangutan hung his head in shame.

"Well, the badger and peacock look okay," an older lady observed.

"Such an odd bunch," said the guy who had given up playing guitar to observe the scraggly group. Santiago played on, not deserting his post. And the pigeons partied on, although no one was paying attention to them any longer except for one woman, the one Luce referred to as Pigeon Lady. She looked over at Ethel, giving her a knowing stare. Somehow, Ethel thought she wasn't as crazy as everyone believed.

"We could have just walked out. All this time wasted," said Polar Bear. "I could have been married to Frida by now."

"I truly wish you were married to Frida right now," Tiger said.

A car with flashing red and blue lights pulled up to the outer edge of the fountain. Two men in blue uniforms got out of the vehicle. "Did someone here report a disturbance?" asked one of the men. The crowd all pointed.

They raised their guns as their eyes grew wide. "Is anyone hurt?" one of the officers asked.

"Hurt?" questioned one man. "Do you really think those animals, if that is what they are, could hurt anyone?"

The other man in blue grabbed the radio from inside

his vehicle. "You're not going to believe what is going on in the park. We have a badger, polar bear, hyena, tiger, orangutan, and peacock. The orangutan is wearing a cap. I think he is a Seahawks fan." There was a brief silence. "Yes, you heard me right," the man continued. "Do you want to send someone from the zoo?"

"There will be more coming," Owen said.

"Then we must do something," said Hyena. "Everything is going so wrong."

"Hyena, I'm surprised at you. When have you ever been the pessimist?" Tiger asked.

"If ever there was a time to be a pessimist, the time is now," Polar Bear said.

At that moment, rats emerged from the drains making their way through the crowd. A new type of panic ensued when men, women, and children started screaming and jumping to avoid them.

Orangutan looked at the policemen; however, his eyes registered to what was beyond the police car. There stood a man in a yellow hat. Or was it beige? At any rate, he took it as a sign. At that point, Owen said, "Run," but not before he removed the books from the burlap bag and handed them to Ethel. He kept the blocks.

When their eyes met, Ethel knew. The boy was not in the plan at all, or not in the way she had thought.

While the others ran, Owen took off in the opposite direction through the crowd, waving his arms and beating his chest, growling. His cap flew off in the process. The screams coming from the crowd were no longer in horror of the rats but of the orangutan that in the dark could have been a gorilla, perhaps even King Kong. No one was taking the time to look back to get an accurate assessment.

Ethel shouted, "Owen!" But it was too late. She looked up to see a boy leaning out an open window with Owen running in his direction. It was Michael. The men in blue saw it too and ran in the same direction, waving their guns as if Owen were the only one, for the moment, that seemed to pose any threat.

All might have been lost if it weren't for the pigeon lady. She began screeching and howling and dancing about, jumping in front of one of the officers, causing everyone's attention to be diverted from Hyena, Tiger, Polar Bear, Ethel, and Badger. The remaining officer was still in pursuit of Orangutan. It wasn't long until Luce and Santiago and all the other pigeons joined in— there had to be hundreds, maybe even thousands; every pigeon in the city had joined in aiding and abetting the escapees.

When the officer tried to forcibly take the pigeon lady into custody, the pigeons swarmed upon the man in blue like a cluster of bees. The officer was swinging his arms and shooting his gun into the air, although it was in vain.

Even with all the commotion, some still had the presence of mind to hold the rectangular objects always glued to their hands up and record the entire proceedings.

More cars with sirens blasting and blue lights

flashing pulled into the park. As they descended upon the crowd, waving their arms at them and pointing while shouting in rather unfriendly tones, scores of rats, more than before, emerged from the sewers.

The people, who once stood in unmanageable caravan type groups, jumped and screamed. Both sexes, Ethel noted.

Tiger stood there, scratching his head. "They are more afraid of the rats than they are of us."

"I thought the rats hated us," Hyena said.

"They don't want us coming back into their home, you nincompoop," Polar Bear said.

Badger shouted, "Come! Follow me. Quickly."

"He's right," said Ethel. "This is our thunder burst. It's now or never."

"What about Owen?" asked Tiger.

"We all know there is nothing we can do to save Owen now," Ethel said.

"We will reconnect in the future. I feel it in my gut," said Tiger.

"Run! Now!" Badger shouted.

More cars pulled up with flashing lights and sirens. The animals made their way out of the crowd with a surge of adrenaline and pounding hearts—heavily pounding in anxiety over the fate of Owen more than due to the extra labor of running. They slowed down their pace once they made it into the safety net of the trees. Still, they ran for a good solid hour. They came to a halt when they reached a creek by some abandoned warehouses.

"We can't drink this water," said Hyena. "It's polluted."

"We must keep moving," said Ethel. "Once we get past the warehouses, we will be out of the city. We will follow the fire roads and then come upon the forest, and by morning, we will be home."

"Home?" asked Polar Bear. "Where Mr. Densworth Lion lives?"

"Yes," she replied.

"Please point me toward North," he said.

With a saddened face, Ethel pointed. "You will not join us in our school, Ted E.?"

"No, I must go home, take my rightful place as heir to the throne and marry Faith." Tears ran down their faces as they said their goodbyes to Ted E. Bear.

They watched with solemnness as Polar Bear made a cane from a tree branch and walked off with the red pouch around his neck.

"Do you think he will make it?" asked Hyena.

"If his sense of direction is better than his romantic inclinations, I think he will," said Tiger.

"I have faith in him," said Badger.

"I will always wonder what was in that red pouch," Hyena said.

The sun was beginning its ascent over the horizon when Luce and Santiago caught up with them. Luce lit on the back of Hyena and Santiago on the back of Tiger, both out of breath. Badger, Tiger, Hyena, and Ethel stopped their weary march and stood static, awaiting news of Owen.

Luce shook her head. "He was climbing up the building where the autistic boy, Michael, lived, when someone from the zoo shot a dart at him. He fell to the ground. Luckily, it was a short fall. He was put on a stretcher and moved into a white van. The police cars blasted their sirens and followed."

"Why did he do it?" Tiger howled.

"To save us," Badger said.

"At least he is not dead," Ethel said it as optimistically as possible. "Please tell us he is not dead." She looked imploringly at Santiago and Luce.

"No, we don't think he is dead," said Santiago. "He has been taken back to the zoo. We followed the vehicles to make sure that was where they were taking him."

"He may not be dead now," said Tiger. "But he will be soon. He is a danger. He tried to kidnap a human child."

"No, they won't kill him," said Ethel.

"How do you know?" asked Badger.

"Because he knows the human language. He can communicate with them."

"What?" gasped Hyena.

"He kept it a secret," Ethel said.

"How can he communicate? He can't speak human," said Tiger.

"No, but he can read their language, and he understands what they say when they speak."

"So, he really knew what was going on back there? I thought he was guessing. But still, they won't know that," replied Tiger.

"He has his blocks—the ones with symbols—the human alphabet. He can use them to spell out words," replied Ethel. "He gave me the books before he departed. He wanted us to have them for the school, but he took his blocks. He thought he would need them to communicate."

"And to think, I tried to talk him out of taking them, saying they would weigh him down. I'm so glad he insisted," said Badger.

"Something's not right." Luce eyed the group. "Where is Polar Bear?"

"He headed north toward his home," said Badger.

"I hope he makes it," said Santiago.

"We can only wish him well now. We will make our way back and start the school. I am more determined now than ever because of Owen. We will construct a statue of him that will stand proudly in front of the school. He will wear a cap and gown and hold a diploma. He sacrificed a lot for us," Ethel said.

"Here, here," they all chimed.

The rising sun spread across their faces, revealing a new strength. They squinted, and their eyes watered as if seeing it for the first time. What was left of their group walked toward the village of Ethel Peacock and Mr. Densworth Lion with a new exuberance.

PART II

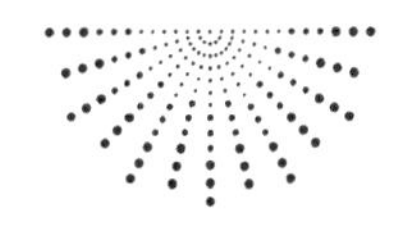

THE RETURN HOME

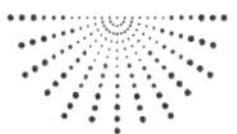

Glenda Lion, exhausted, carried her suitcase up to the door of her den. "Home at last," she said to herself as she fumbled for the key. She used the light of the full moon to aid her search.

She could knock, but she knew Densworth would already be in bed, snoring away. Her mother had warned her about marrying an older lion. One of the things that attracted her to Densworth was his passion for teaching young cubs, something her mother didn't understand. "That's a job for a lioness," she said.

It was Glenda's mother who persuaded Densworth to take the principalship job. Glenda felt he should have stayed in teaching, but the principalship meant more money.

Densworth said he would make it work. He would redirect his passion into making Cub Academy the best school of its kind. "Something great," he had said.

At first, they both believed this, but the job became

an administrative nightmare that drained her mate. They put off having cubs while Densworth was teaching to have time together, and then again when he became principal, until he settled into the job. When they *were* ready, Densworth came home night after night too tired for anything except for eating dinner and falling into a deep slumber seconds after his head hit the pillow.

Even though she was still annoyed at him for forgetting her birthday, she didn't want to disturb his rest. More so, she didn't want her mother's prophecy about their doomed marriage to come true. Despite everything, she loved Densworth deeply.

She dug the key from the furthest reaches of her handbag and opened the door. Candlelight illuminated the main room, enough for her to notice the door was different as she removed the key from the lock. "Has this door been newly painted and varnished?" she exclaimed out loud.

"Yes, dear," said the voice coming from the couch.

"Densworth, is that you? What are you doing up this late?" She looked toward the couch and saw his face was animated by a flood of light.

He came up to her, taking the suitcase from her hand, and ran his other paw around her sleek neck while planting an amorous kiss on her lips.

"Densworth, what has come over you?"

He set the suitcase down, took her by the hand, and led her to the center of the room.

"It is so bright in here. I thought it must be candles, but there are none."

He pointed upward. The full moon was staring down at them.

"Is that a skylight?"

"I thought as long as I was getting the roof fixed, might as well put in a skylight. You must be famished after your trip. I'll be right back."

He disappeared into the kitchen, returning with a tray. He removed the plates from the tray, placing them on the coffee table where a vase of spring lilies sat.

"You must be tired after your trip," he said, patting the couch, beckoning her to sit. Only, it wasn't their same old lumpy couch. It was different.

"This is the couch I've been eyeing at Filbert's Furniture."

"I know, dear."

"But how can we afford it?"

He cut her off. "You let me worry about that, Glenda. Let's eat before the food gets cold."

A rich aroma of food she didn't recognize flooded her nostrils. "What is this?"

"Algae stew. The beavers told me about this new restaurant, *The Seahorse Café*."

"The beavers?"

"It's a long story. I'll tell you all about it after you eat."

After taking her last bite she said, "That *was* delicious. Are you going to tell me about all of this, about the beavers?"

"I have an idea. Why don't we wait until morning?

We can talk over breakfast in the garden." He stood and took his mate's paw, leading her into the bedroom.

THE NEXT MORNING DENSWORTH ONCE AGAIN REACHED for his mate's paw over the patio table.

"I might go away more often if this is what I return to," she said, giggling.

"But I don't want you to go away."

"Honestly, you've fixed up the place so much while I've been away, I don't think I want to ever leave our cozy little den or our backyard. The fence around the garden is so cute. I've always wanted a white picket fence."

"I know you have."

"I believe I might plant some flowers after breakfast."

"That would be lovely. It will look nice for our guests."

"Guests? We never have guests."

"You *want* guests, don't you? Now that we have a proper place to show off?"

"Of course. You know I love to entertain. It is you who never liked having company."

"Should we invite my mother?"

"Your mother!"

"Yes, upon seeing this, she would have to eat crow."

"Dear, there is nothing better I would like than to

see your mother eat crow, but I had another guest in mind."

"Who?"

"I hope you won't get mad, but I've already invited someone. She will arrive around seven this evening."

"She? Who on earth, Densworth?"

"Miss Ethel Peacock."

"A peacock? The teacher at the aviary?"

"Actually, she's a peahen. You're not mad are you?"

"How could I get mad? You've treated me like a queen since I came home last night. And later in bed, I felt like we were young cubs."

Densworth blushed.

"No, I find it unusual. That's all," she said. "Why on earth did you invite a peacock, I mean a peahen?"

Densworth told Glenda about Ethel Peacock's visit to the school.

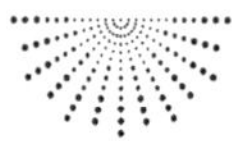

CHAPTER SEVENTEEN

The first animals to greet them were strangers to Ethel. Sounds of snorting and chomping of leaves came from above. They craned their necks to see giraffes.

"Ola Owl said they would come."

"Who is Ola Owl?" they asked.

"Ola is in charge of all the owls. She is a Northern White-Faced Owl. A beautiful creature."

"Yes, the owls decipher the human's language and make the books. They also are the keepers of the ancient wisdom. Isn't that right, Ethel? Ethel and I got to meet her before coming to your tunnel," Luce said.

"Yes, that is right, Luce."

"Please, don't call it our tunnel," Tiger said. "I don't want to ever see that place again."

"Me neither," said Hyena.

"What is that structure up ahead?" inquired Badger.

"That is Betsy Bear's Bed and Breakfast," Ethel

said. "We stopped there on our way to the city. We must stop and pay our respects."

"Yes, we must," said Luce. "She would never forgive us if she didn't meet you."

"She knows about us?" Tiger asked.

"We told her and all the other guests staying there about our quest to visit you. Little did we know we would be bringing you back with us."

"Some of us," Hyena corrected.

"Yes, we are all saddened by the absence of Ted E. and Owen," Santiago said. "And I only knew them for a short while. I can only imagine what you are feeling."

"I hope they are both all right," Badger said.

"We have to keep faith that they are," Ethel said.

"Oh my, oh my," Betsy Bear gasped at the site of Hyena and Tiger, trying not to stare. "Come in, come in. I never dreamed you would be returning with Ethel and Luce. And who do we have here? You have told me about the others. I see a new pigeon. Please, please, introductions?"

Ethel introduced Hiram Hyena, Thor Tiger, Billy Badger, and Santiago Pigeon.

"I am so pleased to meet all of you." She shook all of their paws and wings vigorously. "You must be starved after your trip. The others will want to hear all about it. We have two rooms available, on the house of course. Such esteemed guests. You must freshen up and join us for breakfast, which will be in about forty-five minutes, also on the house. You have time to take a trip down to the lake, take a nice bath, and then freshen up in your rooms. I am so excited. The others will want to hear all about everything that happened since you left us."

THE GROUP SAT AROUND THE TABLE WITH RENEWED confidence and a somewhat more pleasing appearance, although complete renewal might take a month of tender loving care, fresh air, and the forest to heal what had happened to them during their ordeal.

"The Badgers are still with us, but they won't be joining us for breakfast this morning. Mrs. Badger woke up with one of her migraines and will be retiring in her room for a while longer along with Mr. Badger. I'm afraid the Badgers will be checking out today. I think they may head back to the city. But we do have some new guests."

"Oh, I am so sorry to hear the Badgers won't be staying in our community," Ethel said.

"Perhaps I might know them. I am from the city," Billy Badger said.

"I don't know. Perhaps," Betsy Bear said. "But, I think it's best not to be in sight when they check out."

"Why?" asked Badger.

"It's a long, dreadful story. We will explain it to you later," Luce said.

Betsy's daughter, Beverly, came in, bringing a scrumptious pile of biscuits, scones, jellies, and honey. Looking at the protruding ribs of Hiram Hyena and Thor Tiger, she strategically positioned the tray in front of them. "Please eat up. In fact, feel free to have seconds, thirds, even fourths. We have plenty for the other guests. They should be arriving shortly."

"If you'll pardon me a moment?" Betsy nudged her daughter and led her out of the dining area where she wouldn't be heard. "Please see what else we can scrounge up this morning. Eggs, some grits, something that will stick to their bones, although, I don't think one big meal will miraculously solve their ills."

Betsy's plan to fatten her undernourished guests up with one monumental feast was not lost on any of them. By the second tray of food, Filbert Fox appeared.

"Filbert Fox," Ethel gasped. Luce looked at her friend with startled eyes.

"At your service, ma'am."

"I will let you know if I need your services."

Betsy Bear cleared her throat. "Filbert Fox supplied us with a cartload of eggs this morning."

"No doubt," Ethel said under her breath. She knew most looked the other way at Filbert's thievery when it benefited them. Nevertheless, she was grateful for the much-needed sustenance the eggs would give Hiram and Thor. So, she didn't belabor the question of where the eggs might have come from.

Stealing eggs from farmers who lived beyond the nature preserve, among other things, was merely a sideline for Filbert. His so-called legitimate business was a furniture store, the only furniture store in the forest. He had been warned by the owls on numerous occasions that his misdemeanors might put the nature preserve in jeopardy, which in turn would put all of their existences in jeopardy. The little talks obviously went unheeded by him.

"Whatever happened to you two?" he asked, looking at Hiram and Thor.

Ethel's feathers rose in agitation. "I will tell you what happened. These two are heroes. They escaped from the zoo nearly a year ago and have managed to survive, living in the tunnels underneath the city. Last night, they managed to escape through a crowded city park amid vehicles with flashing blue and red lights, and sirens, and men in blue coming at them in all directions."

"It's okay, Ethel," Tiger said, placing his paw on her feathers. "We owe Ethel, Luce, and Santiago a great deal as they facilitated our escape along with Orangutan."

"Orangutan?" asked Filbert Fox.

"Yes, I'm afraid he didn't make it out of the park with us," Luce said.

"Oh, such a shame," Filbert Fox said. His facial expression oozed of sincerity. However, Ethel wasn't buying it.

"There was a polar bear too," Beverly said.

"Yes," Ethel said. "Ted E. Polar Bear. He decided to go north to seek out his family."

"I do hope he makes it. There is nothing more important than family," Filbert Fox said with a genuineness in his voice. While everyone nodded in agreement, Ethel made no apologies in rolling her eyes.

Two baboons appeared in the doorway. "Are we late?" the male asked.

"No, we started a little early. I hope you don't mind."

"No, not at all," the male said. "My wife combed and combed but couldn't quite get my fur the way she wanted. Sometimes it's tiring being a baboon—all the extra grooming."

His wife nudged him, but his eyes fell on Hyena and Tiger. He tried not to stare, but he couldn't help it. "Some new guests?" he inquired.

"It is a long story," Betsy Bear said. "And we are all waiting to hear it. First, let me introduce our newcomers. This is Bertram and Barb Baboon. They run the local grooming shop down the way."

Beverly passed another round of scones and honey and refilled each of their cups with a fresh brew of coffee and tea before taking a seat alongside her mother. She was as eager as anyone to hear the tales of the legendary visitors.

It was two hours later when they finished the retelling of their epic journey beginning with their escape from the zoo, all the things in-between including Ethel's plans of a school, ending with showing up at the bed and breakfast. Ethel concluded with their plans to see Mr. Densworth Lion.

Tiger leaned back in his chair, rubbing his belly, while Hyena burped.

"I was starved, and now I can't eat another bite," Hyena said.

"Same here," said Tiger.

"What an adventure. Reminds me of my younger days," Filbert Fox said.

Before he could offer details, Bertram Baboon jumped in, "Yes, that is quite the tale. We want to do what we can to help. Isn't that right, dear?"

"Yes, you must come to our shop after breakfast. You must be groomed before you show up at Densworth Lion's den this evening. Looking good will certainly help your case when presenting the school to him," Barb said.

"Yes, we will clear all of our appointments. Our customers will more than understand. We offer the works. Steam room, although we might forgo that one, a rich, luxurious bath with sea salts, a full massage, and a complete brush down," Bertram added.

"That sounds nice," Hiram said.

"Oh, yes, we must," said Ethel. "It will do everyone good after our long and frightening journey."

"Might I steal Luce away for a moment before we depart?" asked Santiago Pigeon.

"What on earth, Santiago?" she asked, as he helped her from her seat like a gentle pigeon might.

A few moments after they left, Billy Badger gasped. "Oh, Santiago will need this. He pulled the chain out from under his fur, the one holding the locket and key.

He took it from around his neck and removed a third object—a shiny ring."

"Is that a diamond?" Ethel asked.

"I do think so," Filbert Fox said, leaning in for a closer inspection. Billy quickly yanked it back.

"Does this mean?" Ethel asked.

"Yes, it does. I was merely holding it for him so Luce wouldn't find out. He had a plastic ring that Luce's friend Gloria helped him pick out, but how could I let him give her that when I had found this in the tunnel? It had dropped through one of the storm drains. Humans are such careless creatures, always discarding perfectly good things."

"So, Luce was worried for nothing."

"What?" asked Billy Badger.

"She thought Gloria and Santiago, well, never mind."

"I must hurry. He is taking her down to the lake. He thought it would be the perfect romantic setting to propose."

"They might need furniture soon," Filbert Fox suggested.

Ethel rolled her eyes. "Highly doubtful as they will more than likely move back to the city."

"Ethel, can't we let bygones be bygones? All of this animosity toward me over something that happened a year ago is completely needless. Can't we move on? The owls cleared me of all charges. Where is that namaste spirit of yours?" Filbert Fox asked.

BADGER WAS OUT OF BREATH WHEN HE CAUGHT UP WITH Santiago and Luce. He discreetly slipped the ring under Santiago's feathers and said, "I thought I might take a quick walk around the lake." He rubbed his belly. "But all that food has done me in. I will head back now. I guess we will depart shortly for the grooming shop." He winked at Santiago.

"That was strange," Luce said, watching as Badger walked back toward the bed and breakfast.

"What was strange?" Santiago asked.

"Why did he want to take a walk around the lake? We have done nothing but walk." Luce was still talking when Santiago got down on one knee.

"Luce," he stammered. "This has been a long time in coming, but you are my dream pigeon, always have been since the first day I laid eyes on you." He held up the ring. "Will you do me the honor…"

"Yes, yes, Santiago. A million times, yes."

BADGER RETURNED TO THE BED AND BREAKFAST AND entered the dining room where everyone was still seated. "Mission accomplished," he proclaimed.

A little later, Santiago and Luce entered the dining room. Santiago grinned from ear to ear, and Luce giggled, displaying her ring for all to see.

There were congratulations and well wishes from

everyone before they said their goodbyes. They took the extra gifts of honey from Betsy Bear and departed with the Baboons.

Upon arriving at the stoop of the Baboons' shop, Badger stalled with a dreadful look on his face while he patted the fur around his chest.

"Is something wrong, Billy?" Santiago asked.

"My locket, my key to the city! I must have left them back at the bed and breakfast. It was when I was getting the… oh well. I must go back."

"Do you want me to go with you?" asked Santiago.

"No, no, thanks for offering, but I wouldn't dream of it. You don't want to leave your fiancé. And all of you should get started on your spa treatment. Please, please, not to worry. I will join you as soon as I can." With that, he hurried, as fast as his badger legs would take him, back to Betsy's.

Billy was about to the stoop of the bed and breakfast when he looked up to see two badgers coming out, suitcase in hand. "Pardon me," he said as he stepped up the steps past them. "I'm in a frightful hurry."

Bertha stopped dead in her tracks, as did her husband. "Billy, is that you?" she asked, staring into his eyes in utter disbelief.

"Why, yes, my name *is* Billy."

"Son?" Mr. Badger said.

"Son?" Billy asked, surprised.

"Oh, my, Bradley, he doesn't remember us."

"We thought we had lost you."

"What? You must be mistaken. Not to be rude but

I'm in quite a hurry as I left something behind when I checked out this morning. I must retrieve it and catch up with my friends."

"But Billy, I would know your eyes anywhere," Bertha Badger said.

"Now, dear," her husband said. "Although he does resemble our son, or what our son would have grown up to look like had he lived, it is wishful thinking. A side effect of the migraine."

"Perhaps you are right, Bradley. My head is throbbing so, I can't see straight. I am so sorry." Tears welled from her eyes. Her husband handed her his handkerchief, already soggy. Billy put his paw on her shoulder.

"You said you left something behind?" Bradley Badger asked.

"Yes, a chain I wear around my neck. I hope nothing has happened to it. It holds my two most precious possessions in the world."

"We won't keep you. You look frazzled. I'm so sorry we delayed you." Bradley said.

"No, I'm so sorry, sir. I'm so sorry, ma'am. Any son would be proud to call you his parents."

Billy left them to be on their way and rushed up the steps. He looked over his shoulder to see Mr. and Mrs. Badger make their way down the lane in the opposite direction from which he had come.

"Back already? Is something wrong?" Betsy asked.

"Mrs. Betsy Bear, I'm so sorry to trouble you, but I lost something."

"Oh? I just cleaned the rooms and saw nothing."

"No, I didn't leave it in my room. It must be in the dining room. That was where I was when I was removing the ring. It's a chain with a locket and a key."

"My daughter cleaned up in the dining room. Let me call her."

A few moments later, Betsy's daughter, Beverly, appeared. "No, I didn't see it. I cleaned the dining area, but I wasn't as thorough as usual. Mr. Filbert Fox was getting impatient. I paid him for the eggs. He departed. And then I got busy checking Mr. and Mrs. Badger out."

"Yes, I met the Badgers on my way back. They were such a sad couple."

"Yes, they are. I thought they might stay here in the forest with us, but I think they may have headed back to the city. Poor Mrs. Badger, she still thinks her son will miraculously appear. Well, enough of that. All too depressing. We must check the dining room thoroughly," Betsy said.

The three of them examined every nook and cranny of the room. Nothing. "I'm so sorry," Betsy Bear said.

"I am too. If only I had been paying better attention."

"You have had a lot on your mind. If it does turn up, we will be sure to get it to you. Where might we find you?"

"I'm not sure. I have no reason to return to the city. All of my friends are here now. It could be serendipitous that I lost the chain. What it contained was the past. The locket contained a picture of my family, now long gone. I have come to regard Tiger, Hyena, Ethel, Luce, and

Santiago as my family now. The other item was a key to the city. If I'm not in the city, I will need no key to it."

"You would be so welcome in our little community."

"Why, thank you. I think it would be a good place to make a home."

"I'm sure Miss Ethel Peacock and the others could use you in this school endeavor."

"I am going to dinner with them tonight at Mr. Densworth Lion's den. We will see what happens."

Betsy and Beverly said goodbye, and Badger hurried out the door and down the path, back to where he had left his friends.

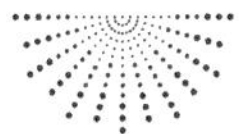

"That boy?"

"Yes, I know, dear. Best not to dwell on it. Might we take a rest under that tree? We have been walking for so long, and you are tired."

"Yes, that would be nice. I know we have been going around in circles. I can't decide," she said while plucking the petals off a daisy. "Do we go back to the city, or do we stay here? Everyone has been so nice to us here. And that young badger we met. I can't get him out of my mind."

"I know, dear. Is your headache any better?"

"Some. Do you see that fox up ahead? Isn't he the one who was staying at the bed and breakfast with us?"

"Why yes, I think he is the same one."

"We must say hello. It would be rude not to."

"Mr. Fox. Mr. Fox," her husband yelled out.

Filbert stopped whistling and stopped in his tracks,

trying to ascertain whether or not he heard his name being called.

"Mr. Fox." He heard again.

Yes, someone was definitely calling his name. He turned to see what looked like badgers making their way toward him. They looked familiar.

"Mr. Fox, we finally caught up with you."

He eyed the weary couple over. The man carried a suitcase. "Have we met?"

"Why, yes. Don't you remember us?" Bradley Badger asked.

"Oh, oh, the Badgers from the bed and breakfast."

"Might we walk with you a while?"

"Company would be nice. Are you going in my direction?"

"Honestly, we are not sure what direction we are going in. We thought of heading back to the city, but it all seems in vain," Bertha said with red, swollen eyes.

"Yes, my condolences. I heard of your plight. I'm so sorry. I'm indeed fortunate to be blessed with many fox kits, all ages. On the other hand, a lot of mouths to feed."

Bertha looked at the ground while her husband stroked her shoulder.

"Why don't you make a new start here?"

"That was the original plan," Bradley Badger said.

"It's a fine little community. Of course, you will need a nice den or hole. I'm sure the badgers living on the East end could set you up. As for your furniture needs, I'm at your service." He reached into his vest pocket pulling out a card, along with it pulling out a chain which fell to the ground.

Bertha shrieked. "The locket on that chain—I know it."

"I found it along the path this morning. I didn't steal it."

"We weren't accusing you," Bradley Badger said.

"Sorry, I'm so used to defending myself. I don't have the best reputation. Some think me rather shady, but if they were in my position, they would understand. What with all the kits I have to feed. Also, my wife's parents recently moved in with us."

"You are most blessed to have such a large family. May we see the locket?" Bertha Badger asked.

He handed it to her. "I haven't opened it. In fact, you can have it. I picked it off the ground for the key. I thought it would be a nice gift for our youngest, Baby."

"Ah, you have a new baby?" Mrs. Badger asked.

"No, he's a year old. I'm afraid we have run out of names." He held it up. "See how shiny it is. Baby loves shiny things."

Bradley scratched his head, raised his eyebrows at Filbert's pronouncement. He couldn't imagine not naming a kit. But Bertha was distracted by the locket. She rubbed her paw over the engraving on the outside. She recognized what had once been a rose.

"It's rather old and rusted. Like I said, I have no use for it if you want it."

Bradley opened the locket for his wife. Their younger, faded likenesses stared back at them.

"This is what the young badger was going back for. I was right all along. He *is* our Billy, Bradley." Bertha Badger wept more, only this time for joy.

Her husband took his wife's paws, laughed, and danced around the forest clearing with her.

Mr. Fox looked at them in puzzlement. "Does this mean you will need furniture?"

"Oh, yes, I think we will," Bradley said. "A whole den full of furniture, two beds for sure." He smiled at his wife.

"We must find him," Bertha said. "Do you know where he was going?"

"Know where who was going?" the fox asked.

"The young badger who was staying at the bed and breakfast."

"The one with the hyena, tiger, peacock, and pigeons?"

Bradley looked at his wife and turned back to Filbert Fox. "He was alone when we saw him."

"Must have been him. He was the only badger other than yourselves I saw at the bed and breakfast. He was at breakfast this morning."

"Do you know where he might have gone?" Mr. Badger asked again.

"They were all headed to *Baboons' Beautification and Grooming Shop*." No sooner had the fox pointed in the direction of the grooming shop, they were off. He shouted after them. "Does this mean I get to keep the key?" But they were nearly running, leaving Filbert Fox in a trail of dust. If they heard him, they didn't bother to answer.

They met a rabbit along the way and asked if they were going in the right direction to the Baboons' place of business. The rabbit told them they were and made a remark, but what she said they didn't know. Being so eager to see their son, they simply shouted a thank you and sped along.

"I so hope she didn't think us impolite," Bertha said to her husband, panting as they scurried along. "She seemed to be complimenting me on something."

As they were running through the woods, he said, "We will see her again and explain it to her, but for now, we must hurry. How is your headache, dear?"

"What headache?"

They rounded a curve and came to a sign on a birch tree that said *Baboons' Beatification and Grooming Shop.* It appeared to be a tree house. "What do we do?" she asked. "We can't climb."

"We ring the bell," her husband said.

"What bell?" she asked.

He picked up a bowl with a wooden mallet setting against the base of the tree. He ran the mallet along the rim of the bowl.

"That sounds so wonderful."

"My dear, you are in such a splendid mood. It warms my heart to see you this way."

"How could I not be?"

Eventually, a soothing sound rang through the air. A

young baboon came down. "I'm sorry we can't take any appointments today. We have esteemed guests."

"Oh, no, we don't want to make an appointment," Bradley Badger said. "We are here to see our son."

"There is a young badger here. Might he be your son?"

"Is he with a hyena, a tiger, a peacock, and a couple of pigeons?"

"Yes, these are our special guests, along with the badger."

They looked at each other smiling. "He is our son," they said in unison. "Might you send him down? But please don't tell him who it is."

The baboon looked at them with a stumped expression.

"We want it to be a surprise. You see, we haven't seen him in many years, that is except for a brief time earlier today."

"Then I must not delay. Right away, sir." The baboon sprung back up the tree in a flash.

"Hello, we meet again," Billy Badger said as he alit from Ethel Peacock's back.

Bradley and Bertha stared at their son with widely exaggerated smiles.

"Is there something I can do for you?" he asked.

Bertha held out the locket.

"Thank you, thank you. A thousand times, thank you. I thought I had lost it. It holds the only picture of my parents." He held it close to his chest. "Where did you find it?"

"It was fate we found it. We came upon a kindly fox in the forest, the one who was staying at the bed and breakfast. He had found it along the path."

Ethel, who was still standing there, rolled her eyes.

"It was so kind of you to come all this way and bring it to me."

"How could we not, son?"

"No, no. I told you before, I'm not your son."

"The locket. Look inside at the picture."

He opened it, although he had seen the picture a thousand times. "The picture has grown quite faded as I've looked at it so much, and the locket has gotten rusted carrying it around in the wet tunnels."

"But you kept it after all of these years."

"It's of my parents…"

"On our wedding day," Bradley Badger finished his sentence.

Billy Badger rubbed his eyes to make sure it was actually them as they appeared to have aged beyond their years. "I thought you were dead. I saw the garbage truck…."

"We eventually made our way back to the city. We floated on a barge out in the ocean amongst piles and piles of garbage. It took a good month before we returned. We looked everywhere for you, son. We camped out at the spot where we last saw you. After several months, I convinced your mother we needed to get away. We traveled from place to place. And then, we heard about the nature preserve. We thought perhaps we could make a home here," Bradley Badger said.

"It is providence that we found you," Bertha said, hugging her son.

"Oh, Mom, Dad, I'm so sorry. I left, thinking you were dead. This is all my fault. I should have minded you."

"No, no, Billy. Don't go blaming yourself," she said. "You were just a young cub."

"You were a rascal." Mr. Badger laughed. "The important thing is that we are together now."

Tears flowed down his cheeks as he reached out to both of his parents. After a long embrace, he said, "We must tell the others."

Ethel flew the three up to the baboons' front office. The receptionist that greeted them at the base of the tree told them to go back to the spa area. All eyes were upon them when they entered. "Hiram, Thor, Luce, Santiago, I would like for you to meet my parents."

"But you always told us your parents were dead," Thor said.

"I thought they were," Billy Badger said. "It's a miracle."

"Indeed, it is," Bradley and Bertha concurred.

"It is a happy day for all of us. I have a good feeling about the future of the school," Santiago said, looking up from the massage table with sleepy eyes as a baboon fluffed up his feathers.

"As do I," Ethel agreed.

AFTER SEVERAL HOURS OF PURE BLISS AT *Baboons' Beautification and Grooming Shop*, they recommenced their journey with Badger's parents. All felt renewed. Badger's parents looked years younger after their spa treatments. Of course, most of their rejuvenation came from finding their long lost son, Billy. The eight of them were ready to face any lion the forest might have to offer.

It was not long before they heard a dog barking in the distance.

"I know that dog," said Ethel. "We will be home shortly. We will have just enough time to rest up before heading to Mr. Densworth Lion's den for supper."

"It's been hours since we ate the feast at Betsy's Bed and Breakfast," Billy Badger said.

"I'm as hungry as a bear," said Tiger.

"But you are not a bear," said Hyena.

"No, but I'm as hungry as one," Tiger countered.

"We all are," said the Badgers in unison.

"HOME, SWEET HOME," ETHEL SQUAWKED WITH GLEE AS she opened the door. She spread her feathers and danced around as she entered the living area.

Ethel opened a window. "It is so musty in here. The place needs airing out after not being home for nearly a week," she said to the others who followed her in.

The space was cramped with herself and seven others. The only ones who didn't mind the intimacy were Luce and Santiago. They had been oblivious to anyone or anything other than each other since announcing their engagement.

"Please make yourselves at home," she said as she squeezed her way into the kitchen area. "I will make us a nice pot of Chamomile tea, something to help relax us before we visit with Mr. and Mrs. Densworth Lion."

The three badgers seated themselves on the couch. Tiger found a spot on the floor while Luce and Santiago perched themselves on the bookshelf, Luce to the right of the statue of Lord Krishna and Santiago to the left. Hyena twirled around looking for a place to sit and spied the chair in the corner. Not being a connoisseur of elegant design, sitting on a tattered, frayed cloth was not an obstacle after being sentenced to a dungeon existence for nearly a year. After that, almost anything was luxurious, even a dusty corner that hadn't appeared to have been touched in years. He removed the stack of *Owl Gazettes* and plopped down. In doing so, he made a heavy *thud* at the same time Ethel returned with the Chamomile tea. The cloth caught under his paw and tumbled to the floor.

Luce gasped, having taken her eyes temporarily off Santiago, not at the sound of Hyena's fiasco but at the rattle of the pot of tea and teacups on the tray that Ethel almost dropped. She quickly turned to see the cause of Ethel's alarm. "Why Ethel, why would you cover up such a beautiful chair?"

"That old thing?" she scoffed.

"Old?" Mrs. Badger questioned. "Why it looks to be new. Looks like it has never been sat on."

Ethel set the tray down on the coffee table and poured the tea, passing the cups around. "You're right. It's never been used. I regret I ever purchased that chair. I meant to donate it to charity, but never did."

Luce knew there was more to it than Ethel was admitting. She squinted an eye while studying her friend over and said, "What gives, Ethel? You are among friends. What is the story behind the chair?"

"You are right. I am among my dearest friends." She took a drink of tea, and the others followed suit. "You may have noticed there is a friction between myself and Mr. Filbert Fox?"

"Oh, yes," Tiger said. "How could anyone not notice?"

"I, for one, found Mr. Fox to be quite agreeable," said Mrs. Badger. "Without him, we would not have found our Billy." She smiled and kissed her son, who sat on the couch between her and her husband.

"Yes," said Mr. Badger. "He was most helpful, not only in helping us to reunite with Billy, but he was most courteous in offering us a discount on our furniture needs." He pulled the card from his pocket. It read *Filbert Fox Furniture for all your future furniture needs.*

"Do not let his sly cunning fool you," Ethel said with a huff. "While I'm joyful that you have been reunited with your son, be wary of any future dealings with Mr. Fox."

"Why so?" asked Tiger.

"Because," said Ethel, "one of my most beloved items went missing right after Filbert Fox delivered that chair."

"Are you suggesting Mr. Fox was responsible?" asked Luce.

"I don't care to admit that I do suspect Mr. Fox of thievery, even though the owls declared his innocence for lack of substantial evidence. I have to speak my truth."

"Not to mention, the chair may be of inferior quality," said Hyena. "Ever since retiring here, something has been chafing against my behind. I think one of the springs may be popping through the fabric." He got up from the seat and dug into the crevice with his paw to find the protuberance. Out came a string of beads. "I think I may have found the problem." He held up his paw, displaying a necklace of sorts.

"My missing prayer beads!" exclaimed Ethel.

"Could that be the stolen item in question? What is your truth now?" asked Luce.

"Oh my, oh my," Ethel said, fanning her feathers, sweat dripping from her forehead.

"We all make mistakes," said Santiago. "Isn't it about time we made our way to Mr. Densworth Lion's den? Do you think I should take my bongos? Would the lions like after dinner entertainment?"

CHAPTER NINETEEN

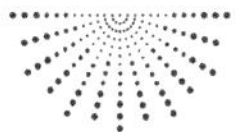

Glenda walked through the den, removed her apron, draped it over her paw, and gave every-thing a final inspection before their guest's arrival. There was another half-hour yet before she would meet this 'proud uppity bird' as Densworth referred to her. Other than Densworth's appraisal of her, Glenda only knew the peahen's name and that she was coming to discuss school matters with Densworth, something about a new school for all animals. Even though he told her about this idea over breakfast, she still could not quite grasp the full concept of it.

She had originally balked at the idea. A wild scheme, she thought. Densworth too, initially, flinched at the proposal, thinking it ludicrous; although now, Glenda sensed he was having a change of heart. Glenda suspected Densworth wanted to do something great before retiring—something radical. This school idea could prove to be it.

Whoever this peahen was, she had some kind of effect on Densworth. Hiring beavers to do all the long-overdue den repairs, putting in the skylight, and buying a new sofa? Perhaps he had discovered just how lumpy it actually was, having been banished to it for a night. And inviting her to dinner of all things? Why was he trying so hard to impress this bird?

They never had company. They never even traveled. There was the one time they had attempted leaving the forest, but as soon as they both got to the perimeter, they oddly became sick and returned home. Some kind of a strange headache hit them both simultaneously. After that episode, they saved all traveling plans for after Densworth retired.

There had been a change in her mate since meeting Miss Ethel Peacock, and she liked it. She was even feeling different herself, and she hadn't even met the bird.

"Vegetarian," Densworth had said. "I'll leave it in your good paws, dear."

Glenda had spent a good part of the afternoon foraging for mushrooms. Rabbit was out of the question, the peacock being a vegetarian. Even if the peacock would eat rabbits, the rabbits lived in fear of the lions and would be hard to catch on such short notice. Mushrooms would have to do. She had no trouble eating mushrooms, but could Densworth? He would have to. With each mushroom she picked, she let the idea of a school for all animals rattle around in her head. The more she thought about it, the more it grew on her, and the more she thought it *could* work.

Would the rabbits and squirrels be a part of it? The squirrels also feared them. When it came down to it, most of the smaller creatures in the forest feared the lions. If this were to work, a whole new way of life would have to come about. This idea would need proper leadership, those with a more amicable attitude. She didn't quite see her mate as pulling that one off.

After getting the mushroom lasagna underway, Glenda looked to see her husband running the feather duster over his books. "Dear, you might want to get that out of sight. A feather duster might be offensive to a peacock." In ordinary circumstances, Densworth would have growled, but ever since she returned from her mother's house, Densworth had taken on a gentler stance with her, the same one he took with his precious book collection.

Although she had never been a jealous lioness, his book collection gave her pause. He always found the time when not reading one of them to peruse them and make sure they were in order and not collecting dust. And now with the new built-in bookcase, the beavers had installed in the corner, she knew Densworth would be a permanent fixture there. She sometimes resented that he was so engrossed in his little corner, the one he called his study. But she considered the alternative and dismissed her thoughts as not jealous but envious that she didn't have a hobby, herself.

All first editions from the owls—he took great pride

in them, the one thing he could show off to company. However, they rarely had company, until today that is. Today was both rare and unique. Rare in that Miss Ethel Peacock was coming and unique in that Densworth winked at her every chance and had trouble keeping his paws off her. Although she acted coy, she relished this new-found attention. She attributed it to last night's full moon, along with all the wine they had consumed.

The smell of the lasagna permeated the air of their small den. She was just eyeing the appetizers—which looked perfect—before jumping at the sound of the door knocker. "She's early." Glenda stashed her apron in the closet and said, "Densworth, you must answer the door, being you are the one who knows her."

"I hardly know her, but as you wish, my dear," he said with a smile.

Glenda fidgeted with her necklace, a gift from Densworth for their first anniversary.

Densworth looked back at her and winked again before opening the door. She knew by his expression that the light from the new skylight she stood under was catching her just right. She could tell he wanted nothing more than to be alone with her this moment. It sent a shiver through her.

"Matilda!" exclaimed Densworth. The shiver subsided.

Matilda bounded through their den. She was a ball of energy but when had she not been?

Matilda looked over Densworth's shoulder and said, "Dear sister, I'm here for a visit." She stopped dead in her tracks and set down her luggage, not one, but two suitcases. This did not look good.

"Oh, I like what you've done with the place." Her eyes traveled around the room and then upward following the beam of light shining down into the center of the room, still casting a halo around Glenda. Matilda's eyes darted to Densworth. "Did you win the lottery or something?" She looked back at Glenda. "Surely Densworth didn't spring for this, the miser that he is."

Everything had been going so well. Glenda had high hopes for this dinner party. Glenda liked Matilda, thought her a breath of fresh air. She wasn't even *her* sister. She was Densworth's sister, the black lion of the family, according to Densworth. He was repeating his father. As far as Glenda was concerned, Matilda was anything but the failure of the family—more like a role model. It's just that now wasn't a good time.

There was friction between Densworth and Matilda. She had come to the forest with them, but they hadn't seen Matilda in months. She took off without saying a word. They chalked it up to meeting a mate (Matilda was impulsive like that) or to some cause she rushed off to join. Matilda was a true lioness liber. She traveled the world, went wherever some rally for lionesses' rights was taking place. Plus, she had stood up to Densworth's father, something Densworth would *never* do.

"No protests anywhere?" Densworth huffed in sarcasm.

"Now, Densworth, is that any way to greet your sister?"

"It's just, Matilda, this is bad timing, *very* bad timing," he said.

"It looks like great timing to me. Did you perhaps build a guest house in the backyard? Looks like you have fixed up the place."

Before Densworth could answer, there was another rap on the door.

"We are having company, Matilda—a dinner guest. Densworth is a little nervous. Please, please be on your best behavior," Glenda said.

"I'm not nervous," he growled.

"Of course not, dear," Glenda said, rolling her eyes.

"Why, Glenda, you know me. I'm always on my best behavior," Matilda said with a mischievous giggle.

Densworth looked at his sister and gave a suppressed growl before opening the door. Ethel stood in full wing spread at the entrance. The three of them stood in awe.

"A peacock?" Matilda whispered to Glenda.

"It's a long story, but you'll hear about it shortly. Why don't you take your suitcases to the spare bedroom and join us after you freshen up from your trip?"

Matilda started to do just that but was caught off guard when the peacock folded her wings and behind her streamed in an unlikely assemblage of animal species in single file. There were three badgers, two older and one younger (they looked to be a family), two pigeons, male and female, the male carrying a set of bongo drums, a hyena, and a tiger. The latter two looked undernourished, to put it politely. They all reeked of essential oils.

Densworth stepped back in surprise as did his mate and sister. Matilda noticed Densworth was at a loss for words, highly unlike her brother, and the expression on Glenda's face was one of worry. "I thought you said dinner guest, as in singular," Matilda whispered to Glenda.

"I did."

"I will deposit my bags and make a quick trip for more food. Be back in a flash." Glenda's face relaxed.

"I hope I am not imposing with the extra guests," Miss Ethel Peacock said, half raising her tail feathers as Matilda spun past her out the door. "I hope it wasn't me," Ethel said.

"Or us," growled Tiger.

"Well," Densworth stuttered, wishing the bird would make up her mind, feathers up or down, although down would be better than up. How they could accommodate everyone in their tiny living space, he didn't know.

"Not at all," Glenda interrupted her husband. "Won't you all come in and have a seat?"

Ethel relaxed her feathers, and they each shuffled past Mr. Densworth Lion, giving him a once-over, and settled into their respective spots as designated by Glenda.

"I guess I should start with introductions," Ethel said. "Seated on your beautiful couch… Is it new? It looks new. It really is lovely."

"Why yes, it is," said Glenda. "A present from

Densworth. He surprised me with it on my return from a visit with my mother."

"Well, it is remarkably beautiful. So bright and inviting," Mrs. Badger said while sinking into the softness.

"This is the Badger family—Mr. Bradly Badger and Bertha, his wife, and their son Billy. They have only recently been reunited with their son, Billy. Such a delightful story, and all because of Mr. Filbert Fox," Ethel said, beaming. "Is that where you got your couch?" she asked.

"Yes, it is," Densworth replied.

"Ethel has a new-found respect for Mr. Fox," Luce said with a smirk.

"Now, Luce, we won't get into that," Ethel admonished with an embarrassed grin on her beak. "This is Luce, my best friend in the world." Luce smiled. "And this is Santiago, her fiancé."

"Nice skylight," said Santiago Pigeon. He looked at Luce, "We really ought to get one of those, dear."

"Yes, we really should, sweetheart."

Ethel continued, "We have Hiram Hyena and Thor Tiger. They along with Billy Badger have a most incredible story to tell you."

"We all have a most incredible story to tell you," Luce added.

Glenda passed the hors-d'oeuvres in the direction of Hiram Hyena and Thor Tiger. "I hope I'm not being insensitive, but are you ill?"

"Have you heard about the animals who escaped from the zoo?" Santiago asked.

"No, we haven't," Densworth said.

"Well, of course, you haven't," Ethel said. "How could you have? It happened in the city, after all."

"I'm afraid we get little news of the city," Glenda said.

"Did I hear there was an escape from the zoo?" Matilda entered the den like a whirlwind, carrying two bags. "I didn't have to go far. I ran into the most delightful rabbit."

"Rhonda, no doubt," said Ethel.

"Why yes, that was her name. When I told her we had more guests for dinner than expected, she was more than happy to help. She also seemed a little frightened. I believe she feared I would eat her. The poor dear bounced all over the place, all the while complimenting me on this or that and telling me about her many children and that Mr. Rabbit left long ago, and she had to raise them on her own. 'God forbid what would happen to them if anything should happen to me,' she said. It took some rather ferocious growls to calm her. She was so relieved I meant her no harm she doled out everything in her cupboard. I assured her it was for a worthy cause. Hope you don't mind. It's all vegetarian. That's all she had."

"Perfect," Glenda replied

Densworth grunted.

"I won't be a moment. Let me set these bags down. I want to hear all about this zoo escape," Matilda said.

They all sat in an awkward silence awaiting Matilda's return.

"I'm back. Please begin," she said while passing cabbage rolls. Hiram and Thor voraciously gobbled them down. "Not to worry, there's more," Matilda said.

"This is Matilda, Densworth's sister. She showed up before you arrived," Glenda said.

"Yes, an unexpected visit," Densworth added.

Ethel began the introductions all over again.

"Please, proceed," Matilda said, making herself comfy as Glenda poured tea.

Ethel began with Luce telling her about the animals living in the tunnels underneath the city. "Learning about these different species of animals working together, I had to meet them. She told me of a hyena." Hiram smiled. "A tiger." Thor waved his paw between bites of a cabbage roll. "A badger." Billy acknowledged his name with a grin. "A polar bear and an orangutan."

"But I see no polar bear or orangutan. And what of Mr. and Mrs. Badger and Santiago Pigeon?" Densworth asked.

"We will get to everything in due time," Ethel said.

They each took turns relating the whole story of their escape from the zoo, about Badger being their savior and leader, at which point Mr. and Mrs. Badger grinned from ear to ear, as any proud parents would, and about meeting Ethel Peacock. They ended with the telling of their escape and of how Orangutan sacrificed himself so that they might be free.

"He used the ruse of a human boy in concocting his plan to make sure the rest of us could escape," Hiram said wiping a tear away.

"Yes, we thought the boy would aid in the escape somehow. Instead, it was Orangutan's plan all along to pretend to abduct the boy from his apartment to create a diversion, throwing them off of our own escape. And he was right. A panic, the likes of which I've never seen before, occurred," Thor said.

"His plan worked," Santiago said.

"When we were out of the city and appeared to be intact and all accounted for, except for Owen that is, Polar Bear said his goodbyes, going his separate way to find his long-lost love."

Santiago put his wing around Luce who cooed.

"It was no surprise to me," Hiram said.

"Nor to me," Thor concurred.

They sat in awe for several moments before Glenda said, "This is a most incredible story."

"Yes, I would have to agree," Densworth added.

"One that will be recounted for generations to come," Matilda said.

"Oh, yes, how could it not be?" they all murmured amongst themselves.

"I don't think our dining table will accommodate everyone. Why don't we eat in here, if that is okay?" Glenda asked.

They nodded their approval.

"Excuse me." Glenda exited and reappeared with a steaming dish of mushroom lasagna. "Matilda says we also have dessert, an apple pie, courtesy of Rhonda Rabbit."

"Here, here for Rhonda Rabbit," Hiram Hyena said.

"It is such a shame about Orangutan," Densworth said. "Owen, you said his name was?"

"Yes, his name *is* Owen. I don't want to refer to him in the past tense. As we said, he was taken away in a van. More than likely he is once again a resident of the zoo," Ethel replied.

"One day, when we regain our strength, we can bust him out," Hiram Hyena said.

"We thought a statue should go up in his honor at the new school," Thor Tiger said.

"School, school," Densworth exclaimed.

"Now, dear, remember your blood pressure," Glenda reminded.

"You were coming here to convince me of a school," he said. "This school has not been decided upon."

"But, we thought…" growled Tiger.

"Oh, yes, we must have a school," Matilda chimed in with a determined look on her face.

"Matilda is the activist of the family. She travels far and wide for the rights of lionesses," Glenda said.

"Oh, do say," Ethel said, impressed. "Where have you traveled to?"

Matilda had a far-off look in her eyes. "Why I can't remember the last place I was. Isn't that odd? One moment I was in the forest, and the next moment I was here."

Ethel looked at her puzzled, as did the rest.

"Well, no mind. I'm sure it will come to me," she said. "But back to the school. I, for one, think it is a brilliant idea. Don't you think so, Glenda?"

"I do," Glenda said. They all looked to Densworth.

"While I am quite impressed by your bravery, a school requires a lot of work, and we will need a much bigger building to house all the animals."

"What about the beavers?" Glenda asked.

"The beavers?" Luce asked.

"Yes, the beavers worked on our den only this past week. They are the ones who put in the skylight. Not to mention Densworth's new bookcase."

"Then, I'm sure the beavers would be agreeable," Ethel Peacock confirmed.

"I believe no one dares to disagree with you, Miss Ethel Peacock," Densworth Lion said with a defeated growl. Glenda smiled.

"Your collection of books is quite impressive. We must have a massive library at the new school, don't you think? You would be the perfect person to oversee that collection, Mr. Densworth Lion. I see you have *The Life of Pi*. It is one of my favorites," Ethel said.

Densworth smiled.

"Seeing that we are all in favor of the new school, I will bring in the dessert," Matilda said, beaming with satisfaction.

PART III

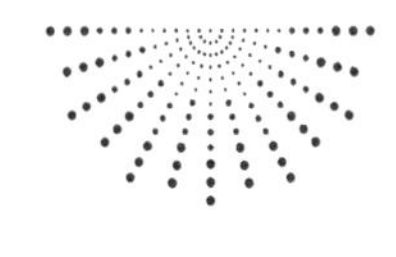

DIVERGENT PATHS

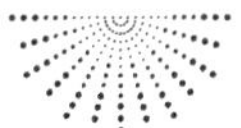

*P*olar Bear stopped at a stream. The reflection staring back at him caused him to turn away in horror and shame. He was shocked at how much he had deteriorated while living beneath the city for so long. How could he not know? He had certainly seen what it did to the others. Had he thought, unlike the rest of his cellmates, he was immune to living under such conditions?

He slurped up refreshment from the stream and lay in the grass, listening to the rush of water, tears flowing from his eyes. He couldn't face his family like this. Most of all he couldn't face F…

Doubts about his decision to leave the group clouded his mind. They were in the same condition as him and had been through the same ordeal as him. They understood. No one would understand at home. Back home, they didn't know about zoos. They didn't know about confinement. And they certainly didn't know about eking by in dark, dirty dungeons beneath a city. They roamed and played on ice floes and swam in clear pristine water—fishing, exploring, and playing. That was how he remembered his old life or rather how he wanted to remember it.

No one would recognize him if he returned in his present state. Would they even remember him? But he had to return to what he once knew as home, if for nothing else but to prove himself, to show his family how he had grown. But had he grown? He had lied to the others. Home wasn't the glorious place he had made it out to be. He was a misfit, pure and simple. Only the humans at the zoo and those back home knew that to be the case.

There was the surgery. Whatever was wrong with his brain, the zoo doctors had fixed. He would always have the scar, but he was smart now—not like before. He rubbed his paw over his splotchy fur. Now that he was out of the tunnels, his fur would grow back. He would have a lustrous coat once again. It would even cover the scar like it had before. He had to hope he would heal. Hope was all he had at this point.

Polar Bear got back to his feet with a plan and renewed determination. He would take his time in returning—catch fish at every stream—fatten up, grow back his once shiny coat of fur, and then he would be ready to face his family and F…. If only he knew her name.

What he regretted most was not being honest with the others. Who was he kidding? Maybe in order to be honest with the others, he needed to be honest with himself. He hadn't been. However, since being with Badger, Orangutan, Tiger, and Hyena, he had matured, or so he thought. He wanted to prove himself to them as well as to his own family. But would he ever see any of them again?

Meeting Ethel Peacock and Luce Pigeon was a godsend. They exuded wisdom: Ethel with her esoteric insights and big dreams, and Luce with her down to earth common street smarts. Why had he always been so rude to everyone? It was a self-defense mechanism, pure and simple.

The others would accomplish this school with or without him. He knew it as well as he knew his own name. His own name—that was another matter of deceit.

Theodore was his proper name. Ted for short. Einstein was a joke—something the others taunted him with, but he had been referred to as Einstein for so long, it stuck. When he returned, he could show that now the joke was on them. If he were being honest with himself, he had to admit the journey home was about revenge as well—revenge for being the butt of their jokes.

He never thought he would see this day, walking freely out in nature. He never thought any of them would make it out of that man-made cave. He promised himself if they did, he would go home. Departing from the others after all they had been through together was hard, but it had to be. It was his test, a way of proving his newly acquired abilities to himself. And perhaps to prove something to his family and the others. And did the polar bear with the name that began with F have feelings for him? A female had never given him a second glance until her. Did he misconstrue her intent? His heart told him it was genuine, and that was in itself a reason to return.

He took out the photograph he carried in the red pouch. It was only a part of a picture—the picture he kept from the others lest they ridicule him even further. She had a beautiful soul. Anyone who looked at him would have to have one, at least the way he was.

The autistic boy had been a source of conflict for him. It wasn't that he didn't like Michael, it's just that he reminded him of how he once was. If surgery could fix him, why didn't the humans perform surgery on Michael?

He smiled, looking down at the fragment of a picture, trying to remember more about her, her mannerisms, her voice. Years had passed. He may not even recognize her, and she surely wouldn't recognize him in his present condition.

The bear, the mate of his dreams, whose name he didn't know had handed it to him before they all ran upon seeing the ship. Her name had been on the picture, but that part had broken off during his capture. All that remained was the letter F. The others were right. He didn't know her name. He only knew it began with the letter F. She was real, not a figment of his imagination. During his time in the tunnel, he had imagined so many different names. Whatever her name was, she was a delicate flower. And she was fabulous to even give him a second glance.

If F did have feelings for him, he could take her back with him. Already, he was thinking of returning to the others. Already, he missed them. If F would consent to be his mate, they both could help with the school. He was getting too far ahead of himself. First, he would have to find her. At this point, he wasn't even sure he could find home.

TED E. HAD BEEN TRAVELING FOR WEEKS, MONTHS—HE didn't know for sure. He lost track of time. At first, he rested every chance he got. Lack of exercise in the tunnels had zapped his strength. In the beginning, the crunch of his bones competed with the growl of his stomach. Eventually, both subsided as he became more proficient at finding food, and all the walking, paired with naps in dense bushy forested areas where he could breathe in all that was natural, restored muscle and strengthened his bones.

As the days passed he began to feel more like his old self. He wept for joy upon seeing the shoreline and smelling the sea air. Still, there were no ice floes as the air was still warm. He stayed as close to the shoreline as possible. Sometimes he sprinted across flat areas, mostly sandy shores. Home couldn't be that much further.

There were brushes with danger often enough.

Before he made his way to the sea, he sometimes had no choice but to travel through human-populated areas. In those cases, traveling by night was the only option.

Once he thought his journey had come to an end when the sun came up. With its rise, the humans stirred in great numbers. They wore brightly colored cloths around their necks resembling ropes or leashes. Luckily, the small, rectangular blocks they were holding up to their faces, the ones they held at the zoo and at the park during the escape, distracted them enough not to even notice him. Or if they did, they thought him a brief figment of their imagination and once again averted their eyes back to the thin, rectangular blocks.

He narrowly escaped the walking human zombies to find himself in a rubble-filled alley with other humans who could have easily been mistaken for human tunnel dwellers. Their stench reminded him of his former days in the tunnels.

This sect of humans had a different form of diversion from reality. One of them held up something in a paper sack, offering to share. Whatever they were drinking took away their fear of him. He looked into their reddened eyes, listened to their slurred human speech, and walked away toward a spot that would serve as a shady out-of-sight day bed. They staggered around in circles giving up on being hosts and settled into their cardboard constructions. None moved from their resting places as he stole away well after the sun lost its shine.

There was another time his journey might have ended tragically. Luckily, the farmer was a bad shot.

And luckily, he had devoured enough fish in the farmer's pond to energize him for a brisk run.

Whenever human civilization was sparse or non-existent, he traveled in a carefree manner on the beach. He swam in the ocean, feasting on fish and sometimes seals. With each day that passed, he felt his strength returning even more, and the reflection that he spied in still pools of water was no longer anything he turned away from in shame.

The area became more rugged, but still, there were always boats to be seen, sometimes along the shoreline, sometimes further out. A fleet of ships was the reason for his retreat into the mountainous area above the shoreline, where he happened upon the family of black bears. There were two adults and a cub roaming outside a cave. The female's first reaction was to shield her cub. At first, the male growled as a sign for him to leave, and Ted E. readily complied and walked away. He hadn't come all of this way for trouble. The black male bear's curiosity got the better of him, and he shouted in his wake, "What are *you,* a white bear, doing so far south?"

Polar Bear came to an abrupt halt and did an about-face. "You know where my kind live?"

He hesitated, looking back at his mate, who had loosened her hold on the cub. When he turned his head back, he said, "Some of our kind have been to the North. They have come back with tales of the white bear."

Seeing the black bears as a respite from the journey,

he asked, "Would you like to hear my most remarkable tale?"

The cub looked at his parents with pleading eyes, although it wasn't necessary. The black bears appeared to be living on their own and were eager to hear any news from near or afar.

"That would be nice. I am called Hobart. You may call me Hob. This is my mate, Henrietta. And this is Henry."

"I am known as Theodore. Please call me Ted."

CHAPTER TWENTY-ONE

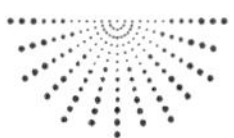

The lights glared in his face as he slowly opened his eyes. He tried to move his arms and legs but couldn't. He looked down to see straps on his chest, legs, and arms.

Someone was standing over him, talking to him. Blurry vision prevented him from making out the human's form. He tried to adjust his eyes, but the lights were bright, not what he was used to.

Three figures in white coats were in the room. He tried to make out their features. His eyes were gradually adjusting to his surroundings. The voice that was speaking was familiar. Molly? Yes, it was Molly's voice.

"Hello, big boy. Finally waking up? Long time, no see."

He was back at the zoo. He must be, but the room didn't look familiar. There were no other animals. Where were Joe and Mac?

"When the zoo called and told me you were here, I got on the first plane. How did you survive this long? Where were you all this time? You look awful. Not to worry. We'll feed you and get you back to your healthy self."

Owen turned his head to the side. The two others in white were coming into view. They weren't the same ones he remembered from back at the zoo. He studied them. They were talking to each other. He couldn't make out what they were saying. Usually, his hearing was astute. He felt dizzy. They had sedated him. He remembered a sharp sting to his side before falling into a net. There were screams and shouting before everything went black.

He remembered Polar Bear telling them how it felt to be sedated. At least he was still alive. But where were the others? He hoped he hadn't sacrificed his own self in vain.

"Do you realize I was living clear across the country when they called? A lot has happened since we last saw each other. I got married. Carlos is a remarkable man. I kind of have you to thank for it, Hector." She held up her hand, waving it all around. The reflection of the shiny stone on the gold ring around her finger hurt his eyes. He squinted and looked away. He had basically known darkness for the past year.

"We met on the night you escaped. I was so down. I had no idea what would happen to you. They finally got the lights back on, and I sat on one of the benches and cried. I was sure you would get yourself killed. Carlos was at the zoo to bring in some chimpanzees. He saw me on the bench. He provided a shoulder to cry on, and the rest is history. There was a search. The people at the zoo thought you might have made it to the Animal Experiment Forest, but there was no sign of you or the others. When there appeared to be no more danger, the search was abandoned, along with my funding. Carlos's specialty is chimpanzees. Spent our honeymoon in Africa."

Molly was still talking when Owen closed his eyes. His head ached. Whatever they had hit him with did a number on him, and he didn't need any more physical torture than he had already endured in the tunnels. He was startled back to reality when one of the male voices got nearer. He was standing right over Owen. Could this be Carlos?

"What are you doing, Molly? Telling an orangutan about your life, like he understands you?" The man laughed.

Owen heard another male laugh. Except he wasn't a man. He was younger, almost a man. Sometimes humans all looked alike to Owen.

"Johnny, did you check on the giraffes earlier?"

Giraffes! He must be back at the zoo.

"They seemed fine," he said.

"As soon as you sweep up around here, you can head for home."

"What about me?" an older scratchy voice asked.

Owen turned his head in the other direction. A man sat in the corner. He was wearing a uniform, but it wasn't blue like the ones he saw in the park. It was brown, and the man had a gun in a holster to his side. Owen knew guns. He jerked, but the straps around his body stopped him from moving very far. *They must think he is a threat.*

"Hector, settle down. It's okay." Molly looked over at the man and the almost man. "He's obviously been through a lot."

"The reason the zoo wouldn't take him back," the man said.

So, he wasn't at the zoo. Where was he?

"I'm off now," said the almost man.

"I'm not far behind you. I need to go home and feed my dog and cats. I'll be back later, Molly. Will you and Bruce be okay alone with him?"

"Sure, we will," Molly said. "Hector and I are old friends. Aren't we, Hector?"

Owen sighed.

A WHOLE MONTH PASSED. THE REASON OWEN KNEW this was because Molly marked off the days and her progress in a notebook she kept. She was always writing things down after interacting with Owen. She usually did it with a smile on her face.

One day she said, "A whole month has passed, Hector." He didn't know if that was a good thing or a bad thing, though he guessed it was good since he was no longer on the table in restraints but in a caged area like back at the zoo except on the inside. There were no other animals. Although he heard them talking about other animals, he saw none.

He was feeling healthier. There was so much food, so much he could hardly keep it down in the beginning. There were pellets intermingled with the fruit and leaves. He picked them out at first but was chastised by Molly. Molly called them vitamins. What vitamins were, he didn't know, but Molly explained that they were good for him. His fur had taken on a new luster and had stopped falling out. In fact, it was growing back. He could no longer feel his ribs. He hoped the others were faring as well. Mainly, he hoped the others were alive.

Molly had begun once again working in sign language with him. She even brought in the alphabet blocks, not the same ones. He lost those during his capture. He wanted to spell out his correct name for her and one day almost did but decided at the last minute to err on the side of caution.

Molly kept talking about this place for animals. It was all some sort of experiment. All he could ascertain was the humans put various wild animals in with the ones already there to see how they would interact. He heard *controlled experiment.* The word *plan* was also thrown around. Owen kept trying to figure out what controlled experiment meant and what the plan was. He thought it best not to let them know he could understand them or partially understand them.

The man, who he thought might be Carlos at first,

was actually Craig. Craig talked about the animal experiment as well. He worked there along with the younger man whose name was Johnny. Neither Craig nor Molly were the ones in charge. That was a whole other group of scientists. Owen had only seen them once. The whole time they were there, Molly bragged on him, "Hector knows this word and that word. We really are making remarkable progress."

They nodded their heads in acknowledgment of Molly's pronouncements but mostly asked Craig about how the giraffes, bears, and lions were doing. There was one lion, in particular, a female they brought back to the lab for a while. They were concerned the dose they had given her had not taken effect. The word *dose* was another word Owen didn't understand. In actuality, there were a lot of human words he didn't understand. He used every sense he had to understand them. He paid particular attention to their body movements when they talked, their facial expressions, and to the tone of their utterances.

Molly's tone had taken a wrong turn over the last week. It wasn't hard to figure out it had something to do with Carlos. Her mate wanted her back home. Everything in Molly's body language, facial expression, and tone sent mixed feelings. He was beginning to understand that what was written in children's books and how what the grown humans actually spoke was worlds apart.

In the beginning, Molly was getting back to the hotel early, someplace she temporarily called home, where she went after being at the lab all day to do something called Skyping with Carlos. But for the past week, she was staying later and avoiding Carlos's calls on her smartphone. Owen had learned about smartphones. The younger man, Johnny, stayed on his all the time and often got yelled at by Craig for being on it so much and not doing his work.

Observing everyone became Owen's strategy. Strategy for what, he didn't know yet. He didn't see much hope in escaping. He had no idea where the nature preserve was that Ethel had talked about. The only places that were ever mentioned were the zoo and the animal experiment center, which they called the *Animal Academy*, and he had concluded that he was in a laboratory which was a part of this animal academy, though he had seen no other animals since being there. So where were these other animals?

Molly began staying late, ignoring beeps that went off on her smartphone. Johnny headed out as soon as the clock struck five o'clock. Owen learned eight o'clock and five o'clock. Five o'clock, besides being the time Johnny almost busted the door down to leave, was the time Craig left to go for a run and feed his dog and two cats. He sometimes came back later and talked to Bruce. He was always showing Molly pictures of them—his dog and cats. They were on his smartphone. He once even showed Owen a picture of them. Owen deduced he had no human female mate. Also, at five o'clock was when Bruce came in. Bruce, Owen learned, was the night guard. Owen pretended to sleep sometimes while listening to Bruce snore. Bruce woke up just before eight o'clock when the others came in and then he departed. Bruce definitely had a female mate. Owen heard her growling sometimes on Bruce's smartphone, although he couldn't make out the growls. Bruce after saying *yes, dear* over and over put his phone back in his pocket in disgust.

Observation had become Owen's routine.

CHAPTER TWENTY-TWO

*B*ernard Beaver scratched his head while pouring over the blueprints. He had finished up all other projects. This one was to take precedence. A month ago he was visited once again by Mr. Densworth Lion. He brought a most unlikely group of reinforcements, his mate and sister, a family of three badgers, a pigeon couple, a hyena, a tiger, and the one who was most definitely in charge, a peacock.

He had to get all of his ducks in a row, although the duck population was declining thanks to Mr. Densworth Lion. Or was it? No one had complained of any ducks missing. Perhaps, the peacock, or rather peahen, had put a halt to it. This peacock had a presence like no other. Bernard Beaver noticed Miss Ethel Peacock could even make the likes of Mr. Densworth Lion shudder. This was in part due to the fact that both his mate and sister gave the peahen their full support.

He didn't dread this project the way he did the

previous one, the den renovations. No, he was thrilled. Never before had a wing of a building been named after him. The *Bernard Beaver School of Engineering* would be his greatest achievement.

Betty, his secretary, said the peahen had a way of turning his head although he didn't notice her criticizing when the peahen said the project manager should be female, insisting Betty Beaver should be the one to lead the construction.

Everyone in the forest was involved in some way. That was due to the backing of the owls. Ola, herself, had come out to inspect the site. The Cub Academy would be expanded into several buildings—a campus they called it. It would be a peculiar school, for certain.

There were to be several stories in some of the buildings. The giraffes were to act as cranes. Almost every creature in the forest was to contribute.

Feeding the workers was a big concern. The bears were providing a major portion of the grunt work besides being major contributors of honey. Filbert Fox promised all the eggs he could procure. Although there were a lot of eye rolls when he volunteered at the last forest clearing meeting, no one protested.

Rhonda Rabbit was in charge of menus and food preparation. She also wanted to be the main social coordinator, but no one saw the need for such a distinction. It was almost dismissed since no one seconded the motion. Then Densworth Lion roared, "Ah, let her be the social coordinator. She will do it anyway."

Glenda, who stood by his side, embraced her mate in

pride at his gesture of making amends with the rabbits. Densworth returned the embrace and cast his eyes at his wife's blossoming belly, and winked.

Santiago gave Densworth a thumb's up, actually a feather's up, and called out, "See you later. Have to relieve Luce. It's my turn to sit on the eggs, although she would gladly take my turn since she uses the time to read *Harry Potter.* Can't put the book down."

YES, BERNARD BEAVER STUDIED THE BLUEPRINTS meticulously. No detail could be left unattended. The groundbreaking was only a week away. Every inhabitant of the forest would be there.

CHAPTER TWENTY-THREE

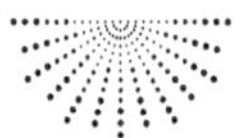

$\mathcal{C}$raig burst through the door. "Something is dreadfully wrong," he yelled. Bruce jerked awake. "Oh, sorry, Bruce," Craig said half-heartedly, his attention directed toward Molly.

But Bruce had automatically moved his hand close to his gun. Owen flinched.

Molly reached through the bars and stroked Owen's head. "It's all right, Hector. Nothing to fear."

"No, nothing to be scared of, O. Boy," Bruce said, removing his hand from the vicinity of his holster. Bruce and Owen had an understanding. Owen wouldn't tell that Bruce slept on the job, and Bruce wouldn't reveal that Owen was smarter than he let on. Bruce had taken to calling him O. Boy ever since what had transpired between the two of them that night. Owen didn't mind as O. Boy sounded more like his actual name than Hector did.

After seeing there was nothing that needed to be

done on his part, Bruce slumped back into his chair and closed his eyes again.

THE NIGHT THAT CHANGED THINGS BETWEEN OWEN AND Bruce happened a few weeks earlier, Molly had re-introduced drawing materials to Owen. The lab walls had turned into an art gallery with Owen's creations plastered to every square inch of available wall space. Molly told Owen his work was a cross between Jackson Pollack and Pablo Picasso. Owen had heard the name Picasso from Ethel. Jackson Pollack was new to him. Molly always left plenty of paper, charcoal, and crayons for Owen before she left for the night. "Never know when the muse might strike," she said.

Molly was staying later as she and Carlos were going through something called a separation. Owen knew he was the cause—the cause of them getting together and the reason they were now apart. Molly had made a brief return trip home and seemed happy when she first came back, but that had changed. He reached his hand through the bars and petted her a lot as her lips stayed mostly turned down. His touch and smile made her lips turn upward briefly.

Owen's smile was much improved since the tunnel days. A special animal dentist had come to see him. He almost didn't mind the sedative they gave him during the procedure since it didn't put him fully asleep. He lingered between both worlds, one in which he heard the dentist rattle on, asking him questions he couldn't answer even if he could speak human language and another in which he daydreamed idyllically of what his friends might be doing. He imagined them in their new school with his statue on the front lawn. He imagined starting an art gallery at the school.

Owen began signing O on his drawings. Molly often commented on his affinity for drawing ovals and zeros on all of his creations.

"What is your fascination with these symbols, Big Guy?"

Molly had an assortment of pet names for him, Big Guy, Big Boy, and Red, to name a few. She loved it when Owen smiled after she bragged about his work. "You are so proficient at these we are running out of wall space."

What Molly didn't know was that Owen was working on a special gift for Molly, her portrait. It was one of the sketches he hid between the rock crevices in the back of his cage. While he did most drawings as gestures, he gave others meticulous attention. These were the ones he hid in the cubbyholes of the rocks. The one he tried to perfect the most was the portrait of Molly.

The cage went back for some distance. Built into actual rocks and landscape, it gave him some sense of naturalness. A gated area separated him from what they called the lab. There was another gate that came down from the ceiling at certain times of the day. Molly or Craig always used sign language asking him to step to the front, and when he did, the gate would come down behind him, leaving him trapped between the two sets of bars. During this time, Johnny emerged through a door that otherwise stayed bolted in the back. He brought in a mop and sudsy bucket of water and cleaned up, usually listening to music through his headphones the whole time.

Owen didn't much like Johnny's music. It created a disturbing vibration. Most of the time, another form of music was piped in through speakers. Molly mentioned names such as Mozart and Bach. Mozart's music reminded him of nature, rippling streams, and leaves fluttering in harmony with gentle breezes.

After Johnny finished cleaning, he took his mop and bucket out of the cage and returned with food. Then he would leave again. The bolt sounded shut, and the middle gate mechanically retreated into the ceiling.

Owen's language skills improved daily. He listened. He learned. One thing he learned was there were other labs with other cages similar to his, housing other animals. When the animals were ready, they were released into the forest, what they called the animal experiment. He knew the animals had to all be studied and treated before being released to the Animal Academy, the other term they gave it. What he didn't know was why the animals were treated. He also didn't know if he was being treated. The only thing he did know was that they wanted the wild animals tamed.

One night after Molly had left, the creative spark hit Owen, and he began writing out his name over and over and then wrote **Not Hector** boldly at the bottom where he would normally put his signature of O. He meant to tear it to shreds but drifted off to the rhythm of Bruce's snoring. The next thing he knew, Bruce was next to the bars, staring down at the paper in disbelief. He was holding a cup of black coffee in one hand, scratching his head with the other.

Molly, Craig, and Bruce drank coffee almost non-stop. Johnny drank something out of a can. Owen gathered it was something that gave them energy, the way bananas gave him a boost. It didn't work too well for Bruce. The man slept more than a bear in hibernation.

That night, though, Bruce was wide awake. Owen picked up the paper, stepped back into the jungle-like area that was a part of his confinement, and tore his masterpiece into small pieces while Bruce spilled his coffee, yelling out, "No!" He shook his head and said, "Don't worry. Your secret is safe with me. They wouldn't believe me, anyway." He walked to the closet to retrieve the mop, the whole time shaking his head.

He mopped up the spilled coffee, mumbling, "Whatever animal experiment they're doing around here isn't right. No, not right, at all."

～

"WHAT DO YOU MEAN?" ASKED MOLLY. "WHAT'S dreadfully wrong?"

"Something is not right with the animals. I did my routine inspection this morning. Something uncanny is going on. They are all acting odd, different species coming together. Like the lion lying down with the lamb. Except the lions, bears, giraffes, foxes, rabbits, beavers, and squirrels weren't lying down. They were conferring with each other. The whole scenario appeared to be friendly."

"Isn't that what you want?" asked Molly.

"Yes, but there were others there, some in the group we didn't put there."

"I realize the smaller animals were already a part of the forest. But didn't we treat the lions and bears so they wouldn't be so hostile?"

"Yes, but there were two new ones."

"Oh?"

"Yes, a hyena and a tiger," Craig said.

Owen perked up and pressed against the gate.

"From the zoo?" Molly exclaimed.

"Yes, they have to be the animals that went through the park that night—the ones we thought didn't survive."

Molly looked at Owen who was wide-eyed.

"If I didn't know better, I'd almost think he understands us," Craig said.

Molly used sign language, "Do you understand, Hector?"

Owen remained silent, his eyes darting back and forth between them.

"A polar bear also escaped that night. Did you see a polar bear?"

"No, I didn't. Maybe he was too far gone and didn't

make it." Craig hesitated. "The thing is, the hyena and tiger looked to be healthy. And they weren't being aggressive. None of the smaller animals seemed to exhibit any feeling of threat from them."

"You said the water was treated?"

"Yes, to keep the ones already heavily dosed calm. There is no way such small amounts could change animals so drastically that haven't been through the process."

"You know Hector was with the hyena and tiger that night in the park," Molly said.

"Yes, and the big fellow went wild, veering off in a different direction, attempting to climb an apartment building."

Molly looked over at Owen. "You don't suppose…?"

"Suppose what?"

"It was a ruse to help the others escape?" she said, all the while staring at Owen.

Craig looked in Owen's direction, too. "I think he's smart, but I don't know about that. No, I think he panicked. What if he had taken the boy who lived there as a hostage, or even worse, killed him."

Owen looked down, shaking his head.

"Call it woman's intuition, but he understands us."

"He only signs simple things. He couldn't possibly understand us, could he?"

"The boy was standing at the window you know."

"Yes, it was a close call," Craig said.

"It was almost as if the boy was waiting for Hector," Molly said. "The newspaper said he was autistic."

"I don't understand. Are you implying something?"

"Maybe he and Hector could communicate. Why did he go to that particular window? When they interviewed his mother, she said Michael, I believe that was his name, loved animals. She said he seemed to understand them. That's why she took him to the zoo so much."

"Possibly you could conduct a study. You've been looking for a new grant opportunity. But what about Carlos?"

"If that were to happen, Carlos would come here."

"Oh, he would? I thought you two were at a stalemate over your careers, neither one of you willing to budge."

"That's true."

"I think you could change his mind if you wanted to. Never underestimate the power of female persuasion," Craig said.

"How would you know since you are of a different persuasion?"

Craig laughed. "But all of that aside, there were other anomalies."

"Like what?"

"There was a peahen and two pigeons in the group."

Owen rattled the bars as soon as they said that, causing Bruce to stir. He robotically got up from his chair and walked toward the coffee machine.

"We really need to bring a cot in here for him," Craig said, shaking his head.

Molly, only slightly amused, kept her serious stance. "That is odd. Pigeons live in the city. And you didn't place the peahen there before I came?"

"No, we didn't. I used the telephoto lens this morning and got some pictures." He pulled out the memory card and held it up. "Let me get these loaded to my computer, and we can look at them together." He went into his office with Molly close behind.

Bruce stopped on his way back from pouring himself a cup of coffee and stood to face the orangutan. "You wouldn't know anything about this would you, *Owen*?" Bruce whispered through the bars after Craig and Molly were out of earshot. "Well, I'm off now," he shouted as he walked toward the door but not before turning and giving Owen a thumbs-up.

CHAPTER TWENTY-FOUR

The three black bears lived as hermits, if you could classify a family of three as hermits. The way Hob explained it to Polar Bear was, the humans came into their forest with machinery and trucks, leveling everything in their path. They had no choice but to leave.

"They destroyed our habitat, our food sources. What else could we do but steal *their* food? Even though we were only taking their discarded food, for the most part, they took revenge. It is we who should have been taking revenge. After all, it was they who took away our home.

"They had guns. Henry's parents were killed. Several of the bears were. Henry just happened to be with us when it happened. He doesn't even know we aren't his real parents. He was so young when it took place. I guess you may have noticed we are somewhat old to have a small cub?"

Polar Bear nodded his head and let Hob continue with the story.

"The bears scattered, all heading further into the wilderness—what was left of it. We happened upon this nice cave and stayed here. It was almost time for hibernation, and it seemed like a safe place. We lost track of where the other bears went. We supposed, hoped, they all found various safe places to go into their winter sleep. We only awoke a month ago. We liked it here and decided to stay awhile before trying to find the rest of our clan."

"That is a tragic story. I have had my own brushes with humans, too many of them."

"We would like to hear about them. You said you had a remarkable story to tell," Hob said.

"Perhaps you would allow me to stay a few nights and rest up before resuming my trek?"

"We would welcome the company. We haven't left to find the others because I thought it a good idea to teach Henry how to survive on his own in the wilderness, but Henrietta misses her friends. We were talking about setting off to find them when you appeared."

"If you are not Henry's parents, what relation are you to the cub?" Polar Bear asked. "It seems odd his name should be Henry, so close to your mate's name."

"Henry was named after my mate. We are Henry's grandparents."

· · ·

Two nights turned into many as the three bears made him a part of the family. The three bears became four bears. Hob, Henrietta, and Henry, over a period of two months, had filled the void Polar Bear felt from no longer being with his friends.

When the four of them weren't scavenging for berries and insects, Ted E. wove rich details of his life into tales far into the night.

"You're the best storyteller ever," Hob and Henrietta said.

"Yes, the bestest," Henry exclaimed.

Unlike before, this time he was completely honest, neither exaggerating nor minimizing his experiences. His accounts were filled with emotion that often brought the four of them to tears. He told the true story about F, showing them her picture that he carried in the red pouch, about how the other bears made fun of him, and about how a surgery they performed on him at the zoo corrected whatever was wrong with him.

Polar Bear exhibited extra caution each time he removed the picture from the red pouch as Henrietta loved to look at it so much. She got all teary-eyed each time, saying, "I do hope you find her. There is nothing like true love."

Henry showed a remarkable curiosity in his scar and liked to run his paw across it. Polar Bear let him. There was something about the young cub's touch that made him eager to be a father himself. It didn't hurt that each time Henry rubbed his paws over the spot, he said, "You are the bravest bear I have ever met."

They all agreed his coat had grown back enough to fully cover his scar. Still, Henrietta applied special herbs to it on a daily basis saying it would help the scar disappear altogether one day.

Henry never tired of hearing about Ted E.'s adventures and had all the stories memorized. He looked up to Hyena, Tiger, Badger, and Orangutan so much that he bragged to his grandparents that one day he would set off and attend this school for all animals to which Hob replied, "And if you do, you will be the first bear in our line to attend school, the greatest school ever for any animal."

Having never seen a peacock, they were amazed at the description of Miss Ethel Peacock. Henrietta was in awe of the city-dwelling pigeon, Luce. Henry thought of Santiago as a celebrity and wanted to learn to play the bongos.

"Maybe someday," his grandfather said.

ON SOME DAYS, AFTER BOATS WERE NO LONGER IN sight, the four of them went down to the shoreline. Humans, wherever they traveled, left behind an array of garbage, some of it edible. Hob and Henrietta were always overly cautious when they did, after their previous encounter with humans. When there were no signs whatsoever of humans, they swam and played together, as if they were the only creatures on the planet.

Being with them reminded Polar Bear of the days

before his capture on the ice floe. Ted E. taught Henry how to fish. The cub looked up to Ted E. so much that the family named him as Henry's godfather.

"One day I hope to have a cub just like you," he told Henry. "But first I have to find F."

Months passed. Polar Bear felt so at home with the bear family he put off continuing on his journey—that is until Mother Nature reminded him it was time to leave. Brisk winds blew in from the ocean. The bears tasted the first snowflakes on their tongues. While Hob, Henrietta, and Henry became more sluggish with each passing day, the colder air enlivened Ted E.

They embraced each other in tearful goodbyes.

"I hope we can meet again, my dear friend," Hob said.

"As do I," Polar Bear replied.

"Please be safe," Henrietta said, putting another pouch around his neck. "Some dried berries and fruits for the trip. You will find your true love. I know you will."

Polar Bear bent down and rubbed his paw over Henry's head. "You mind your gra…" He caught himself and looked up at Hob and Henrietta.

"We thought we would tell him before we go to sleep."

Polar Bear looked back down at Henry. "Be a good cub. I know you will."

Henrietta and Henry watched sleepy-eyed as he departed, and when he was out of sight, they retired to their cave for the winter.

"Maybe we will see him come spring," Henry said.

"Maybe, son," Hob said.

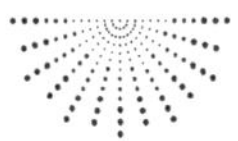

CHAPTER TWENTY-FIVE

"It's been eventful around here the last couple of days, huh, Hector?" Molly said it absent-mindedly as she tapped on her smartphone. She and Carlos were on the mends. He knew from her increased smiling.

Owen had even met Carlos, in a manner of speaking, as Molly started Skyping with him after hours. She held up her phone so that Owen could see what Carlos looked like. Owen wasn't impressed. Why did Molly want such a scrawny male? She told Owen to say hi, which he signed. She told him to smile, which he did.

When Owen first heard that everyone was safe and so near, he was excited. He thought he might be released to join them, but that didn't seem to be happening. He took to moping. Even Johnny, who didn't notice much of anything, noticed.

Did his friends know what this place was? Even he didn't know for sure. For what purpose were the humans placing the animals here? If it was to get along with each other, which was happening, why weren't the humans happy? Was it because the animals were doing it on their own? After heavy contemplation, he concluded that had to be it. If there was anything he understood about humans, they liked to be in control. He also understood they feared. It was because they feared they needed to be in control.

What would they do if they knew he understood them and could communicate better than he let on? If *he* could do it, then all the animals could do it. That would cause more fear and more control. He dare not risk letting them know. Soon, they would have to release him to the forest with the others.

Molly patted him on the head. "I'm afraid I will have to say goodbye by the end of the week. This was only supposed to be temporary. I have to go back. My marriage depends on it. Also, what grant money I had for working with you at the zoo ran out a long time ago. I tried to get an extension, but I'm not showing any progress, and without progress to report, the ones in charge won't let me stay."

Owen cast his eyes downward. The other scientists were coming by daily ever since Craig reported what was going on in the forest. Molly tried to get Owen to perform for them. He wouldn't. If he showed them what he knew, he was certain they would never let him loose to live among his friends.

"I'm sure you are wondering why I called this meeting," Ola said from her perch on the tree. A clump of leaves hung down, casting a shadow over part of her face, adding even more of an air of mystery.

The morning had begun with a burst of sunshine although clouds now hung over the forest clearing. All morning, the animals worked at a furious pace, attempting to make as much progress as possible before the impending thunderstorm.

They nodded and mumbled amongst themselves, some scratching their heads, those who could, in puzzlement at the interruption. Thanks to the beavers' everwatchful eye and instruction, work was ahead of schedule. But animals, being animals, could tell when a period of rain that would last for days was coming. It was built into their internal radar.

Cornelius Owl merely had to put his wing up to his

beak to hush the baffled congregation. Ola spoke in an ominous tone, "We are being watched."

At the pronouncement, there were gulps and whispers. Once again, Cornelius raised a wing, and silence ensued. All eyes were upon the owls, perched in various branches of one of the oldest oak trees in the forest, but in particular, the eyes were upon Ola, who remained in the shadows.

"The humans suspect," she said. Owls tended to talk in terse sentences.

Ethel Peacock stepped forward. "Suspect what?"

"What they suspect is unclear, but they are watching us with keen interest."

The owls, also, often spoke in riddles.

"What is your advice?" Densworth Lion came forward and stood beside Ethel.

The owl turned her head in all directions, perusing the crowd. "My advice is to stop the construction of the school."

One enormous, low-pitched groan came from the crowd.

"But we are halfway there. We must stick to a stringent schedule if the school is to be completed by next semester," Bernard Beaver proclaimed.

"Indeed," said Ola. "But if the humans see us as a threat, and the humans most always see animals as a threat, especially certain ones among us, they will act. How they will act, I don't know. But be forewarned. Whenever humans fear something or someone, they act irrationally."

"Surely you are not saying we should *abandon* the school project," Hiram Hyena said.

"No, we will not give up what we have worked so hard for," Ola said.

"Then what shall we do?" asked Thor Tiger.

Ola ruffled her feathers and once again turned her head in all directions. "They watch us even now," she said. "What we must do is scatter, recommence our lives before all of this began. The rains are coming. Beavers, go back and build your dams. Baboons, groom yourselves in your usual manner. Bears, acquire honey; rabbits, attend your gardens; squirrels, gather nuts, and Ethel Peacock, Luce and Santiago Pigeon, Hyena and Tiger, you must stay out of sight, for you were not placed here like the others. After the rains, I will send word. Any further meetings cannot be held out in the open."

"Placed here?" murmured both Hiram and Thor.

The animals talked among themselves in whispers until Cornelius flapped his right wing and said, "Go now."

They reluctantly obeyed.

BACK AT ETHEL'S NESTING AREA, ETHEL PASSED CUPS of tea around. Hiram and Thor sat silently. Luce and Santiago watched as their three hatchlings waddled toward Billy Badger who dangled a worm before them.

"I, for one, would like to know what is going on,"

Thor Tiger said. His voice was clear, and his orange coat with black stripes appeared lustrous. The forest agreed with him as it did Hiram.

"I must have an audience with Ola to see what she knows," Ethel said.

"But it will be dangerous," Luce countered. Luce was always the worrying mother hen these days. And Santiago was the doting, protective father.

"Perhaps, but we've come this far," she said.

"We can go with you," Hiram said, looking at Thor.

"No, no," Ethel said. "Ola said for you two to stay out of sight. The owls have never led us astray. We must trust their judgment."

"Yes," Badger said. "The humans could be watching us now. What would they think, seeing a peahen, hyena, tiger, badger, and family of pigeons together?"

"Badger is right," Ethel said. "We must all go our separate ways for now. I will see Ola and find out what specifics I can and report back."

CHAPTER TWENTY-SEVEN

Ethel crept in and out of bushes, staying off the main path, as she made her way to the owl sanctuary. She suspected the man with the dog and cats was the root of the problem. While everyone out of habit steered clear when he did his early morning and evening inspections, she noted in the last few weeks he had been lingering longer, taking his time, aiming his camera with the long projection in the front toward the preserve. Normally, the animals would proceed with added caution due to this, but they were letting their otherwise keen animal guard down, all because of their exuberance for the school. If anything were to happen to them, it would be all her fault. After all, she had been the one to bring them the idea of the school.

There had been some doubts at first. She realized a lot of the smaller animals embraced the idea of the school out of self-preservation. Most lived in fear of the lions. Rather than live in dread of the lions, they saw it as a way to work together with them. Some were suspicious, thinking it was all a trap, a way for the lions to lure them in since the school was an expansion of Cub Academy.

She walked along in deep thought, squeezing her feathers close to her side. She labored over the pros and cons. She had never once given credence to the thought there could be cons until now. Ethel had always been one to forge ahead with an idea she received either in a dream or in meditation. Wasn't such an idea divine?

The animals were now working together. Although she preached to them about the advantages of vegetarianism, she knew they all had their inherent vices. The lions still ate rabbits. Or so she thought. Why had no rabbits ever complained or reported one of their own as missing? There were many odd things. The bears never seemed to have a shortage of honey, no matter the time of year. And why had the lions or bears never ventured beyond the forest? She knew that sometimes the forest ranger took animals who were sick out of the forest and returned them when they were better. Or was that what was really going on? She had asked Matilda again, several weeks after the dinner party, about her adventures, and she abruptly changed the subject, saying it was all a haze. Normally she would have thought something was terribly wrong, but the completion of the school left no room for anything else on her mind.

She looked up to see that she had reached the owls' headquarters. She made her way up, passed the owl offices, and entered Ola's reception area. "I'm here to see Ola Owl," she informed the secretary.

Dorothy looked up at her, noticeably miffed. "Ola is not to be disturbed," she said, looking back down at her ledger.

"But this is of utmost importance," exclaimed Ethel, raising her feathers.

"Everything is of utmost importance at the moment," Dorothy scoffed.

"Won't you even announce my presence?"

"No," Dorothy said bluntly.

"Well, I never," Ethel said as she turned and bounded down the hallway.

She fluttered around outside the headquarters' entrance, not knowing what to do. Then the idea hit her. "I must see Filbert Fox. If anyone is sly enough to outmaneuver Ola and help, he is."

She traveled down the path with a determination. This time she didn't bother to hide. This was not an area usually inspected by the man with the dog and two cats. In fact, the more she thought about it, she realized it was the lions, bears, and giraffes he paid the most attention to. Filbert would be the most likely to know what the man was up to since it was in that direction he went when he stole the eggs, that is if Filbert Fox was even stealing the eggs. That first day she went to see Mr. Densworth Lion, they were having chicken for lunch. Why chicken? Did the chicken as well as the eggs come from the farmer? Why were the humans letting this happen? Ethel entertained all kinds of theories as she walked along the path.

Up ahead she saw the sign, *Filbert's Furniture Store.* One of his teenage kits told her he was at home and gave her directions. She traversed along, noticing the woods got thicker. She spied a hole in the ground. By the description the kit gave her, this must be it. She tapped her claw on the wooden doorway covering the hole. Nothing. Maybe he wasn't at home after all. Just as she was about to turn and head back, the door opened. Out popped Filbert holding a toddler.

"Miss Ethel Peacock!" he exclaimed. "To what do I owe the pleasure?" He wiped away some drool off his shoulder the toddler had deposited. Filbert, known for his fancy dress, was wearing a vest with holes, and his fur was going in every which direction. Noticeably embarrassed by his appearance, he looked away.

"And who is this?" Ethel asked.

"This is Baby."

"Baby, an odd name."

"Please, please come in," he motioned.

Ethel twisted and squeezed her body down the tight hole, adjusting her eyes to the dim lighting. She expected Mr. Filbert Fox to be living in style. She found quite the opposite. His den was as unkempt as his fur. All ages of kits scurried everywhere. Mrs. Fox appeared from a corridor, her paw on her stomach.

"Company? Dear, why didn't you tell me we would be having company? I would have straightened up the den."

"It's a surprise visit," he said, setting the toddler down.

"No worries about the mess. I'm quite the messy person myself," Ethel lied. "When are you due?"

"Any day now." She stood for a moment, totally thrown off guard by someone other than foxes in their den. "Where are my manners? Can I get you something? We seldom ever have company. Not even my mother. Both my parents were living with us but recently moved out."

"She's afraid she'll have to babysit," Filbert snarled.

"No, nothing. I just ate," Ethel lied again. "I'm here on a most urgent matter."

"Do say," Filbert said. "Please have a seat."

Ethel sat down on a worn chair and immediately jumped up. His mate ran to the rescue as fast as her condition would allow. "Here let me take that. The kits leave their toys all over the place. I'm sorry."

"Nothing to apologize for."

"This is my wife, Florence," Filbert said.

"I'm most pleased to meet you."

"I am the one who is pleased. Your reputation precedes you," she said with a smile. "How is the school going? I'm afraid I haven't been able to help… well, as you can see."

Filbert's voice took on an authoritative tone, "Kits, all of you go outside and play, right now."

"Even Baby?" one of them asked.

"No, not Baby. He can stay here."

"I'm here on a most urgent matter," Ethel said while

watching the kits scamper off. "Did I say that already? Yes, yes, I believe I did. I'm afraid I've been a bit flustered over certain happenings as of late."

"Please tell us what this is about," Filbert said. Florence took a seat beside him.

"There is something strange going on. You weren't at the gathering today, I noticed."

"No, I wasn't. I was afraid to leave with Florence so close and all."

"I totally understand."

"Do you mean with the humans?" Filbert asked.

"Why yes, I do. How did you know? That is why I'm here. I thought if anyone might know, it would be you. I'm right, aren't I? I just came from Ola Owl's office. Dorothy would not let me near her. I went almost immediately after the speech she gave this morning."

Filbert stared with a blank face. Ethel craned her neck, awaiting some news on Filbert's part.

"Dear, maybe you should tell her."

"Tell me what?"

"That the owls are not the benevolent benefactors they proclaim to be," Florence said.

"Now, dear," Filbert admonished.

"It's true, and you know it. With all of this stuff with the humans that has come to pass, the other animals really must know."

"Know what?" Ethel insisted.

"The owls have secrets too," Filbert said.

His wife groaned and grabbed her stomach. "It's time."

"I'm afraid I have no expertise at all when it comes to delivering fox kits," Ethel said.

"We do," they both said in unison.

"Perhaps, if you would be so kind to watch Baby and keep the other kits out while Filbert helps with the delivery?" Florence said.

"Here, dear, let me help you to the bedroom." Filbert took his wife's arm.

They slowly made their way down the hall. Ethel looked at Baby who was chasing a ball along the floor of the den. "I guess it's just you and me. I have no idea how long it takes a mommy fox to deliver." Ethel rolled the ball toward Baby.

A thunderclap sounded, followed by loud pellets of rain hitting the roof of the den. With that, all the kits came tumbling down through the hole.

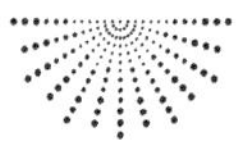

CHAPTER TWENTY-EIGHT

Polar Bear was floating on a piece of ice, his belly full from catching and eating seals all day. He drifted off to sleep as the ice drifted along the water. A loud clunk awakened him. It was the ice hitting another piece of ice. He opened his eyes to see a group of bears staring down at him. He gazed upward at their faces. One of them was his brother. He started to say something, but his brother spoke first, "Who are you?"

He rose to his feet. He had left scrawny with below-average intelligence. Now he both outweighed and towered above his brother by several inches and felt he could match him in wit any day. He slung his neck around, releasing a spray of water and growled. The others stepped back.

"I am Theodore." Polar Bear smiled, reaching his arms out to his long lost brother, but his brother stood with a puzzled look.

"Theodore? I once had a brother named Theodore," he said.

"I am the same Theodore."

The others gasped.

"Can't be." Polar Bear turned. It was his cousin Ralph who spoke. Ted recognized the beady eyes. Ralph had been the loudest and most voracious teaser.

"You aren't my brother. My brother is dimwitted."

With Wilford's continued rejection of an embrace and acknowledgment of their kinship, Theodore dropped his arms. "Take me to see my mother and father," Theodore demanded and growled. The group took another step backward in unison.

"Come this way," a female voice said. She appeared to be the only one not intimidated by him or his brother.

Theodore stood transfixed. Could it be her? She had grown from her teenage self and was even more beautiful than he remembered.

"This is my wife, Cora," Wilford said.

The hope he momentarily felt dropped like a rock to the pit of his stomach. It wasn't her after all. But it looked like her. Were his eyes playing tricks on him? Or maybe her name did not begin with F at all? If it was her, how could she not remember him? But then, if it was her, she was married to his brother. The point of whether or not she remembered him was moot.

"Whether or not you are my brother remains to be seen," Wilford said.

"Yes, we all saw his brother die before he was taken off by humans," Ralph interjected.

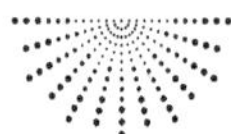

CHAPTER TWENTY-NINE

"Is everything ready for the transfer?" Molly asked.

"Yes, Molly. Quit worrying so much. Hector will be fine," Craig said. "The van is on the way now. You're so down. I realize you will miss Hector, but aren't you excited to be reunited with Carlos again?"

"Of course, I am. It's just I had such high hopes for Hector."

"Hopes for what exactly?"

"I honestly don't know. Perhaps that we could communicate better. We were doing so great. Or so I thought. He still only signs simple things. I thought we might move on to more complicated communication, but ever since all the buzz around here about the animals acting so unconventionally, Hector has changed as well, and not for the better."

"Yes, they are still acting bizarrely. I feel something

is about to give. I don't know what, but something. I will miss you, but now would be a good time to leave. They might scrap this program, altogether. You put everything you have into that orangutan and for what? I do believe your affection for him is more than for Carlos."

"Craig, how can you say that?"

"You've been here for months, apart from your husband. You're supposed to be newlyweds. You're married to your work. But then, from what I can tell, he is too, or he would be here beside you."

"That's what anthropologists do."

"You both study animals. Can't you come to a compromise?"

"He studies chimpanzees. I study orangutans."

"The two can't be combined somehow?"

"Perhaps, but he's teaching. He just got tenure. Thus, our dilemma."

"Wouldn't Carlos rather be out in the field?"

"Sure he would."

"You two need to work this out."

"I know we do. We've committed to a long discussion involving our future together. I will have time to make sure Hector gets settled in at the zoo before my flight leaves tonight, and then Carlos and I will settle in what direction our lives are going to take one way or the other. I really think it will be okay with us. We *do* love each other."

"Then don't look so down."

"It's just that I've been with Hector since he was

born in captivity at the zoo. It's almost as if he is my child."

"Maybe that's the solution."

"What?"

"Maybe you and Carlos ought to have a little orangutan or chimpanzee of your own, or maybe even a human baby."

"Craig, you are so funny."

"That's why everyone loves me."

"Let's change the subject. Earlier you were saying the animals are acting bizarrely again?"

"If you insist."

"I do."

"Well, bizarre is right."

"Are you talking about the different species congregating as if they were one species and the smaller animals not being afraid of those above them in the food chain?"

"Yes, and the fact that all that has stopped, the congregating, that is. Once they were all friendly. Now, they're not. Only that part has changed as far as I can tell. The lions still don't hunt the other animals."

"Why would they? I thought you gave them plenty of food to protect the wildlife already there?"

"We do. But still, things aren't right. Even though the lions weren't hunting or killing them, the smaller animals used to fear the lions. They don't. And it's almost as if they know we're watching them, and because of that, they have purposely stopped socializing with each other."

"Maybe you are imagining it. Possibly things are back to normal."

"Yes, in a way, but, this didn't happen until we stepped up our observation of them. It's like they know something is going on. It's eerily suspicious. Wouldn't you say?"

"What kind of drugs are you putting in the water? Do you think that has something to with it?"

"Could be. I just deposit it and observe. What's in it is above my pay grade. Anyway, with the new developments, my orders have been to temporarily stop."

"That's probably for the best. Still, I think you are being paranoid. At any rate, I'm just glad Hector won't be subjected to it, whatever you are doing to those animals."

They both turned as Owen perked up at the sound of the name, Hector.

"You see, he knows when we are talking about him," Molly said. She walked over to the bars. "You know. Don't you, Big Boy? Today is our last day together. The van from the zoo will be here soon."

Owen jumped and pounded and rattled the bars.

"None too soon," Craig said.

"What's wrong? Don't you want to go to the zoo?"

Owen jumped up and down wildly.

"What has gotten into him?" asked Craig.

"He definitely knows something is going on, me leaving and him being transferred from this facility to the zoo," Molly said.

Owen held up his hand and tapped his index and middle finger on his thumb repeatedly.

"No? No to what, Hector? What is it, Hector? You don't want to go to the zoo? Is that it?" Molly asked. "That has to be it," she said to Craig. "Zoo is one of the words he knows—the one I taught him as home. I wish we had the computers we worked with when we were at the zoo."

Owen retreated to the back of his enclosure and brought out a paper and handed it through the bars to Molly.

"Oh my God." She looked up at Owen. "Hector, this is me. You drew this?"

Craig walked over. "That is darn good, not his usual childlike drawings. I wouldn't say it was equal to Renoir but pretty darn impressive. He even got your mole. Do you have a mole?" He studied her face.

Molly scowled and flicked off a piece of debris from the drawing.

"Oh, my bad," said Craig.

Owen motioned for some more paper and a crayon. Molly went over to the table and returned with them. Owen placed them on the floor and wrote out **Owen** not Hector in simplistic kindergarten style and handed it to Molly.

Both she and Craig gasped. They looked at each other.

"This changes everything," she said.

Craigs eyes got big. "I see some major funding."

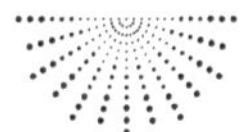

olar Bear stood before his parents. "Theodore, is that you?" his mother asked.

"Now, dear, don't get your hopes up?" It was his father who spoke.

"It can't be my brother, Mother. This bear is not dimwitted at all."

"Shush," his mother commanded. "I would know those eyes anywhere. A mother always does. This is indeed Theodore."

Theodore embraced his mother. He stepped back, seeking some recognition from his father, who was scrutinizing his new demeanor. He moved his gaze over Theodore's body, stopping at his eyes, peering into their inner depths for a prolonged period, as if inspecting them for the whereabouts of a future king. He placed his paw on Theodore's shoulder, breaking into a wide smile. "Son, we thought you dead. But you have returned to us.

You have not only returned to us, but you have returned a different bear." His father looked out to see a crowd had gathered. "Prepare a feast. This is a joyous occasion. For the son we thought dead, is alive."

His brother's snarl over the pronouncement did not escape Theodore. The younger brother he once looked up to as the older brother was no longer the same. Or was it him? In his former condition, he could not see it. Wilford, not him, was assured to step up as heir to his father's throne. With his return and his new fitness, both mentally and physically, this was no longer the case. How did he not see this before? But then, he was seeing everything with different eyes now—the same soul but different eyes. The ignorance had been removed and along with it the innocence. A shiver of regret over the latter crept like a kundalini awakening, a term Ethel might give it, through his body.

THEODORE SAT AT THE HEAD OF THE TABLE, A PLACE OF honor—his mother on one side of him and his father on the other. Wilford sat to his father's left and his mate, Cora, across from him. He could not help but stare at Cora, thinking she was the one he had pined for all this time. He noticed Cora was also ogling him, but then, why wouldn't she? He *was* the guest of honor.

"Dear Brother," Wilford said with more than a tinge of sarcasm, "you must tell us where you have been for so long."

"Yes, please do tell us," Cora said. "What is it like coming back from the dead?"

"Now, Cora, he obviously did not die. My mate is particularly interested in such matters—life after death."

"Yes, I do admit to it. But I am more interested in the change that has come over your brother. I remember him…," she hesitated.

"When he was dimwitted?" Wilford finished.

"Wilford," his mother admonished. "We will not have such talk here. I never liked it when you and Theodore were cubs. I particularly don't like it now. And what of your wife?"

Theodore looked at Cora.

"What your mother means, Theodore, is that my twin sister, Fable, suffers from the same affliction that you once had, perhaps a milder version."

"Fable? Twin?" Theodore exclaimed.

"Yes, do you remember her?" Cora's eyes widened.

"Dear, how could he remember your sister? I'm sure he remembers little, considering his previous condition," Wilford scoffed.

"No, of course not. I'm sure you couldn't. She has always tended to avoid group activities." She glared at Wilford. She knew that others poked fun at Fable, and she saw how it hurt her.

"It is better that she excluded herself as she couldn't keep up with the rest—always the last to get the joke," Wilford said.

"You mean the jokes that were about her?" Cora tensed up while placing her paw on her stomach.

"You remember not being able to keep up, don't you, Theodore?" His brother displayed a grin.

"Enough!" Theodore's father said, pounding his fist on the table, frowning at Wilford. A somber silence rippled like a wave down the long table, almost causing the wine the server was pouring to stop midstream. After the silence, Wilford picked at his food, pretending his father's admonishment didn't affect him.

"I'm sorry," Theodore said, looking down at his untouched plate of food. "Sorry that your sister sees the need to avoid others," he said, looking at Cora. "And yes, I do remember the jokes." Theodore looked at his brother, not in anger but in pity. Wilford cast his eyes away.

"We must not dwell on it. This should be a happy occasion. A toast," his father said, holding up his goblet. "To my son, who will one day be your ruler. May his rule be one filled with wisdom."

"Here, here," echoed those at the table, all except for Wilford, who continued to pick at his food.

"Please, please, eat," said his mother after everyone placed their goblets on the table. She placed her paw affectionately over Theodore's while displaying both a smile and watery eyes.

"Now, dear Brother, you must tell us what happened to you. I'm sure everyone is as curious as I am," Wilford said, pretending his father's rebuke hadn't happened.

"Theodore has had a long journey. He should eat and rest first," his mother said.

"Mother, I am not weary at all. I would like nothing more than to tell of my journey. It has been a most spectacular one."

THE POLAR BEARS LOOKED TO THEODORE IN AWE AS HE began the tale with waking up at the zoo in an enclosed area inside a building, under observation by a group of humans in white coats. Again, he was put to sleep. He woke up in pain with his head bandaged. The humans had performed some type of surgery on him. All he knew was that after the pain subsided, which took several weeks, his thoughts came to him clearer than ever before. He felt smarter, more alert. He could reason. Yet, a part of him missed the simplicity of the way his life was before. Everything was more complex.

After the white-coated humans quit coming in to observe him and check the wound, at which times he was sedated but not to the point he slept, they moved him to another enclosure. Only this one was out in the open, and there were other animals. He stood and turned and asked that his mother might pull back the fur from his neck to show everyone the scar. Reluctantly she did, and everyone gasped.

"Not to worry," he said. "Although I can't see it myself, I am told it is much better. That is because of Henrietta."

"Henrietta?" his father asked. A brightness shone in

his father's eyes. "Is Henrietta your mate? Where is she? You must introduce us."

"Yes, dear Brother, is she in hiding?"

Theodore growled and touched the red pouch that hung around his neck. "I have no mate. Henrietta is a black bear who I met later on my journey. I will get to her," he looked at his brother in anger.

"Son, please do continue if you don't need to rest."

"No, Mother, I am fine."

Theodore told of the night the lights went down at the zoo and of the mechanical failure that led to a brief opportunity for escape.

"You must explain *zoo* to us," one of the cubs at the table said.

"Yes, yes," the others echoed. "We have never heard of zoo before."

"It is something I hope you never encounter," Theodore said. "Animals of all types are collected, the way I was from your midst. They are put in various cages on display for humans. Day in and day out humans, in all shapes and sizes, came and gawked at us from the other side of the bars."

They looked at Theodore in shock and wide-eyed amazement.

"But some of us were fortunate enough to escape, if you could call it fortunate. For we went from one prison to an even worse confinement."

All looked at Theodore like hungry children wanting more of his story, even Wilford.

"As I said, there were others who escaped with me. There was an orangutan, a tiger, and a hyena."

"We do not know of these animals," his father said.

"You wouldn't, dear Father, for these animals do not live in the colder weather." Theodore sighed. "These animals, unlike myself, were born in captivity at the zoo. They hail from areas all over the world. This earth is much bigger than we can even imagine. In a way, I have been blessed to see a small part of it and to make friends with creatures other than my own kind.

"The orangutan, tiger, and hyena told stories handed down from their parents of what it was like to live in the wild before they were captured like myself and brought to the zoo. They longed for that life in the wild, even though they had known nothing but the zoo. It was instinctive with them.

"I have learned much during my journeys. I have seen the differences between animals and humans. Animals are instinctive, intuitive. We connect with nature. Humans avoid these attributes. They consider them inferior."

There were *ooh*s and *ahh*s as everyone looked around at each other, not believing what they were hearing.

"Believe it. It is true. You have had few dealings with humans. The ones you see farther north still act to some degree with instinct. It is not true the farther south you go. But I digress with this philosophical thinking about animals versus humans."

Theodore's father smiled. "The Theodore we knew before could never have come to such conclusions."

"And yet, we loved that Theodore just as much," his mother added. Theodore placed his paw upon his mother's.

Theodore continued with the story, telling about the escape from the zoo, about living underground for nearly a year, of how he met Ethel and Lucy, and how they helped them to escape from their underground captivity, and about the school for all animals that Ethel wanted to start. During the telling, there were questions —many questions. With every gap in the telling, someone had a new question for Theodore.

"A badger?" one of the cubs asked.

"A small creature, a burrower of holes. That small creature took charge and led us to safety. We owe our lives to Badger, not only for saving us on that fateful night we escaped from the zoo, but for keeping us alive. Badger adopted us as his family, for he lost his own family tragically."

"There is always hope," his mother said. "He could be reunited with them. You came back to us."

"Perhaps, Mother," Theodore said, not wanting to spoil their happy reunion with the incident of how Badger's parents met their demise.

"Oh Theodore, all you went through," his mother said, clasping her hands over her heart.

"It was hard, Mother, but in looking back, I don't know if I would trade it. For a lot of good came from it.

I gained remarkable friends—the best friends a bear, any animal for that matter, could ever have." Tears welled up in his eyes. He looked over the crowd, all strange faces to him, even those of his parents and his brother. The only face that felt like home to him was that of Cora's. Except it was Fable he was seeing and not Cora.

A small cub shouted out, "What did you eat? Were there seals and fish in the tunnels?"

He told about how Badger brought them food and about the different eating habits. He had to explain vegetarianism to them. He told them what a peacock looked like and talked about Luce and Santiago. There was much about a city he had to explain.

"A city is a place where humans live. Humans live much differently than we do. They have different structures for everything—structures they go to during the day, different structures they send their cubs to, separate from the structures they go to, and structures they sleep in during the night. Conditions of nature must be right for them to venture outside. In warm weather, their herds were thick at the zoo. In times of cold weather and rain, their herds were sparse. It is during the cold weather that most retreat to their buildings to hibernate. Humans are fragile creatures. Because they are fragile, they fear a lot of things, nature being one of them."

Theodore took a drink from his goblet. He laughed. "Humans fear such inconsequential things, small things." He told about the rats that lived underground.

"The rats thrived in this underground existence. The rest of us did not. With each passing day in the tunnels, we grew weaker, to the point even the rats who we chased down as food could outwit us. We had no fresh air, no sunshine, no nature from which to draw upon. All of our strengths diminished greatly. We became shells of our former selves. The fur fell in clumps from our bodies. We slept most of the time. We could not differentiate night from day." Seeing the anguished look on his mother's face, he decided to not elaborate any more on his physical condition.

"I'm afraid I was the sorriest of the lot—in attitude. After the surgery, I became proud and arrogant. I am ashamed to say I bragged to the others about my former life. For they did not know about my affliction or the surgery that corrected it. For certain, they saw the scar, but they did not question. They were, *are*, my best friends, and to my shame, I was dishonest with them. They also poked fun at me, for a matter I won't go into, but if I had been forthright with them, it would not have happened." Theodore raised his paw to his red pouch.

"Dear Brother, please tell us about the pouch you wear around your neck."

Theodore growled. "I cannot and will not at this time. But I *will* continue with my story."

The others murmured, "Yes, please go on."

"There were times even when we hid in the tunnels. For they were not completely free of humans. We knew the humans must surely be looking for the animals that escaped from the zoo. There were men in hats. They sometimes worked in the tunnels. Humans used noisy machinery to do their work. And there were the human cubs. These were the outcasts and rejects of their kind. There was one in particular who was the way I was before. I found out his name was Michael."

"Did the parents not care for their cubs?" one of the cubs asked in amazement.

"They cared, but in a different way. They controlled their young. But some were hard to control. This one, in particular, was hard to manage. He sometimes escaped from his parents, but they always found him. In most cases, the ones who turned out different were sent away, but this one for some reason was not. Badger could communicate with this one. The human boy was instrumental in our escape plan, in one respect." Theodore held his head down and sighed at the remembrance of Owen's sacrifice.

"Yes, yes, tell us how you so heroically escaped, dear Brother."

"Yes, you must have been in great danger," Cora said to her mate's dismay.

"Yes, danger was always a factor." He told about that chaotic night in great detail, finishing with, "The men in blue took off after Owen, allowing us enough time to get out of the park and go somewhere safe. It was then, with reluctance, I said my goodbyes."

"And then you came home," his father said.

"Not entirely. I started out toward the North, not knowing if I would find my way back or not. One of my lowest points was upon seeing my reflection in a stream.

How I was still alive, I didn't know. The others fared no better. Yet, I was determined to regain my health and my strength. I traveled slowly, resting, catching what fish I could along the way. I sometimes had no choice but to go through the human cities. Whenever danger prevailed, you could be sure humans were in the vicinity.

"I finally made it beyond the confines of the most populated human areas. Still, I always had to be on guard as I found that humans have a tendency to encroach on the wildest of territories in an effort to tame it and make it their own."

"How can nature be tamed?" one of the cubs asked.

"You would have to ask a human that. But on with the story. One day, I encountered a family of black bears. I told them about my adventures. They were eager for any news because they had been driven off their own land by humans. This family of bears, Hob, Henrietta, and Henry, took me in as their own."

"Ah, the Henrietta you mentioned, earlier," his father said.

"Yes, the same. Henrietta was good with herbs and helped me back to health. I ended up staying with the bears until it was time for their hibernation period. Reluctantly, we parted. I walked and walked, and now I am here."

Those around the table sat in awe. If a pin had dropped at that moment, it would have been as climatic as an ice floe crashing down.

"That is quite the story," his father said after taking a pause to properly digest it all.

Thunderous applause echoed off the ice floes. Everyone clapped vigorously except for his brother who patted his paws together in slow motion.

"With that, I do believe I am tired. I will take my leave now and shall see everyone in the morning."

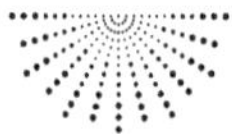

Ethel watched as both fox kits played. After being named Godmother to both Baby One and Baby Two, how could she not keep a watchful eye on her protégés? She had taken it upon herself to supervise their education. With less to occupy her time since the school had been put on temporary hold, she instructed the two kits in rudimentary schooling which also gave Florence Fox some time to herself.

Baby One and Baby Two did not quite set right with her. Since she was already seeing to their education, she saw fit to rectify their lack of designation. "They must have names," she told Filbert and Florence.

"We would like to name them after you and Luce, but since Baby One and Baby Two are both males, it would not seem proper."

"I am most touched," said Ethel.

"You are our hero," Florence said.

If Ethel could have blushed, she would. Instead, she

spread her wings in all of their glory, nearly knocking over the kits in her exuberance. She quickly dropped the wings back down to her side.

"Tell me," she said. "Do you have any other heroes?"

"All of your group, the ones who escaped, are our heroes."

"Then might I suggest you name them after the two male members who did not come back with us—Owen and Theodore?"

Florence looked at Filbert who readily agreed.

"Baby One shall be called Owen, and Baby Two shall be called Theodore."

They unanimously smiled, even Owen and Theodore.

Ethel *ah hemm*ed. "We must get to the business at hand. I have given it a few weeks considering Baby Two, I mean Theodore's birth, but we must get to the bottom of what you hinted at with the owls."

"Oh yes, the owls," Filbert said. He took in a heavy breath and let it out. "Please be assured, I do not want to degrade the owls in any way. They have kept watch over us most… how do you say?"

"Watchfully," Florence piped in.

"Yes, watchfully," Filbert said, rolling his eyes. He sat up more erect. "Yes, dear, that is indeed a good word. The owls watch. They see more than we can. They understand the human's language."

"But you, dear, are sly." She snuggled up next to her mate, letting out a sultry purr. Filbert grinned.

"You were saying, Filbert?" Ethel coaxed.

"Yes, well, they know what the humans are doing here."

"And that would be?"

"The only thing I've heard is that this whole forest is some sort of experiment. That is, it is not exactly a nature preserve in that they leave us alone to progress as we normally would on our own."

"What do you mean?"

"All I'm saying is that you might want to be careful where you quench your thirst."

"I don't understand?"

"The humans add things to the lake."

"What things?"

"Some chemical is my guess. I have seen them do it, put some other liquid in it, something green. I was first alerted to it by Mr. Thaddeus Tortoise. He has been here longer than anyone. If you want to know more about what is going on with both the owls and the humans, you might ask him."

Ethel sat back in her chair, eyes wide, amazed at this new revelation.

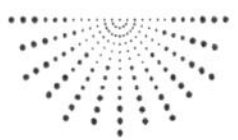

CHAPTER THIRTY-TWO

Ethel traveled down the path in haste, looking to the right and left. She didn't know where Thaddeus lived. She asked everyone along the way. No one seemed to know. Different ones said, "Oh, here and there."

"I usually see him right before a rain," one of the baboons told her.

"He was in my shop last week," said Sebastian Squirrel. "Always pays in cash. Doesn't believe in credit. Old school. Well, what can I say? He's been around for a long time—longer than any of us."

"If you see him, please tell him I was looking for him," she said, trying to depart. But Sam had to inquire about the school, in particular, if there was any news on who might teach the creative writing class. Ethel assured him he would be among the first to know before closing the door behind her and once again heading down the path.

"Oh, where oh where could he be?" she said to herself, half out loud.

"Oh, where oh where could *who* be?" Out sprang Rhonda Rabbit.

"Thaddeus Tortoise. Have *you* perhaps seen him?"

"Why, yes, I have."

"I do hope it was recently."

"Why, yes, most recently."

"And…?" Ethel waited.

Rhonda wrinkled up her nose and pointed. Ethel looked in the direction of her paw and saw Thaddeus relaxing in Rhonda Rabbit's garden.

"He often comes by for a light snooze. He finds my garden most serene."

Ethel let out a sigh of relief. "I hope it is okay if I wake him. I really must talk to him on a most urgent matter."

Rhonda's ears perked up, and Ethel realized her faux pas. If Rhonda were to get wind of this, it would be all over the forest. The owls would know before Ethel made it back to her nesting area which was only a hop, skip, and jump away. She must think quickly.

"Rhonda Dear, that acorn stew you brought to the groundbreaking—it was most delicious. Might I have the recipe?"

Rhonda smiled, fluttered her whiskers, and dropped her ears. "I don't a have a recipe. I could tell you."

"Oh, I'm horrible at remembering such things. Do you mind writing it down?"

"I suppose I could. Do you have something I could write it down on?"

"No, I'm afraid not on me. Might you go back into your hole, find some paper, write the recipe down and bring it out to me?"

"But you said you needed to speak with Thaddeus on a most urgent matter."

"Perhaps it wasn't as urgent as I thought. After thinking about that delightful stew, I find *it* is the most urgent matter."

Rhonda's cheeks turned pink. "Well, I suppose. I will hurry."

"Take your time, dear. I can wait. Oh, and the recipe for the carrot cake too, if you don't mind," Ethel called out as Rhonda hopped toward her hole.

As soon as Rhonda's tail was no longer in sight and down the hole, Ethel bounded toward Thaddeus and knocked on his shell.

"What, what?" he exclaimed. He looked up. "You are blocking the sun."

"Thaddeus, I really must speak to you."

"I'm here. Speak."

"No, not here. Could you please go back to my nest with me?"

"Do you have a garden as nice as this?"

"Well, no."

"Then, speak now or forever hold your peace. I'm old, and I don't want to move."

"It's about the owls. It's about the humans, something they are putting in the water."

Thaddeus roused.

"I see I have your attention."

"I admit you do."

"We cannot talk here."

"I know. I know. Rhonda. Not the best one for keeping secrets. Lead, I will follow."

"We must hurry before she comes back up."

Ethel looked behind her to see Thaddeus lagging far behind. She backtracked. "Won't you let me carry you?"

"I thought you would never ask."

They were a good way down the path when Rhonda erupted from her hole. "Ethel?" Rhonda called out.

Ethel covered Thaddeus with her feathers. "I'm sorry. I'll be back. Remembered I left something on the stove."

Rhonda looked around. "Now, where did Thaddeus take off to? Thaddeus," she called out.

"I HAVE NEVER BEEN INSIDE YOUR HOME. I SEE YOU LIKE color all around you, not only on your person. I'm rather dull myself."

"Oh, I wouldn't say that. You see and hear more than most. Why I had never thought of that before I don't know."

"Lots take me for granted."

"I won't make that mistake again," Ethel said. "Might I offer you some tea?"

"That would be nice, and if you have something to go with it, something other than carrots or cabbage rolls, that would be nice, too."

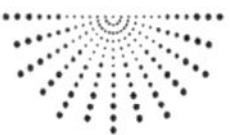

CHAPTER THIRTY-THREE

*E*ven though Owen was sad he wasn't reunited with the others, was glad to be back with his parents. All three wept tears of joy at their reunion. He spent the next couple of weeks telling his parents about his adventures as well as relating them to the other primates. Even Joe and Mac were in awe.

Besides the humans in white coats who came to study him, the zoo was attracting record numbers. The orangutan that had escaped and been on the run for so long, was the star attraction. Still, Owen practiced at being on his best behavior since some thought he might still be a threat. Owen noticed one man who showed up at the zoo almost every day. Owen had a funny feeling about him but couldn't name it.

Just as all the hoopla about Owen's capture was dissipating and the zoo's busy season was winding down, Owen looked up at the thinning crowd and saw a familiar face. He jumped up and down, pounding on his chest, and signed Molly. She waved back at Owen. Molly wasn't alone. The scrawny human specimen, Carlos, was standing beside her. They both waved from across the bars. Molly glowed. Owen's mother came over. "She's with child, Owen."

Owen noticed the slight lump in Molly's middle section.

IT WASN'T LONG UNTIL OWEN WAS MAKING REGULAR visits to the lab.

"We are back for good, Owen. Ever since you showed me the picture you drew of me and wrote your name for me, I knew I had to get back to you. After showing Carlos, it took little convincing him we should work as a team. I will be working with you, and he will be working with the chimpanzees. Perhaps you could introduce us." She laughed. "Feels funny not calling you Hector. I have called weekly to check on you."

Owen signed love.

"Oh, Owen, I love you, too," she said, signing.

OWEN SAT BEHIND A GLASS PANEL WITH A FLAT-SCREEN monitor on the wall looking out at Molly and Carlos on the other side of the glass. Molly looked at her husband and said, "I'm so excited. We've never had equipment so sophisticated." She looked back at Owen, signing and speaking, "When you are ready, Owen, tap on the glass."

Owen tapped, and Molly tapped on her computer, revealing identical screens for herself and Owen. Both screens showed columns of something akin to hieroglyphics resembling what they represented. She erased all the symbols, except for one, and picked out the one that stood for apple so that it was the only symbol on his screen. She went back to the screen that showed the symbols. "Now, Owen, can you tap on your screen the symbol for apple? Like this." She tapped randomly on her screen first, and Owen did likewise, matching the symbol she tapped.

Carlos slid a cup of sliced apples through an opening in the glass divider. She went down the list: banana, baby... Molly rubbed her belly and pointed to it. Owen smiled. She continued. Bird, ball, chair, child, drink, elephant, fire, giraffe, hyena... Owen got excited at seeing the picture of a hyena. "Do you know this one, Owen?" He looked through the glass with a gentle face and smiled, signing yes.

Molly turned to her husband who was standing over her shoulder. "A hyena was one of the animals he escaped with that night."

"The stories he could tell if only he could," Carlos said.

"We'll get there. I'm sure of it."

He rubbed Molly's shoulder and bent down and kissed her in acknowledgment. Owen jumped up and down. "He feels things," Molly said.

"Of course, he does," Carlos agreed.

"I'm hoping for the day we won't have glass or bars separating us."

"It will happen," Carlos said, smiling.

Day after day, both Molly and Carlos worked with Owen. After learning rudimentary words, they introduced Owen to the alphabet. Molly worked with Owen in the morning, alongside Carlos. After lunch, Carlos brought in one of the chimpanzees, held up a banana, and signed. He continued, using other objects, signing each. By mid-afternoon, Molly usually left for home as her doctor cautioned her not to overdo it.

At night, she and Carlos compared notes.

"I taught him to spell Hector before he escaped. How he knew how to spell Owen, I have no clue. If he knew how to spell his name, he must know more."

"The foundation that gave us such a generous grant to pursue it is counting on it. We'll figure it out, sweetheart. In the meantime, we need to be thinking of names for our baby."

"How's it going?" Carlos asked, bringing his wife a green drink.

She sneered. "I'll never get used to the taste of this."

"I bet Owen would like it," he said, looking through the window. "Has all the stuff he likes."

Molly held her nose and drank it down. A new symbol came across Molly's screen. It was a cup with a straw. Owen pounded on his chest. "He's thirsty, too." Carlos laughed. He handed Owen a cup of juice through the opening.

An intern came in. "Thought you might like these."

"What are they?" Molly asked.

"The books you used with Hector, I mean Owen, when you worked with him before."

"Thanks. Set them down over there."

"How about lunch?" Carlos asked. "The weather is nice. We could walk down to the jungle canteen. They have those big salads you like."

"I am getting so sick of salads."

"You have to eat healthily," Carlos teased.

"I know."

"We'll leave as soon as they come to put Owen back in his environment with the other apes."

"Oh, is that what we are calling it now?" Molly asked.

"Molly, we've been over this. We can't set Owen free."

"We could take him to the forest, where the other animals are."

"Only if the zoo agrees and if all parties sign off on it."

"I wrote certain things into the grant, not specifically that. I wanted to leave it broad. But a trip to the forest could be construed as part of the grant. You know, to see how he interacts, especially upon seeing the other animals who escaped from the zoo."

"Well, that will not happen until we write up our

quarterly report. Besides, aren't you afraid of what they might be doing at the Animal Academy?"

"I've talked to Craig twice since we've been back. The animals are no longer being taken out of the environment for injections. Nor are they adding anything to the water. They have managed to tag a few, in particular the badger that was with them that night in the park. They haven't caught the hyena or the tiger. To be safe, they have closed off all possible escape routes out of the forest, the ones not bounded by water, so they won't end up back in populated areas. They are letting things take their own course and monitoring the situation daily."

"And no trouble?"

"He doesn't report any. They are still providing food for the wilder animals."

"Where are Morris and Alf? I'm starving."

"They'll be here."

"What kind of books did they bring us?" she asked.

Carlos picked them up from the table and perused through them. At the sight of the books, Owen jumped up and down.

"Do you remember these books, Owen?" Carlos passed one over to her. She held up *Curious George*. "I remember this one. It was one of your favorites. Hmm, we had several *Curious George* books. They're not all here."

"You know, we will get to start our own collection of these books soon," Carlos said.

"You will have our child reading before he's two years old." Molly smiled, patting her tummy.

"Doesn't hurt to start early," Carlos said.

"What about this one? Could this mean something?" Carlos held up *Owen the Orangutan.*

Owen jumped up wildly and tapped on the book symbol on his computer screen which caused it to appear on Molly's screen.

"I think we have the answer to how he got his name," Carlos said.

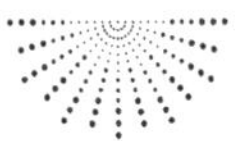

CHAPTER THIRTY-FOUR

"This is my sister, Fable," Cora said.

"Hello, Fable." Theodore smiled with both affection and pity. Was this what the others felt for him so long ago?

She looked up shyly at Theodore who was a head taller than she.

"My sister doesn't get many visitors."

"Come to think of it, I don't think I got many in the past either."

"But your parents are the rulers. Although we protect Fable as much as possible, you had every advantage."

"You are right, Cora. But it is as if some of those memories have been erased, or I remember them differently. The memories I had sprouted from a simple mind." He hesitated. "Do you think I might be alone with Fable?"

"Certainly. Just know she might not understand everything you are saying."

"I will speak to her from the heart. She will understand that."

"Oh, by the way, I wanted to tell you how much I enjoyed hearing of your adventures last night. You spin a remarkable story—from the heart," she said smiling. "You should write them down for all animals to read. For all the animals who will attend the school, the school for all animals. I like the sound of that."

"I do, too." He smiled. "I had never thought of it, but that is a brilliant idea of writing it all down."

Cora smiled and left them.

Fable stood on the ice floe, watching the fish swim by. The image of her he had carried with him for so long had grown dim, and he saw it with a simpler mind. Most would turn away, but it was Fable who had given him the courage to go on each day and to return to his home. But home wasn't the way he remembered it. He left as an outcast but returned as a hero.

The only thing still troubling him was his brother, the brother who had always protected him before. That was the way he remembered it. He was young then, and things aren't always the way you recall them. In the past, he was never a threat to his brother. Now he was.

"Do others taunt you, Fable?"

She turned from staring at the fish. "Taunt?" she asked.

"Tease. Do the others tease you or make fun of you?"

She shook her head. "I don't know. I don't think so. Cora looks after me."

"I can see she does. Cora is a good sister."

"Yes," she replied, once again turning her head and watching the fish.

"Fable is a beautiful name," Theodore said.

She blushed.

"I still have what you gave me on the day I was captured."

Fable looked at him with a puzzled expression. Theodore pulled the red pouch from under his fur.

Fable gasped. "My pouch! I thought I had lost it."

Theodore's heart sank. He brushed the disappointment aside, knowing he was once the same way.

"Do you know what Fable means?"

"No," she said demurely.

"It means story. Your sister reminded me when she said I should write down my story."

Theodore sighed. He wasn't sure what else to say to Fable. This reunion was nothing like he had envisioned, but then life didn't turn out the way most expected it to.

He was glad he came back, but he knew he couldn't stay. This was no longer his home. There was a time when he would have been home anywhere, the time before the surgery. He would have adjusted, not knowing any better. There was a time he wanted to take Fable back to meet the others, to be a part of the school. Now, he didn't know. But he did know he wanted to go rejoin the others.

"Fable, do you mind if I keep this?" he asked, holding up the pouch.

"It's okay," she said and turned once again to watch the fish.

In the weeks that followed, Theodore's father groomed him for kingship. Celebrity status was heaped on Theodore. The opposite sex vied for his attention. Female cubs, way too young, either giggled or swooned in his presence. Young cubs clamored for more stories. The male bears, close to his age, all wanted to be seen with him. Even Ralph was calling him his long-lost friend much to his brother's chagrin. When Wilford wasn't gritting his teeth, he doled out off-handed remarks and wisecracks.

Wilford's jealousy was creating a rift in his marriage. Seeing Cora's sadness left a knot in Theodore's stomach. It also didn't help that ever since his return, his parents catered to his every whim, although he was doing his best not to ask for much. Still, his mother seized every opportunity to make up for lost time, imagining needs that Theodore didn't have. Cora said it was a mother's guilt for not having been able to save her son on the day he was captured. "I ought to know," she said. "I often feel guilty for not being there as much for Fable as I should, and now that I'm pregnant…"

"You're with cub?" Theodore exclaimed.

"Yes, you will be an uncle."

Theodore smiled. "Fable will be an aunt."

"Yes, she will."

"And Wilford will be a father," he said.

"I know you are worried, but you are not seeing your brother at his best. He is going through a period of conflict. He had so many things he wanted to accomplish as king—good things. I only say this to you because I see in your eyes you don't want to be king."

"It shows?"

"Yes, you long to return to your friends, don't you?"

"Yes, I do. I no longer belong here. You are the only one who recognizes this."

"Oh, no, it's not that I think you don't belong. You would make a wise ruler, and you would grow to love your subjects, as they would you. In time, Wilford would even grow to accept it. But you would be divided, always yearning to go back to your friends. You went through a lot with them, and the bond you formed with them is strong."

"My brother must have some good qualities. Otherwise, you would not be his mate."

She smiled.

"You know, Theodore, that day you talked to Fable, you caught her on a bad day. On most days, she is high functioning." Cora paused. "I see all the unmated females throwing themselves at you. You don't seem to be interested. I wonder…" Her voice trailed off.

"It's not that they aren't attractive."

"But there is someone else, isn't there?"

"There was someone else."

"The night you told us your story and you clasped the red pouch, I recognized it."

"You did?"

"It was Fable's, wasn't it?"

"Yes, I carried it with me for all those years. It gave me hope," he said, clutching the pouch once again.

"She remembered giving it to you that day. She told me so, the day after you visited her."

"She did? But she said…"

"She was not at her best on that day. When you told your story, do you know what intrigued me the most?"

"What?"

"The school for all animals. You know what I think my sister needs?"

"What?"

"A change of scenery—one where she will be accepted on her own merits. A place where she can contribute." She looked down in reflection and back up. "Do you think Cora could learn at this school?"

"Possibly." A tear rolled down Theodore's eye. "I needed to come back, but you are right. I long to be back with my friends. I don't fit here. I think I did fit at one time, in an odd sort of way. My father wants me to take over as soon as possible. I thought I wanted this at one time, but all of his words of duty and responsibility go in one ear and out the other. The only responsibility I feel is to my friends and the school they want to establish. Besides, ever since I've been here, I've been so cold." He hugged his chest with his paws.

"Cold?" Cora asked.

"I've lost the insulation I once had. Maybe in time, I would get it back, but I'm not sure if I want it back." Theodore looked down at the water. He saw his and Cora's reflection. It could have been him and Fable staring back. That image made him smile.

"What is it, Theodore?"

"Cora, do you think… I mean, if Fable were to agree, would you give us your blessing?"

Cora smiled. "I would, but you will need to ask Fable yourself."

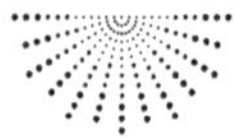

CHAPTER THIRTY-FIVE

"It is confirmed," Ethel said.

Ethel, Hiram, Thor, Billy, Luce, and Santiago sat together under a rocky recess camouflaged by a thick overhanging branch. Winter was setting in, and there was no foliage to hide them like in the spring and summer.

"We won't be discovered here?" Thor asked.

"We shouldn't be. Thaddeus said this area was out of range for the human's telescopic devices. And we came at different times not to arouse suspicions."

"What can we do?" Santiago asked. "We are no match for the humans."

"Aren't we? We have the advantage. Billy can understand them to some degree."

"I only understand the ones who are special, in particular, the boy, Michael. We have not seen him since we left the city."

"If only we had someone like him, an intermediary," said Ethel.

"But we don't," Thor said.

"We will have to make the best of what we have," Hiram said.

"It is so," agreed Luce. "We must start with what we do know."

"That's what I love about you, sweetheart. You always take the logical approach," Santiago said.

"What we do know is that the humans have been putting something in the water or have been in the past. But Hiram and Thor, according to your observations, they haven't been doing it lately?"

"No," they agreed.

"And the dog was trying to warn us all along. According to Thaddeus, he barked every time his master put something in the lake. We also know that some strange things have been reported about the lions and bears in particular. I have questioned Glenda and Matilda but not Betsy."

"You weren't too aggressive with the questioning, were you?" Luce asked.

"No, I was clever. I began by telling them about India, relating how I got to this country. I steered them to the subject of travel and asked them about their own adventures."

"And?" Badger asked.

"The thing is, they only seem to remember their existence in the forest. Once Glenda said they thought about traveling but suddenly became sick. And then,

Matilda, who is known for her globe-trotting, changed the subject whenever I inquired about her adventures. What is indeed suspicious is the blank stares they both exuded when I asked them. I changed the subject to avoid any distrust on their part."

"That was wise," Luce said.

"Have we heard of any other similar stories?" Ethel asked.

Badger hesitated. "I'm not sure, but I seem to have some missing time."

"Please explain," Thor said.

"The problem is, I can't. One moment I was on my way to see my parents, traveling down the path. It was noon. The next thing I knew, I awoke from being asleep, in a different place, and it was almost dark. My parents were frantic. They were looking all over for me. You can only imagine, having lost me once. My mother is still not over it."

"Badger, you should have reported this to us," Ethel said.

"Yes, you should have," the others echoed.

"Do you think the owls had something to do with it?" Luce asked.

"No, I think it was the humans. Thaddeus also said the humans take the animals from time to time and later return them. I have my suspicions that is what happened to Matilda. On my flight from India, I wore a tag around my leg for identification. I think the humans have tagged you. I think most all of the animals here are tagged in some manner, something we can't see. For all I know I could be tagged, but I have no missing time."

"There is nothing on my person," Badger protested.

"Not on your person, *inside* your person," Ethel said.

"Humans can do that," Luce said, nodding her head. "I have lived in the city long enough to know."

"I have too," said Santiago.

"Does anyone else have anything to report?" Ethel asked.

They all shook their heads.

"Badger, I'm afraid you cannot meet with us for the time being."

Badger hung his head as low as it would go, being that it was already low to the ground. "I understand. I am a danger to the group. I was probably selected because I was among the escapees."

"I fear you are right. We are all in danger. We must continue to lie low, not congregate in large groups. And now with all the foliage absent from the trees, we are even more susceptible."

"That means a further delay in the building of the school," Thor said. "It has already been postponed so much."

"I'm afraid so. No one hates this worse than me," Ethel said.

"Perhaps the beavers," Santiago said.

"Yes, we were in the middle of constructing the engineering school," Hiram said.

"And I so wanted to begin the statue of Owen," Billy Badger said.

"As do we all," Ethel said. "But if we don't proceed with due caution, the school will never happen. I do have to give credit to the owls as they are wise about that. Still, they are not telling all. And I plan on getting to the bottom of it."

"How?" asked Badger.

"I am leaving right after this meeting. If I have to, I will camp out at Owl Headquarters until Ola sees me. She can't hide from me forever. If there is nothing further, we will adjourn this meeting."

They lingered in silence, reluctant to move from their spots and each other's company.

"Cold weather has settled in. Do you realize we have been in the forest now for almost as long as we were in the tunnels?" Thor said.

"Still, we are no closer to the school," Santiago said.

"No, that is not true," Ethel said. "It is partially built. It will get completed. We must have faith."

"I wonder how Ted E. and Owen are doing," Hiram said.

"Luce, Santiago, I know Owen wasn't at the zoo when you flew back to check, but that was before your hatchlings were born. Now that they are older, might you make another trip and see if there is any word?"

"We were talking about doing just that the other day. I know you have your hands full with your two fox godkits, but would you care to watch our three as well?" Luce asked.

"They are all my godchildren. You know I love babysitting."

"Then, we will leave first thing tomorrow morning," Santiago said.

"I will send word when we will meet again. The meeting will be held at a different place. Badger…"

"I know. I won't be meeting with you."

"And remember, everything we discuss is to be kept secret," Ethel reminded them.

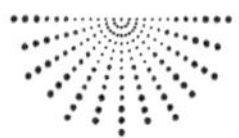

CHAPTER THIRTY-SIX

"This is nice. We haven't had a night out in a long time," Molly said.

"I'm so glad we are taking this time for ourselves," Carlos said.

"We've worked hard. Our sponsors gave us high marks on the quarterly report."

"We have more than that to celebrate," he said, bringing his glass of wine up against her glass of sparkling water. "At our last check-up, the doctor said our baby boy is doing fine."

"Cheers," Molly said.

"Cheers."

FIVE CHILDREN ACCOMPANIED BY TWO ADULT supervisors entered Molly and Owen's inner sanctum. Mrs. Briggs spoke, "Children, this is Molly."

"Hello." Molly made no physical contact as she was advised against it. She was given a complete set of instructions and profiles on each of the children who would take part in the study.

Mrs. Briggs, a special teacher, and her assistant, Miss Cooper, would be present at all times.

Michael was among them. Molly had specifically sought Michael out. His mother who had full custody since the divorce was reluctant at first, but Molly had convinced her he would not be in harm's way. She had said, "Mrs. Carroll, please be assured, I would never put Michael in danger in any way. As you can see, I am with child, myself." This had been the trump card in persuading Michael's mother to sign the consent form.

Molly walked over to the glass enclosure and asked that Owen be brought out. Three of the children, two boys and one girl, erupted into smiles. One of the boys who smiled was Michael. Molly was sure Owen and Michael recognized each other. Molly wanted to use Michael exclusively for this part of the study, but her sponsors insisted on at least five participants.

All the children except for Michael had been working with sign language. For this reason, the grant sponsors thought it odd that Molly wanted Michael but conceded to her wishes since she was determined to include him in the study.

The two children who remained unmoved in facial expression walked up to the glass, followed closely by Miss Cooper. Mrs. Briggs stayed a few steps back with the other children.

All the children were non-verbal. Molly asked Owen to sign hello. All but Michael signed hello back.

"Are you hungry, Owen?" Molly asked.

Owen made the sign for food. Molly asked what he would like to eat. Owen turned to the computer screen on the wall and touched the sign for banana. Michael's eyes lit up. Molly handed Owen a banana through the opening.

"Do you want to ask Owen if he wants something to drink, Michael?" Molly asked. "Here, can you touch this drink symbol on the screen?" Molly motioned him over to her screen careful not to make physical contact. Touching any of the children, except in the case of an emergency, was strictly forbidden.

Michael looked up at Molly and put his finger on the picture that displayed a cup and straw. Owen immediately touched his own screen where the symbol for yes was. Michael's eyes lit up again. Molly was elated that Michael picked up on communicating through the computer with Owen so quickly. She took a drink to Owen, sliding it through the glass opening, and they watched as he sipped the liquid.

All of the children adapted to working with the special computer program designed for them and Owen. They had worked with computers in the special school they went to.

This continued for one hour each day until Christmas break began for the children. Molly was glad to have the break herself. The pregnancy caused her to grow more uncomfortable with each passing day.

On New Year's Eve, John Carlos, a healthy seven-pound-one-ounce boy, was born.

PART IV

REUNITED

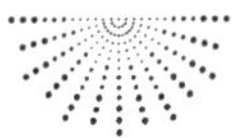

*P*olar Bear embraced his parents once again, this time with a tearful goodbye. Fable, his new wife, stood by his side. Many thought his behavior odd. He returned a hero and could have picked any bride he wanted, someone to sit beside him on the throne. His rightful succession to the throne, he also rejected.

His brother, although not unhappy to see him go, was as puzzled by his actions as any. But upon Theodore's departure, Wilford fiercely hugged him and bade him a safe journey. That was the Wilford he remembered.

He turned to Cora. "I will take good care of your sister. You must promise me to take care of my brother. See to it he rules with wisdom when the time comes. If anyone is capable of guiding him, it is you."

Cora, with tears in her eyes, embraced both Theodore and Fable. "Fable, you will be fine. I know you are in good hands with Theodore," she said to her sister.

They turned from the saddened crowd that had gathered to see them off and began their long journey to the forest.

Theodore turned to his bride. "Fable, you are about to have the adventure of your life."

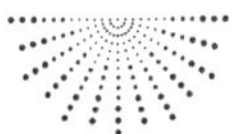

CHAPTER THIRTY-EIGHT

Ethel trekked to the owl's headquarters every day for a solid month, at different times hoping to catch them off guard. She abstained for several days in hopes they would think she had given up. She returned late one evening when the ground was heavy with snow to see Ola flying from her sanctuary.

Ola shrieked when Ethel lifted off in full-wing spread—full enough to block her path.

"I knew this day would come," Ola said, tumbling to the ground.

"You're not hurt, are you?" Ethel asked.

"No, I'm fine." She dusted the snow from her feathers. "Well, let us not stand out here in plain sight. Come up to my office where we can talk in private."

Ethel followed.

"I'm afraid I have nothing to offer you as everyone has gone home for the day."

"That's okay. I'm not in the mood for niceties. I would rather we get down to business," Ethel said.

Ola took a moment to compose herself. "I suppose to say you have questions would be an understatement. And you are angry."

Ethel's silence confirmed her displeasure.

"Sometimes knowing the human words is a curse. Do you know what a Petrie dish is, Ethel?"

"No."

"It's a shallow dish that scientists use to study organisms. We are organisms. Humans also are organisms, although I dare say they do not think of themselves in that manner.

"Humans are always studying animals. They study us. They eat us. They hunt us for pleasure. We are the subject of their experiments. They use us in studies as test subjects before subjecting themselves to something that may do them harm. We are expendable. Especially rats and mice.

"But then, sometimes they protect us. We are the lucky ones. Peacocks are revered where you come from, and here, you are a beautiful creature—an ornamentation for humans' pleasure. Humans are not apt to harm something pleasurable to look at or something that is not worth eating. Both of us fall into that category. Owls are a protected species. When our numbers get low, humans pass laws and inflict penalties on those who would do us harm. Other animals are not so lucky, as you well know. Humans breed animals to eat and hunt them down for sport.

"Think of this forest as a giant Petri dish and of all the creatures in it as one big experiment. That is the dish half-empty way to look at it. The dish half full way would be we are a group of protected animals. There is a fine line between which way you want to look at it.

"You know about zoos. This is somewhat like a zoo. The difference is the animals here do not know they are confined. It is the zoo of the future."

"We are not confined. Luce flew in to see me. We both left together to seek out the animals who escaped from the zoo."

"Make no mistake. Animals here are confined. They don't know it. Animals that don't know they are confined will act differently. They can be studied better as to how they react in a natural environment. Sure, zoos try to make the environment natural, but animals don't for one moment buy it, and how could they with humans gawking at them day in and day out? The smaller, non-threatening animals, so far, are free to come and go."

"So far?"

"Even we owls cannot predict what actions humans may take. Oh, we can come to educated assumptions based on previous behavior, but sometimes, *often*, their conduct is erratic. Have you ventured to the far side of the forest, the one where service trucks come and go?"

"No."

"Few have. By instinct, animals make their homes away from such areas. There is a sign at the entrance. The sign says *Animal Academy: An Experiment in*

Animal Behaviors, followed by the name of the research corporation. There is another sign that says *Danger Keep Out.* That sign was added later.

"This research corporation has ties with the zoo. Animals are exchanged back and forth. In some ways, it is a more humane way of imprisoning animals. The corporation was started by animal activists. Everyone here thinks of it as a nature preserve, and that *is* how it began. This goes back some fifty years. Thaddeus Tortoise was in mid-life when it started. He can tell you a lot about the olden days. The corporation has changed hands since it started."

"Thaddeus told me about the water."

"There were already residents here, the smaller animals: rabbits, foxes, squirrels, tortoises, and birds, we owls among them, to name a few. Deer made up the largest population at the time. It was natural. It was nature. But as with most things, especially nature, humans can't leave well enough alone. They always see some way to improve it. Lions, bears, giraffes, and baboons were added later—in stages. But they couldn't put aggressive animals in with the gentler ones. Thus, the tampering with the water came about.

"The baboons came first. While baboons can be aggressive among their own kind, they aren't usually aggressive toward others. They are also both omnivores and herbivores. I surmised the humans were building up to more aggressive animals.

"From there, they brought in lions. They were

sequestered to the far end. And the bears, who came later, to the other end.

"You know about the injections, the tagging, the water?" Ola asked.

"Yes," Ethel replied.

"I can see by your eyes you are putting it all together, all into perspective."

"Why?"

"Why is the eternal question. Why anything? Didn't the yogis, at the ashram you came from, sit cross-legged pondering that all day long?"

"Yes, I dare say you are right."

"Are they any closer to the answer?"

"None of us are. Why did you not tell all the animals this sooner?"

"I have lost many a night's sleep over this very question. The time wasn't right. The owls would be dismissed as lunatics, not wise at all." Ola laughed. "We had to keep up our mystique, after all. But there is much more to it than that. We weighed the pros and cons. How would the animals react if they were told? Could there be a rebellion? Would all chaos break loose? Although, I'm not one to take the humans side, for the time being, what the humans were doing seemed to be a solution."

"You mean a solution to the problem they created in the first place when they mixed species here that were not natural to the environment?"

"Yes, but that point is somewhat moot now. Would

you go back and erase it all if you could? Would you delete the friendships and experiences you have had?"

"No, I can't imagine not having met everyone I've come to love so dearly."

"Exactly. As far as not letting everyone know, in actuality, the time is never right until answers are demanded. When the animals want to know the truth, they can handle the truth. It is the same with humans. We are all organisms in a Petri dish. The question is who is studying the humans, but then that is above my pay grade.

"Speaking of pay grade. That is a human expression. We animals in some ways are becoming too much like the humans. I see that. I think even you see that. The humans don't see it, though. They see something else.

"The humans only see different animals congregating and co-operating, and they perceive this as a threat because it is something they are not controlling. Yes, they wanted the lions and bears more docile. But they don't have any concept of what is actually going on. Take, for example, the bears—the ones who run the bed and breakfast. They live in an abandoned human house. I am surprised the humans have not torn it down. I fear it is only a matter of time. The humans only see bears and other animals going in and out, sleeping there, and swimming in the nearby lake.

"As for the lions, why the humans wouldn't even dream of lions having an actual school for cubs. No, they see lions out in nature, under trees, playing with their young. The squirrels they see as animals who collect nuts and junk.

"The humans see what they want to see, what they expect to see. Have you been reading the *Harry Potter* books we translated?"

"Yes, almost finished with the last one. I've been reading them to the fox kits. I find the books most fascinating."

"Think of the humans as Muggles. They can't see the magic of the animal kingdom."

Ethel nodded as if in revelation.

"Let's talk about the school for a moment. A school for all animals? Don't get me wrong. I still think it is a good idea. It's a revolutionary idea born out of the desire to evolve. My concern is that we are becoming too much like the humans. What would you call that, Ethel—animals acting like humans? Kali Yuga for animals? On the other hand, this idea of a school where animals work together could lead us into a golden age. The animals may have started getting along via an artificial means, but I think both you and I know it has gone far beyond that. We don't give enough credit to the true human and animal spirits. They are much stronger than we can even imagine. Perhaps it is fate, the course we are taking."

"You've given me a lot to think about," Ethel said, rising from her seat.

"Don't think too hard on it. It can mess with your psyche."

"What is the answer?"

"The answer? Even we owls are not that wise."

Ethel started out the door, then turned. "Ola, all these manuscripts and ancient artifacts you have, what good are they? What do they tell you?"

"They tell me once there was a great golden age, and that humans got along, and animals got along, and humans and animals understood each other and lived in peace. All creatures were in tune with nature. They also tell me that time is coming again soon. A spark will ignite it. Perhaps, Ethel, you are that spark."

"Ola, you flatter me. I hardly think…"

"Peacocks are by nature prideful. The fact you are expressing humility denotes change is coming."

"Alf and Morris haven't brought Owen yet?" Molly asked.

"No, Alf called, and said they were running a bit late, something about the zebras," Carlos said.

Carlos had taken over much of the work since the birth of their baby. Molly flitted in and out, working around John Carlos's naps and feeding times. There were days Molly didn't visit the lab at all.

"Will the children be in today?"

"Only Michael. Spring break, you know. His mother is bringing him in since Michael gets agitated if he doesn't get to see Owen routinely."

"Have you noticed how much of a bond even Michael's mother is developing with Owen?"

"Oh, yes, hard not to see it."

"She views Owen as the interpreter between them both. Who would have thought?"

"I know, and she was so reluctant when I first approached her about this program."

"And look how well it has worked out," Carlos said.

"I'm sorry I'll miss them, but you know how cranky John Carlos gets if I don't get him down for his nap."

Carlos kissed his wife while holding his son's tiny hand up to his.

OWEN SAID GOODBYE TO HIS PARENTS AND WAITED FOR the van that would take him to the other side of the zoo where he met Michael on an almost daily basis. Owen looked forward to it as much as Michael did.

Alf drove the van, and Morris handled the transfer of Owen to the other part of the zoo where the lab was situated. They went through the same ritual each day. He would lead Owen, in restraints, into the backside of the building where he would enter with him into the glass cubicle through a back door. Just before entering, he would remove the restraints and slip him a banana, which was totally against the rules, and say, "Our secret, Owen." Owen always gulped down the banana in one bite. He knew better than to let Molly or Carlos see. He smiled his big toothy grin and handed Morris the peel.

This afternoon Morris opened the doors on the back of the van. Both Morris and Alf would apply the restraints. Morris also carried a Taser in case of any unforeseen incident. There had never been one. Owen was always eager to go to the lab, and transferring Owen to and from was Morris's favorite part of the day.

It perplexed Morris to see Owen cast his eyes downward each time he placed the restraints around Owen's ankles and wrists.

"Oh, what the heck," Morris said. "We'll leave them off for today. We both know you don't need them."

Alf looked at Morris and said, "Are you sure about this?"

"Alf, you never saw this. Why don't you go back to the van and wait? I'll take full responsibility if anything goes wrong."

The walk from the truck to the back entrance and down the hallway to the back door of the enclosure fronted with glass was no longer than several feet. On most days, Alf sat in the van during the transfer, talking on his smartphone to his mate. Owen wondered why he wasn't today. It reminded him of the early days when Molly and Carlos used to talk on the phone.

Owen sensed something different in the air this morning. Everything was off—no restraints, Alf not on the phone. But then came the familiar ringtone. Alf looked at his phone.

"Go ahead, talk to her," Morris said.

Alf, instead of getting back into the van stood on the sidewalk and talked. No sooner than Owen and Morris entered the building a loud boom shook the structure's foundations. Fire shot out from a storage room. It contained chemicals. Some debris hit Morris, knocking him out. The flames licked at Owen's back as he bent down and dragged his handler by his collar out the back door they had come in.

Owen placed Morris in the grassy area off the sidewalk where they had entered the building. Alf was running toward them and screaming at Owen, but Owen ignored him and went back inside. Michael, and maybe Molly, would be inside.

He went down the hall, bypassing the door he normally entered. The second door, the one Molly, Carlos, and Michael entered was blocked by rubble from the explosion. Even though the fire alarm was blaring in his ears and water from the sprinklers was coming down, Owen heard them yelling and pounding from the other side of the door.

With the strength of seven men, Owen used his long arms to remove the debris. Carlos, Michael, and his mother came rushing out, going in the opposite direction of the flames with Owen behind them acting as a barrier, pushing them along.

Once outside, no one thought anything of Owen standing there alongside the three of them, not even Michael's mother who sometimes asked if the glass enclosure was enough protection. Owen reached down for Michael's hand, which he gladly gave him.

"Michael doesn't like anyone touching him," she said, surprised.

"Owen isn't anyone," Carlos said.

She nodded.

MOLLY TREMBLED WHEN SHE HEARD THE NEWS. SHE and John Carlos left the building only an hour earlier than the incident occurred.

It was attributed to no specific group. There had been protestors in the beginning—those who thought Owen should not be returned to the zoo, some of which didn't think Owen should be allowed to live.

The man apprehended for the incident had been one of the original protesters who advocated euthanizing Owen, saying he posed a threat. When questioned, he swore he had acted alone. He admitted to coming to the zoo regularly, calculating the best time to strike. He swore he thought no one was in the facility on that day. He swore it was merely a scare tactic.

Molly was frantic. "He could have killed all of you. If it weren't for Owen... I don't even want to think about what could have happened. John Carlos would have had to grow up without his father."

CHAPTER FORTY

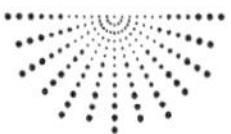

The city council, who commissioned the statue of Owen, meant it to be placed at the zoo entrance. Instead, it was positioned in the center of the forest. Why the center, Molly or Carlos didn't know. But it was something both Michael and Owen communicated through the computer screen and sign language. Both were adamant about it, and both became highly agitated if another location was even suggested. In the end, the foundation over the grant, and also the ones footing the bill for the statue, said if the work they were engaged in were to come to fruition, then the wishes of Owen and Michael must be met.

Molly, Carlos, John Carlos, Michael, his mother, city and zoo officials, along with some press, traveled to the Animal Academy where Owen was to dwell temporarily, depending on how things went and what the foundation decided, for the unveiling of the statue. There were twelve armed guards with tranquilizer darts stationed on the outskirts of the event, should the need arise. There was after all lions, tigers, and bears as well as a hyena in the mix somewhere in the forest. However, the biggest fear was a protest group. Molly wasn't too concerned about the animals. She got the distinct impression from Owen there was no need for alarm.

One of the twelve guards was the same policeman who had chased after Owen that night of the escape. He had obtained special permission to be there. Without fear, he walked up to Owen and handed him the baseball cap that got lost that night in the confusion. Owen took the cap with his endearing grin, placed it on his head, and signed thank you. The policeman saluted Owen and walked back to where he was stationed as a guard.

The ceremony ended with no disturbances. Some said the forest was eerily quiet. Others described it as mystical. Humans sensed the animal inhabitants watched the ceremony with reverence and awe.

Molly's heart was divided. Tears formed in her eyes. She handed John Carlos to her husband. Owen bent down and she patted him on the head and hugged him as far as her arms could reach around his body and said, "This is your new home for the time being. I hope you like it here. Somehow, I think you will. I believe you are among friends."

THE HUMANS DEPARTED. WHEN IT WAS DEEMED SAFE, every creature living in the forest came out from their hiding places. Ethel, Luce, Santiago, Hyena, Badger, and Tiger embraced Owen heartily. There was not a dry eye in the forest.

Densworth Lion stepped up and extended his paw. "At last we meet."

Every animal, one by one, came up to pay homage to Owen. He greeted each with a big smile, wearing his retrieved baseball cap and standing beside his statue.

Rhonda Rabbit was jabbering away when a hush fell over the crowd. They all turned to see Polar Bear coming toward them. He had a female polar bear by his side, followed by three black bears, two older and one younger.

"So, she really does exist," Tiger whispered to Hyena.

"I think we can finally recommence work on the school," Ola Owl said with a satisfied sparkle in her big eyes.

ACKNOWLEDGMENTS

A special thank you to my beta readers, Lisa Kramer, author of *P.O.W.ER*, Brenda Killmer Ricker, who is working on her first book, *Charlie Saves the Monkey Ship,* Barbara Chambers, Elissa Strati, author of *First Street Church Romances,* Erin McIntyre, author of *The Red King Trilogy Books,* Kim Daniels, Linda G. Hatton, Susanne Larssen Chetkowski, Haylee Ayers, and Charlotte Dombroskas.

A special thanks to my editors, Emerald Barnes and Anne Wills.

And, to my husband, Chris.

J. Schlenker, a late-blooming author, lives with her husband, Chris, out in the splendid center of nowhere in the foothills of Appalachia in Kentucky where the only thing to disturb her writing is croaking frogs and the occasional sounds of hay being cut in the fields.

For more information:
https://www.jschlenker.com/
jschlenkerauthor@gmail.com

Jessica Lost Her Wobble

A Novel Tea Book Club Selection, 2017 Wishing Shelf Book Awards Finalist, 2014 William Faulkner-William Wisdom Writing Contest Finalist, and recipient of a 5 Star Readers' Favorite Award.

At mid-life, Jessica, after many upsets, moves to an island for contemplation of her life and to make a new start. While there, she reflects back on her beginnings in the early twentieth century in England, her move to New York City, and marriage at a young age, while making friends with a girl half her age. This friendship opens up a new world for her and helps her explore her own soul. Jessie becomes a part of the island otherwise known as a local as she reinvents her life there and finds love. But all is not as it seems.

"Jessica Lost Her Wobble" is J. Schlenker's first novel.

Review Excerpts: "Let me get this out of the way.. Buy this book and read it!!" "Exceptional book. I would give it 10 stars if they were available." "This is a book that must be read to the end, meaning all the way through the last big surprise epilogue. I didn't see it coming and it changed the whole texture of looking back on this well-written novel."

The Color of Cold and Ice

A recipient of the IndiBrag Medallion.

Sybil has dreams; the prophetic kind, although interpreting them correctly is another matter. Her latest dream involves her sister Emerald, who wants to pursue her art once more and move on with her life after losing her husband. John, once felt he was making a difference as an ER doctor, but finds himself slipping away in his Manhattan practice as well as in his marriage. Allison, John's wife wants to change her ho hum existence with John into something spectacular. Mark, Allison's brother, a struggling musician, wants to quit rambling in life and find his purpose.

The cold changes everything.

Review Excerpts: "I loved the way colors were the background that all of our lives are made of, and how they became an intricate part of the story…" "Color of Cold and Ice is a beautiful story of strangers brought together through a series of life changing events and their journey to find happiness."